# FLOPPING

## in a Winter

## Wonderland

Also by Jason June
*Jay's Gay Agenda*
*Out of the Blue*
*Riley Weaver Needs a Date to the Gaybutante Ball*
*The Spells We Cast*
*The Magic You Make*

# FLOPPING

## in a Winter

## Wonderland

### JASON JUNE

**HARPER**
*An Imprint of HarperCollinsPublishers*

Library of Congress Control Number: 2023948457

ISBN 978-0-06-326008-5
Typography by David DeWitt
24 25 26 27 28  LBC  5 4 3 2 1
First Edition

To Zach, for being the best big brother a kid could ever hope for:
I love you, broface.
And to Andrew, for being the best little sis a gay could ever
hope for: Merry Christmas, you filthy animal.

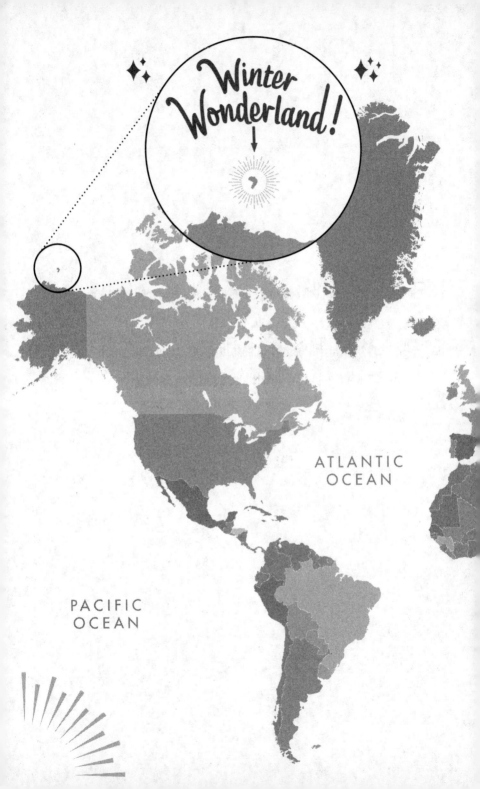

Winter Wonderland!

ATLANTIC OCEAN

PACIFIC OCEAN

ARCTIC
OCEAN

PACIFIC
OCEAN

INDIAN
OCEAN

# Aaron

"So we've got about half an hour until fireworks, both literal and maybe even metaphorical." Casey mimes making out, wagging his tongue back and forth. He makes the weirdest moan sound too. It's a mix between a printer getting jammed and a golden retriever whining when he's hungry.

"If those are the sounds you make when kissing Raquel, I'm surprised you've made it this long together," I say.

My brother pushes me, fake affronted, until his forehead furrows into an innocently concerned scowl. "Wait. What?" He snatches his phone from his pocket and his fingers fly across the screen. **Babe. Do I make weird sounds when we kiss?**

If she says yes, I know Casey will be devastated. My brother's been in love with love since he first realized what it was, crushing on Disney princesses and pop stars until he was old enough to date. He dove headfirst into love in the sixth grade when he lent the new girl, Raquel Strickland, some lunch money. They've been together ever since, over eight years. They're both sophomores at UC Irvine, and they've never been apart for longer than *three days*. They are the *epitome* of codependent. Casey can't do a single thing without bringing Raquel up. They've even got a ship name: Rasey. And they use it in a "cutesy" (read: disgusting) way whenever they're about to have sex.

*"Bro, go for a walk. We need a little Rasey time."*

I throw up in my mouth every time he says it.

With the text sent, Casey glances at his home screen, which shows that sunset was at precisely 4:44 p.m. Thanksgiving fireworks on Newport Beach always start exactly one hour post-sunset. People come after stuffing their faces with turkey and plop onto the beach and *ooh* and *aah* while they think about all they're thankful for. At 5:17, we're nearly to the start, upon which Casey is convinced I will have my first kiss during the romantic bursts of colored light. With whom, exactly, doesn't really matter to him, just that it happens. This stretch of sand is packed with locals and SoCal tourists, one of whom is allegedly going to go down in the history books of Aaron Merry's life. *My* life.

"Anybody nearby piquing your interest?" Casey asks, his hazel eyes scanning the crowd underneath his mop of disheveled dark blond hair. "What about him? Just look at the way he fills out those undies."

I follow his gaze to the very ample ass of a guy in a brown Speedo with red, yellow, and orange feathers protruding from the butt like a turkey. "I don't know. He's really dressed for the holiday. You know how I feel about people being too on the nose with a theme."

Casey rolls his eyes. "I'll never live down telling you to go to prom with Bereted Barry, will I?"

"Mais non."

Prom was yet another event where Casey thought he was going to find me my first kiss. *One Night in Paris* was the theme, and I was a sophomore while Casey and Barry were seniors. Barry had just been dumped by his boyfriend, and Casey thought the romance of the night would be the perfect way to get Barry out of his funk and me out of my relationship dry spell. Does it count as a dry spell if you've never actually been in a relationship? Either way, Casey's so in love with love that it's been his life's mission for me to feel the sparks too.

But that prom wasn't it. Barry *was* cute, but one look at the beret he wore and there was no way I was going to kiss him. It was all just too eager. Like, what if the theme had been *Under the Sea*? Would he have come dressed as a crab or had sequined scales on his jacket? I couldn't stop thinking of him trying to kiss me with fish lips, and it was all over for the rest of the night.

"Wait, bro, what about him?" Casey nods to a guy whose

face is buried deep in his phone, his skin illuminated by the glow of the screen. "He seems the right amount of disinterested."

"But look at that scowl." As if to emphasize my point, the guy scrolls farther into whatever it is he's looking at, and those furrows only get deeper. Grand Canyon–level deep. "He looks like he has *opinions*."

Casey crosses his arms. "You mean like yours, right now?"

"At least I'm commenting on what I'm seeing with my own two eyes. I bet he gives his hot takes on every Reddit thread there is but doesn't actually *do* anything." I can't stand a person who wants to rant and rave about what they read online but has no idea how to act in real life.

That's how it continues for the next twenty-seven minutes. Casey finding someone in the crowd, me turning them down for a plethora of reasons: "Can you imagine what his breath will taste like after he finishes that turkey leg? And who brings a turkey leg to the beach?" "He literally just fist-bumped his friend, Casey. *Fist-bumped*." "They're wearing a tank top *on Thanksgiving*, and the shape of their chest hair looks like the Bat Signal."

After the thirteenth person I quickly turn down, Casey's whole body slumps. All six feet eight inches of him weighed down, his feet sinking into the sand. "This isn't going to happen, is it?"

I scan the crowd one more time for good measure. "No. It's not. Sorry, Case."

The first firework goes off in a shower of golden sparkles, the boom putting a resounding period on my statement.

Casey looks up into the sky, bursts of red, orange, and blue highlighting his face. "I guess I just thought the holiday would change things."

I quirk an eyebrow. "How so?"

"Thanksgiving is all about people coming together, grateful to be in each other's lives. I thought you'd find a guy who you'd be thankful gave you your first kiss." He hooks an arm around my shoulders and pulls me in. He's so freaking tall that my head fits right into his armpit. Not my favorite place, but I've always had a soft spot for his overly sappy brotherly love. "There's no one more independent than you."

He isn't wrong. Love, relationships, and attachment just aren't my thing. I wouldn't call myself aromantic or asexual, although I'm super supportive of folks who are. I'll never forget that time in PE sophomore year when I was so attracted to a passing senior, I had to pretend to have explosive diarrhea so I could run back to the locker room before everyone saw the hard-on making its presence known in my swimsuit. I've had crushes on a couple guys too, complete with daydreams of what it would be like to be in a relationship. But anytime those thoughts come barreling unwelcomed into my head, I stamp them right back down. I don't want to kiss anyone. Or date anyone. Or ever say the dreaded L-word. I've been telling myself that so long now that it's pretty easy to find reasons why no one is worth it.

Here's the thing: when you kiss, or date, or *love*, you lose your entire sense of self. It happens literally every time I see someone else my age start dating. We've all seen those friend fights where one friend dumps the other because they're suddenly coupled up and have no more time to hang out with anyone from their life before they *fell in love*. It's bad enough when you get super attached to friends, letting your whole identity get wrapped around whether somebody else likes you. But with love, it's that times a thousand.

So, I prefer my time alone, basically in all walks of life. I don't do teams, I don't do BFFs. I only do activities I can depend entirely on myself for. SAT tutoring, singles tennis, treasurer of the ASB because I ran totally unopposed. No attachments to anyone or anything, except Dad and Casey. I don't want to have to rely on anybody, but I definitely like for others to be able to rely on me. I'm the constant. I mean, think about it. No family, no friend group, no organization has ever been able to peacefully exist without one person in there who can fix everything.

And that's me. Because sooner or later, someone's bound to have an emotional crisis, and without me to pick up the pieces, things won't go smoothly. It's weird—even though I don't put out the vibe that I want friends, kids at school always find me to help them get through their breakups.

A freshman came up to me last year when her girlfriend dumped her and said I was known as the Robot, the guy who could look at anybody—even the most snot-streaked, tearstained, heartbroken mess—and tell them exactly why they are better off single. She needed a robot—everyone does. Emotions get in the way. In *all* walks of life. I was able to keep my cool when the ASB found out thirteen hundred dollars was missing from our accounts and nearly made us lose our DJ for homecoming. A few impromptu car washes and some budgeting finesse, and voilà! Homecoming saved. When Mom left and Dad was a mess, I was the one buying groceries and making dinner for weeks, or checking that bills were paid. If *everyone* became a wreck, nothing would ever get done, and then the situation would get much, much worse.

That's what I'm for. Robot to the rescue.

The last burst of fireworks fizzles into nothing, and Casey uses his giant body to shield me from the crowd as it disperses. He's always got that caretaking instinct, honed during his time interning for Newport Beach Family Services. He spends time with foster kids waiting for their next placement. His outrageously wholesome dream is to become an adoption agent to help as many children and families as possible. He brings that tender energy to everything he does, like now, as he hovers over me while we're jostled from side to side with the hustle of bodies. But no matter how hard we're bumped into, nothing can make gargantuan Casey move.

"Keep your eyes peeled, bro." I've always loved the way Casey calls me "bro." It's not in that hypermasculine, let's-pound-our-chests kind of way. It's a sweet, endearing way of pointing out to everyone that we actually are brothers. It makes me soften every time, if only a bit. "Just because the fireworks are over doesn't mean you can't still create some of your own."

Casey fully doesn't support my need to be single. He's just convinced that I haven't met the right guy yet, and if he's not constantly vigilant, he'll have failed me as a brother. If we were home, it's about this time that I would convince him we should watch yet another made-for-TV Christmas movie—his absolute favorite, whether or not we're in the holiday season—so he could obsess over some fictional characters' love lives instead of my own. There is nothing Casey loves more than Christmas. Well, Raquel for sure, but he's just completely obsessed with the holiday, which means it's all we'll be talking about now that Thanksgiving is officially over.

"Maybe next year, Case."

My phone buzzes with a text, and I open it to see a homemade meme from Mom. She's imposed her face over a cooked turkey. Only she's put it in between the drumsticks instead of where a head should be. In big white block letters, she's written, *I'M STUFFED. MISS YOU.*

Nothing says love from afar like your mom's face over a turkey's vagina.

Casey smiles at his own phone, but I know it's not from one of Mom's signature memes. That goofy grin is reserved only for Raquel.

"Gotta get some Rasey time in, bro," he says. "Mind if I take the car?"

I shake my head. We drove the couple blocks to get here only because we each had one slice too many of pumpkin pie. There's no walking when you're that full.

"Cool. Catch you back home." He takes off, his inordinately long legs getting him to the parking lot in no time flat.

Which leaves this robot exactly how he likes it:

Alone.

# Kris

Nathaniel pushes me against the wood siding of Santa's Workshop, hard. His scruff scratches my skin as he shoves his tongue down my throat. His right hand's in my hair while his left cups my ass, creating this bizarre sensation of my right butt cheek heated by his warmth and my left ice-cold as it presses against the chilling pine. My whole body is a whirl of sensation: hot, freezing, scratchy, booming all around from my heart pounding in my chest and the blasts of fireworks in the sky. When it's this late in November, the Elves love to set the daily fireworks off at 10 a.m., just to mess with the mainlanders who can't believe it stays so dark here. Where else in the world could you get a post-breakfast firework show on the day after Thanksgiving? A few places on mainland Alaska, and *definitely* on Winter Wonderland, our tiny island an hour's flight north.

"You're so hot," Nathaniel slurs into my mouth, his tongue smashing against mine between each word. He tastes like hot chocolate.

"You are," I breathe back, then slam my lips against his. This is my favorite thing about kissing: how different people are at it. Some are slow and gentle, others are fast and hungry, and Nathaniel's going at me like a polar bear who hasn't eaten in months.

Nathaniel throws his other hand under my butt and lifts me up, pressing his whole body against me while I wrap my legs around him. Even through his snowsuit I can feel a fairly solid bulge pressing against me.

"Merry Christmas to me," Nathaniel says as he presses harder, everywhere.

"It's the day after Thanksgiving." I cringe as soon as I say it. Rule number one of Winter Wonderland is to never let the magic of the holidays slip. I mean, why else would someone visit a year-round Christmas island off the coast of Alaska if they didn't want the delusion of Yuletide sparkle?

Not to mention making Nathaniel fall for that sparkle is what could finally let me reach the goal I've been working *my whole life* for. Okay, maybe not my whole life, but at least for six years, after it really sunk in that there are no gay Santas in all of Winter Wonderland. An entire Christmas theme park island with Santas of every race (as there should be)—and even churches of every denomination for those who celebrate Christmas for the merriment but have other religious traditions—yet no Mr. and Mr. Claus in sight. It'd be the ultimate irony if kissing this guy just right would be what helped me finally change that. And Uncle Toby would appreciate the fact that it's what finally let me avenge him.

A red firework reflects off the snow, creating a soft pink glow that only adds to the heated blush of Nathaniel's cheeks. He pulls back to look me in the eye. I can't tell if the look is concern or worry or adoration or what. When his tongue's not down my throat, he's so unreadable.

Is he going to say it? *Is he going to say it?*

"Kris, I lo—" Another succession of booms cuts him off, making him glance up as more bright blossoms of color join the mass of stars in the dark Alaskan sky. It really is so romantic. This has to be the moment.

I grab his cheeks with both hands, pulling his head toward me. Only I'm pressing too hard, smooshing his face so his lips are kind of fished out.

"You were saying?" I ask.

I need him to say it.

Nathaniel bites his lip like he's nervous. I bet he's wondering if he could possibly feel this way, if he could possibly fall so hard so fast.

But I know he has.

"It's okay," I whisper. "You can tell me anything."

He swallows, his Adam's apple bobbing down his throat torturously slow. It makes me want to lean in and kiss his neck, but that would be distracting. No more distractions. *He has to say it.*

"Okay." Nathaniel nods, takes a deep breath, and goes for it. "I lo—" Here it comes. "—ve my boyfriend. Back home. We were on a break, but he called before breakfast and wants to give our relationship another chance."

My entire body sags. I would fall to the ground if Nathaniel wasn't still holding me up. It's saying something that he can hold me at all. I'm six foot one and have considerable glute muscles thanks to all the skating and dancing we do on the island. My legs drop, dangling on his sides like limp noodles.

Nathaniel doesn't seem to notice. "If I don't get back with him, I'd totally kick myself for losing the best thing that's ever happened to me."

I finally plant my feet on the ground and push him off. He has the nerve to drop the L-bomb, but not on me? "You just wanted to cram your tongue down my throat one last time before telling me you loved somebody else?" I shove past him and stomp down the alley.

"Wait, Kris." Nathaniel's feet crunch in the snow as he hurries to follow. "Where are you going?"

"I'm over this."

"But I thought—we were just having fun, weren't we?"

I shrug. "It was a little sloppy, if you ask me."

"You didn't seem to mind yesterday. Or the day before that. Or the six days before that either."

"Yeah, well, I guess not everyone's who you think they

are. I bet your boyfriend thinks *you're* better than you are."

Nathaniel's forehead scrunches in confusion. "But we were on a break. This was just a fling. A holiday fling."

"So you won't mind if I just *fling* myself on home then." I turn around and walk backward, waving sarcastically. "So long, Nathaniel. Thanks for nothing."

My sixth boy of the year, and yet another epic failure. It's not that I was in love with any of them, but I definitely need one to fall in love with me.

It's the only way I'll get to meet Kris Kringle in the flesh.

The Winter Wonderland founder mocks me with his megawatt, white-bearded smile as soon as I get home. Mr. Kringle was born with the legendary gift-giver's name and his looks to boot. A card with his very Santa-esque mug sits on the dining room table, next to a giant basket filled with Winter Wonderland memorabilia: hats, gloves, Below Zero jackets that are deceptively thin, thermal underwear, and more, all embroidered with the cursive WW logo inside a silver snowflake. Workers on the island—a.k.a. Elves or Wonderers or townies—are always given new gear around the holidays. Dad sits right beside the stash, grading tests as the island's resident science teacher. He looks up when he hears me shut the door.

"The Big Man sent a delivery!" Dad says, using the chipper Winter Wonderland tone that's the complete opposite of my current mood.

"I can see that." I nod toward the basket.

"What?" Dad eyes the overflowing gifts, confused. "No, not that. Big Man!" He holds out an envelope covered with enormous loopy script that I'd recognize anywhere.

*Big Man*, Dad's nickname for his older brother. "Uncle Toby!" I take the letter from Dad and see my name spelled out in curls and swirls. Well, not my name exactly, since Uncle Toby addressed it to *Kristopher Bright*. My name is legally just Kris, but Uncle Toby said he was always a Full Name Gay. "Kristopher" became payback for me calling him Uncle Toby all his life, but in my defense, *Tobias* is a mouthful for a baby. Toby stuck because when I tried to switch to the full, I always tripped up on it.

Kristopher,

I'm kicking this letter off with some Christmas cheer. I got cast as Santa! Albeit a mall Santa, but at least it's something. When I told my new boss I used to work in Winter Wonderland, she hired me on the spot. Now I'll pull day shifts in the "North Pole" (it doesn't even come close to WW, but it still feels like home) and continue to do nights at the shipping center.

You wouldn't believe how warm it is in Chicago this time of year. A whole thirty-one degrees! I walked outside in shorts, and folks looked at me like I'd lost my marbles.

*I miss you and your mom and dad more than you know. It feels weird without all that Bright-ness in my life, even more so knowing this will be our first Christmas where we're not all together. But I know that we'll be reunited somehow. Onward and upward!*

*How's the end of your semester looking? I can't believe you're just six months away from graduating. I feel like we put you in your first baby elf ears just yesterday.*
*Merry Merry,*

*Uncle Toby*

It's always touch and go whether his letters that come every two weeks with the Wonderland bimonthly mail delivery will put me in a good or bad mood. Today, it's bad. He's always upbeat, but his letters just hit home how different life is without him on the island.

"How's Big Man?" Dad asks as he doodles a Christmas tree with a huge star on top next to the A+ he just graded.

"Good," I say. "He got a job as a mall Santa."

Dad finally catches on to my flat tone. He looks up from his paper, setting down his gold Sharpie. "I know it's tough, Kris. But this is what he wanted."

I scoff. "Right. What *he* wanted."

"You know what I mean. Tobias chose to leave. He wasn't asked to."

"He might as well have been."

"Kris." Dad sighs. "I can't have this argument again. I know it's hard for you to understand why he left, but—"

"You're right, Dad," I say, my mouth stretching into an apologetic smile. It's entirely forced, but I know that Dad is fooled by my fake sincerity because I've had to use it more often than I'd like the last six months. Besides, you don't take acting classes five days a week to hone insta–Christmas cheer and not learn a thing or two. "I'm sorry. I just miss him is all, but I shouldn't take that out on you. I'll snap out of it. I promise."

With that, I hustle upstairs to my room, where I can safely let the act drop. Because it's not hard for me to understand why Uncle Toby left at all.

He was forced to.

There was a rare Santa opening, the first in almost ten years, and Uncle Toby tried out. He was a shoo-in. Not only does he have that bear Santa build, but he's been naturally silver-haired ever since he turned forty. Plus, he lives and breathes Christmas, good at every single holiday-related activity, and was even a head woodworker at the Wonderland Toy Factory. I mean, Santa delivers toys to kids around the world, and Uncle Toby makes them? He was born for the job.

He made it to the top two before getting cut. No one

Ho Ho Ho–ed better than him; no one could improvise with guests with so much whip-smart and family-friendly banter. It was clear to anyone who saw the contenders that Uncle Toby was meant to be Saint Nick.

But Uncle Toby had one condition. Throughout the audition process, he made it clear he wanted to be the first openly gay Santa on the island. The hiring committee told him that was against company policy, referencing the stance they made clear in a press release a few years ago when the absence of any Wonderland LGBTQ+ representation was brought up on social media. In the company's eyes, it wasn't discrimination, because they'd still hire Uncle Toby, they just wouldn't let him "turn Santa gay."

Uncle Toby walked. Not just out of the competition, but off the island. He couldn't face knowing he was truly the best and was still pushed aside because of outdated attitudes.

I don't blame him in the slightest.

I just miss him.

So I've made it my mission to get him back. It all hinges on the Race, my grade's annual competition to see who can get a guest to fall in love with them first. Because inevitably, some tourist always falls in love with us.

It happened for the first time to Nicky in the eighth grade. A sweet braces-wearing boy mistook having his first kiss with her under the mistletoe to mean he was madly in love. He told Nicky as much, to which she had to say the feelings weren't reciprocated. He threw his sparkling cider on her. We thought it might be a one-off, but one day later, the girl Chris was paired with for sledding races dropped the L-bomb after they won. Once it happened to Rudy the day after that, we knew this was more than a fluke.

We started calling ourselves the Fling Ring thanks to all the visitors who—even after professing their love—ended up only being flings. That's not to say that we didn't enjoy kissing or going on dates with the folks who came and went. It's just that we all knew these wouldn't be real relationships because our suitors were holiday drunk. Not, like, actual drunk, because this all started when we were thirteen, but the second everyone comes here all the lights and music and Christmas cheer go to their head. We see it for the ruse it is, since we're in on the massive production and have been our whole lives. We're the first generation of kids born on the island, but we missed out on the gene that makes you fall for Christmas magic, because *we* are the ones making that magic.

Being the Fling Ring was all a joke until Anjelica moved to Winter Wonderland a few months after we created the name. Anjelica Pérez-Kringle is the one and only heir to the Kringle's Krafts billions as the daughter of Kris Kringle and supermodel slash former Miss Colombia Sasha Pérez. She's also my best friend, so I've heard all about the trouble she got up to on the mainland. To prevent Anjelica from sneaking into more clubs and crashing yet another Maserati, Kringle made his only daughter move here, to this little island in the middle of the Arctic Ocean, where there was really only so much trouble she could get into. If she's good enough to make the Nice List, he flies her back to their Manhattan penthouse apartment for our short "spring" break, the second half of February, and lets her bring one of us with her. She thought it was so hysterical that these lovestruck tourists were falling for us that she made it a game. The Race. Whoever gets a visitor to confess their love to one of us first gets to join her for the entire break, an all-expenses-paid trip off this chunk of rock.

Winning the Race would get me in Kris Kringle's *home*, and face-to-face interaction with the man who founded this place is the only thing I haven't tried yet to bring Uncle Toby back. Kringle hand-selected everyone who moved to this island when it opened, my parents and Uncle Toby included. Hearing from folks firsthand what the holiday meant to them, what their current living situation was like, were all taken into consideration. Kringle's known for having the biggest heart, and I need to remind him of that. But he rarely makes it to the island now. The multibillion-dollar craft company he founded that allowed him to buy this uninhabited hunk of Alaska and create a nonstop Christmas theme park has grown so big, it became too much for him to handle alone. A board was established, and they make all the business decisions. Although Anjelica insists they still defer to her dad on questions of holiday cheer, which is why I'm hoping if I can convince him to bring back Uncle Toby, we just might be able to make it happen. All I've got to do is get a guy to fall in love with me so I can win the Race. I'll get to see Kringle and convince him to take up this fight with the board. I'll be able to say to his face why Uncle Toby *and* gay Santas are so important for Winter Wonderland. I mean, how do you turn down a wholesome kid who's even named after you when they ask for your help at your dinner table?

Nathaniel's out, obviously, in terms of helping me reach my goal. I can't waste my time with selfish idiots who'd go on vacation and have a fling behind their boyfriend's back, anyway. I don't know what I was thinking. Things are getting desperate.

There's got to be a guy out there, somewhere, who will love me.

# Aaron

"I was wrong all along, Jake." The voice reaches me on the street as I get out of my car. I know it's coming from the backyard, through the open doors of what's supposed to be the guesthouse but has become Casey's bedroom. "I don't need New York. I don't need my high-stakes job. The only thing I need for Christmas"—dramatic pregnant pause where you know the camera is zooming in on this lovestruck heroine's eyes welling with tears—"is you."

Hopeful violin music swells, and I cringe. Not only from just how cheesy these made-for-TV holiday movies are, but because if another neighbor complains about how loud Casey blares his Christmas media (movies, music, holiday baking competitions, you name it), Dad's going to go Grinch on his ass and kick him out. Casey says the magic of Christmas and the magic of love are natural partners. *I know.* I've eye-rolled so many times at Casey that I think I've seen him more from my peripheral vision than looking at him dead-on. But because of this perceived perfect pairing, Casey never takes his Christmas decorations down. This is the one month of the year when the rest of the house actually matches, thanks to the lights wrapped around our home and the two palm trees out front, and the inflatable Santa who now waves jovially next to the mailbox. Every other month, it's year-round Christmas for Casey with the guesthouse aglow, and he's always in a sappy Hallmark-channel mood.

It's really annoying.

But I'm the robot that keeps everybody's life together. Maybe my brother's fallen asleep, unaware of how loud his movie's playing. Either way, I better book it to Casey's Christmas Casita before Dad can get to him first. I take the side gate, the fastest route to the backyard. Casey's Christmas lights are lit and blinking, and his life-size Mrs. Claus is dancing next to the open sliding-glass doors. As the credits start to roll on whatever terrible movie just ended, the screen backtracks to the main menu and scrolls through more holiday streaming options. So Casey's definitely awake.

Little white puffs start bursting up and over the couch. At first I think Casey might have added a fake snow machine to his Christmas collection. He always talks about how much he misses snow when he comes back from the slopes. He and Raquel returned from an overnight trip to Mountain High Ski Resort just this morning, so it wouldn't be shocking if snow was on his mind. But as I get closer, I see those little white balls aren't fake snow at all. They're tissues. Used, balled-up, soaked tissues.

That's when I hear it in the silence of Casey choosing his next movie.

Sniffling.

He's crying.

I've literally never heard him cry in my entire life.

He's just not that kind of guy. He might get a touched tear in his eye from whatever it is he's watching, but never a full-on sob. He's happy-go-lucky, everything's-always-coming-up-roses Casey.

"Case?" I lean over the back of the couch to see him sprawled out, shirtless, and in his Frosty the Snowman pajama bottoms. Even more crumpled-up tissues cover his torso. "Casey, what happened?"

My brother throws his hands dramatically over his face, and the remote careens straight for my nose as it flies from his fingers. Thank god tennis taught me how to move fast. I duck out of the way just in time.

"She broke up with me!" Casey cries. "We're through. I-I-I can't believe it, Aaron. I'm s—. I'm si—. I'm sing—. I can't even say it."

"Single?" I offer, only to be met by an ear-piercing wail. "Sorry. Just trying to be helpful."

"I never thought this would happen, bro." His sweet use of the title reminds me that I'm going to have to be the one to help him out of this funk, because if not me, who?

I step around the couch and sit on the largest of Casey's three white ottomans that when stacked create a snowman. "Did she say why?" I ask.

Casey takes his hands from his face, his tearstained cheeks bright red. "She said she needs to see what else is out there. She told me on . . . on the car ride back."

Casey breaks down into another torrential wave of tears. This is what I was talking about when you get close to people. They can completely wreck you.

You'd think with Raquel being such a presence in our lives for almost a decade that I'd have some connection to her too. Or maybe that I'd feel a sense of loss with this news. But nope. I always saw her as my brother's girlfriend, and even appreciated that she kept him occupied and happy so I wouldn't have to worry about him so much. I'd let them do their thing and make sure our family kept on ticking.

But honestly? I am surprised. Raquel always came across just as lovestruck and codependent as my brother. But I guess Casey's the only needy one now, and it's up to me to fix him.

"She dumped me like she'd already moved on," Casey says, staring into the distance while he relives how it all went down. "Like there was no changing her mind, Aaron. She must have—" He squeezes the words past the lump in his throat. "She must've met someone else. I think it's that guy Stefan from work. I knew it was weird that they were doing so much inventory at Subway. It's meat and cheese and veggies—you either have it or you don't!"

He sobs again, pushing one of his used snot snowballs against his face. As Casey blows, a message pings on my phone from Mom:

**Hey, haven't heard from Casey since I sent him my Thanksgiving text. How's your brother doing?**

They always do this. Casey and Dad had pretty much the same reaction when Mom left: they shut down. Case never cried; he was totally emotionless. Anytime Mom calls, he always says he's busy, and if he ever replies to her texts, it's basically one-word answers. So they end up talking through me, and I guess I'm happy to be the middleman if it keeps the peace, but right now I can worry about only one of them at a time.

"She belongs here." Casey holds a hand over his heart, and I can picture all the times Raquel fit perfectly into the crook of his arm, her head nuzzled against my brother's chest. "She won't even let me try to make it right. I'm already blocked on everything. Texts, DMs, all of it. Eight years down the drain."

"Oh, Case." I lean forward and pat his shin. It's awkward and stilted. I'm not super great at physical comfort. "How can I help?"

"There's nothing you can do," Casey says. "This isn't something that can be fixed by a checklist or, or, or, like, analyzing your way out of it or whatever. This is love, bro. You can't put a Band-Aid on a broken hear—"

Casey's phone blares to life, cutting him off. He shoots up from the couch, a look of hope in his eyes. But we both realize the ringtone is wrong. If his phone rings with "All I Want for Christmas Is You," it's Raquel. All other callers get "Rockin' Around the Christmas Tree."

But "Rockin'" isn't playing. "Walking in a Winter Wonderland" is. I've heard it a million times before, but never set as his ringer.

I lean over the coffee table, trying to get a view of his phone. "Who is that?"

Casey's mouth falls open as a lone tear slides down his cheek.

"Winter Wonderland!" Casey shouts. "*The* Winter Wonderland." His hand shoots out and he grabs the phone, right before it would've gone to voice mail. "Hel—" He hiccups. "Hello? Yes, this is Casey Merry. Uh-huh. Uh-huh. Yeah, it is a perfect last name for Christmas. Haha. Uh-huh." His eyes get wider by the second, then, "Wait, what?" He puts his phone on speaker. "Can you say that again? I just want to be sure I'm not making this up in some post-breakup fugue state."

"Oh, sweetheart," a feminine voices croons, oozing genuine empathy. "I'm so sorry to hear that. It sounds like this trip was perfectly timed then. Nothing like a little Christmas cheer to mend a broken heart. My name is Sandra, and I'm calling from Winter Wonderland to inform you that we had a booked guest pull out at the last minute. You've been selected in a lottery from our wait-list to take their place. You and your family will receive an all-expenses-paid trip to Winter Wonderland, the planet's only year-round Christmas island. This opportunity is good for our Twelve Days of Christmas package from December fourteenth through the twenty-sixth."

Casey's eyes are wider than the snow globe collection he has perched in bookshelves along the wall. This is the most coveted of Winter Wonderland packages. To actually get to celebrate Christmas *on Christmas Day* at the world's premier Christmas theme park? Even I know this is a get, and I'm the kind of guy who couldn't care less if Christmas were a thing.

"We've had a number of folks chosen before you turn us down because of previously scheduled holiday plans. But as long as you and your family are available, we'll have tickets overnighted to you. We'll need you to confirm within the hour. I'm sorry it's so last-minu—"

"We can make it!" I yell. That kind of emotional outburst is so unlike me that my cheeks instantly blaze. In a much more acceptable tone, I say again, "We can make it. Count the Merry family in."

Does spending the better part of two weeks in a constant state of Christmas sound miserable to me? Yes. But seeing Casey so devastated, I know it'll take something huge to knock him out of it. This seems like the most pragmatic thing to do.

"Oh, terrific!" Sandra cheers. "We can't wait to see you. I'll send over all the details right now. Just to make sure I have the correct email address, is Christmas Casey at Gmail dot com still accurate?"

Casey looks dazed, nodding at his phone like Sandra can see him.

"Yes," I say. "That's right."

"Fantastic," she trills. "We'll see you in just a couple weeks. Merry Christmas!"

She hangs up while Casey's mouth hangs wide open.

"You won the lottery," I say. "You've wanted to go to Winter Wonderland your whole life." It's been open for more than twenty years, but the tickets are way too expensive. Casey's always held out hope he'd someday be selected through the lottery, where the island pays for families to visit when someone backs out of their reservation. And now it's actually happened.

Casey looks to the mantle, where picture upon picture of him and Raquel sit side by side in holiday frames. He turns to me, tears in his eyes again, and grabs my hands.

"It's a Christmas miracle."

# Kris

"The song says, 'make the Yuletide gay,' and yet not a single boy who likes boys decided to pop into Winter Wonderland this last Twelve." I smack a palm against the handcrafted wooden cafeteria table. "I'm as good as losing this bet."

Other Chris nods along. "I know what you mean, man. Not even a glance my way this session. I swear poop scoop duty is cursed. No girl wants to kiss a guy they only see shoveling reindeer shit all day."

The gingerbread-decorated swinging doors burst open as the rest of our senior class marches into the cafeteria like their lives depend on it: Nicky Chen, Nick Berg, Noelle Marshall, Dasher Chadha, and Rudy Jankowski. I scan their faces to see if any of them looks triumphant. Noelle, no. Nick, no. Nicky, neither. Dasher looks pissed. And poor Rudy seems like he might cry. The tip of his pale nose gets bright red whenever he's upset, like the universe really wanted him to live up to his namesake reindeer.

But as terrible as it sounds, my heart skips a beat seeing all their scowling faces. It looks like no one had some tourist's undying love professed to them during the last Twelve. Visitors don't just stay for one night; they come for a full twelve days of Christmas so they can really escape into a holiday fantasy. A fantasy that usually results in mainlanders telling at least one of us that we're their soulmate.

Rudy plops onto the bench across from me and Chris. "Before anyone says it, I know I look like Rudolph." He pulls a Kleenex from his pocket and gives a big, wet blow into it. "That girl I paired up with caught a cold, and here we are." His eyes water a bit before he lets out a massive sneeze. "No love, but a lot of making out."

"Lucky," Chris mumbles.

"I was *this* close," Dasher says, holding his thumb and pointer finger just millimeters apart. "I thought I had it perfectly planned out at the MistleToast. We slow-danced to *every single slow song*, I positioned us perfectly under the mistletoe *five times*, and all she did was jam her tongue down my throat." He slams his messenger bag on the table before sitting next to Chris. "I feel so used."

Nicky huffs. "Do not even get me started on the caliber of boys we had to choose from. Disgusting." She glances between Chris, Rudy, and Dasher. "You should be ashamed of your straight-boy kind."

Noelle points at Nicky. "That part. I had to tell some guy *my eyes are up here* three times on Day One before I just threw in the towel."

We all turn to Nick for his tale of failure, but his head is buried in his phone. When he finally feels the pressure of six pairs of eyes on him, he looks up. "Oh, uh . . . I guess I just wasn't in it that much. I don't really need to win because . . . New York's not that great."

The rest of us moan, and Chris reaches across the table to throw one of Rudy's used tissues at Nick.

"Of course *you'd* say that," I snap. Nick not only won the first and third years of the Race, but his parents go off-island for the entire month of June every summer. His parents are the head Wonderland doctors, so their salaries are definitely higher than most of our parents'. Nick's been to New York, Tokyo, Los Angeles, and Orlando. Each year he comes back, and when the group's dying for stories on what the real world is like, he just shrugs and says, "It was fine."

Other than Noelle, who won the second Race, the rest of us have never left the island. Eighteen years old, and I've only ever seen the same forty square miles of planet Earth. I think for most people, it'd drive them bonkers, being stuck in the same place their entire life. I don't really mind it. I can see the literal boundaries of my world, and there's comfort in that. But the others hate it. They're desperate to win because they're desperate to see firsthand what life is like somewhere else. It's not cheap to get off this island, and most of our parents work for only minimum wage plus their guaranteed health care and faux-gingerbread housing.

Noelle adjusts the red and green headband in her coils. "If we don't get our act together, Anjelica won't be taking anybody to New York."

"My thoughts exactly."

We all look toward the gingerbread doors to see Anjelica there, poised as ever. Her light brown skin is covered in head-to-toe red, following the Winter Wonderland mandate of wearing only red and/or green on opening day for a new batch of visitors. She's got a red turtleneck bodysuit tucked into red leather pants, capped off with red Louboutin stiletto boots (that even have a red sole). The only thing not red is a green Fendi clutch, from which she pulls a tube of bright red lipstick to reapply. "You're all better than this."

She marches over to our table, the heads of the other three classes following her too. But Anjelica doesn't flinch or flaunt at the attention. She's got this magnetism to her that none of us can resist, this confidence that's undeniable. It's why I gravitated to her when she moved here three and a half years ago. That, and Christmas *doesn't* run in her blood, despite being Kringle's only kid. The open defiance makes me love her. She's my best friend and she knows it, but neither of us tries to voice that out loud because we both know she's just going to leave when we graduate in six months, while I stick around in Winter Wonderland.

As Anjie hovers over our table, she takes one quick look at Rudy and arches an eyebrow. "Rudy, baby, you're Patient Zero. If you infect everyone before the next guests even get here, we'll have no one to blame but you for ruining the last round of this competition."

You'd think after a worldwide pandemic we already would have thought that, but we were so focused on how we'd each failed in our own way, no one realized how Rudy could ruin it for all of us. We scramble to get up from the table, and Rudy covers a cough as he stands first. "I get it, I get it," he says. "I'll stop by the Ho-Ho on the way home." Winter Wonderland likes to give cutesy names to potentially Christmas buzz-killing necessities, like a hospital. It's called the Ho-Ho-Hospital to make customers think of Santa instead of the compound fracture they might get in an ice-skating accident. Islanders call it the Ho-Ho for short.

Anjelica twinkles her red-manicured fingers. "Love you." She doesn't say it like a Grinch. You can tell she means it; she just knows how to get to blunt business. Like she does now, when she takes an apple-cider-scented sanitizer and sprays it all over Rudy's former seat before taking it herself. "Speaking of love, what is with all of you? We've never made it to *Christmas* without anyone becoming the object of some mainlander's affection. I guess I should call Hugh Grant right now and tell him that love actually *isn't* all around."

Everyone groans while I give Anjelica some serious side-eye. "Oh god, Anjie, no."

"You know our golden rule is no Christmas puns," Noelle adds.

It's this thing that happens when you grow up in Winter Wonderland. Our parents moved here because they were obsessed with the holiday. They eat, sleep, breathe, and *pun* Christmas. We've lived around it our whole lives, so it's not magical to us. It just is. But even though she's the daughter of Kris Kringle, Anjelica knows a whole world that's entirely un-Christmas, so she still thinks it's clever when she drops a "fun" pun. We all think it's sappy-parent-level cringe.

"Oh, excuse me," Anjelica singsongs. "I don't think you'll mind my cleverness so much when I sweeten the pot on our deal."

That gets everyone to shut up.

Anjelica leans in, the rest of us scooching closer. "Daddy's up to something. Something big. A *second* Winter Wonderland. He's scouting locations to buy an entire neighborhood in a major city that will be Christmas all year round. But as soon as word gets out about job openings, you know what will happen."

"They'll be flooded with applications," I say. It's exactly

what happened when Kris Kringle called for the first Wonderers to move to the island. Hundreds of thousands of Christmas fanatics applied for the positions to work here.

Anjelica grins. "Exactly. Imagine how great it would be if you could impress him right to his face and prove you can bring the soul of Winter Wonderland to the new location. I mean, you've lived here your whole life. Who better to lead the way in a second spot?"

"I could live in a city," Chris says. "A city full of girls."

Nicky clears her throat.

"Sorry," Chris corrects. "Women."

"And on the mainland," Dasher adds. "We could go anywhere we want on our time off."

Anjelica's offering them the perfect way to get off the island for good. Mainlanders assume that should be easy. They think we can just hop a flight on Kringle Air to whatever city we want and go from there. But the thing is, that just doesn't happen for the majority of Wonderers. When our parents got the opportunity to move here, it's like they won the lottery. A job for the rest of their lives, one handed directly to their children too, and that health care and housing extend to their kids, and their kids' kids, and so on. Kris Kringle wanted to create a true feeling of family on the island, and with his serious Santa complex, he wanted to provide what he saw as the greatest gift of all. My parents were so grateful that they named me after him. The job placement was especially needed for them because Mom had just been forced to shut down her bakery, and Dad was getting fewer and fewer substitute-teaching gigs.

What our parents didn't realize was a gift for them feels like a prison for most of their kids. Before Uncle Toby left, I would have said I wasn't one of those people; I liked the comfort of knowing I'm good at everything here. That we had a place here. The wider world is a massive unknown, and why would I want to voluntarily throw myself into something I may potentially bomb in? If I can get Uncle Toby back here, everything will be perfect again. But now that the Race comes with the potential for a life outside the island, I know my class-mates are going to go extra hard to get someone to drop the L-word this next Twelve.

And if they do it first, I may never see my uncle again.

Nick, of course, doesn't care about the added stakes. "*That's* the best you can do to sweeten the pot?" He scoffs. "Seriously, the mainland's overrated."

"Shut up!" Dasher, Chris, Nicky, and Noelle all shout.

"But the only way to get that job is by using your Christmas magic to make someone fall in love with you," Anjelica says. "For the winner, the trip to New York will give you a taste of your new life once you get the gig."

The bell for classes rings with the opening notes of

"Jingle Bells." The other tables all hop up, while us seniors sit in stunned silence.

Finally, Chris's face breaks into his full-toothed lovable himbo smile.

"Oh, it's on."

# Aaron

Kringle Air is a trip. Each seat is a cushy, lie-flat business-class pod reconfigured to look like Santa's sleigh. Curly gold writing swirls across the maroon sides to designate seat assignments. Red and green accent lights reflect off the sparkly walls and floor, which look like they could be made of tinsel or, like, North Pole magic or something. "It's Beginning to Look a Lot Like Christmas" plays over the speakers, mixing with *oohs* and *aahs* every time someone walks through the boarding doors and takes it all in.

It just gives me a headache.

I plop down into seat 4A and dig through my backpack for my pill case. Casey glances over from across the aisle, knowing my overly planning ways mean I've got a supplement in here for everything he could need. "Can I pop a melatonin, bro? I was up all night, too excited for our trip. I felt like a kid before Christmas." He laughs, but it's not as loud or carefree as usual. Still, it's a start. I think the

Christmas spirit is slowly but surely helping him move on. Or maybe he's trying to spare us the truth and really was awake crying his eyes out because this fantasy is coming true but Raquel's not in it. "That's pretty on the nose, huh?"

"On the *Rudolph* nose?" a syrupy sweet voice says, followed by the jingling of bells. I look up to find our flight attendant—whose name tag reads *Zelda*—pointing to a bright red clown nose—er, reindeer nose, I guess—and hamming it up. She's got jingle bells for buttons and a candy cane pen poised over a notepad. "Anything to drink before takeoff? Hot cocoa? Eggnog?"

"Eggnog, please," Casey orders.

"Just water for me," I say.

Zelda gives the briefest of frowns before jotting down our drinks and looking at Casey with a mischievous grin. "How 'bout some extra Christmas cheer in your nog?"

"Yes, plea—"

Dad reaches through the open partition between their sleighs to whack Casey on the shoulder. "You're not twenty-one, big guy." To Zelda's credit, with Casey being so tall and having so much facial hair, he's always looked about five years older than he actually is.

"Just the virgin eggnog for him," Dad says. "And I'll take a cocoa with peppermint schnapps if you've got it."

"Right away, sir." Zelda heads to the galley while I grab a pill for Casey from the slot labeled *M* for *melatonin* and from *A* for *Advil* for me. We gulp them down when Zelda hands us our drinks. Casey picks up his seat's Christmas tree–shaped remote complete with ornament buttons and flips through the in-flight-movie options. The farther he gets through the list, the deeper his scowl gets.

"What is it?" I ask.

Casey stabs his tree at the screen. "I've got a memory with Raquel for every single one of these." He pulls up *Elf.* "She'd always answer the phone screaming *Santa!* like Buddy does." He highlights *The Grinch.* "She taught herself how to apply body makeup so she could turn me into the Grinch for a Whoville costume contest." Then *Love Actually.* "And I promposed using the giant flash cards from this. *To me, you are perfect.*"

I've heard him say that line to Raquel a million times. He slinks back in his chair, tears welling in his eyes again.

"Hey, buddy," Dad coos. But his eyes go wide as he realizes he said the infamous elf's name. We both know it'd be easy to accidentally push Casey deeper into Raquel regrets. "I mean, sport." Dad glances at me and cringes. "It's going to hurt, and that's okay. You've got to feel that before you move on."

"Yeah, like you did?" Casey says with a little too much venom, which really isn't fair to Dad. He was left just like Case and I were when Mom decided she didn't like her life anymore. She was tired of Southern California, tired of her job heading up an insurance company, tired of family life in general, I guess. She told us she was moving to Wisconsin to work at a cranberry bog, and whoever wanted in could join her. It was so sudden, so spur of the moment, it didn't feel right. Dad agreed with me. We liked the sun and the availability of things to do in Orange County, not to mention Dad loved and still loves his gig as a Realtor selling the beach home dream. Casey was the closest to going with her. The thought of getting real snow every year heavily appealed to him, and cranberries are used in so many holiday things that he was pretty torn. But love won out. He couldn't leave Raquel. So Mom left us all, divorce papers sent to Dad a few weeks later.

Dad was stunned; we all were. But Dad's surprise turned him into a zombie. It's not that he was depressed, necessarily. It was more like he didn't know how to do things around the house: couldn't fold a sheet to save his life, could barely boil water, failing at all these things that were a breeze for Mom. Dad's great at turning a dilapidated old bedroom into a stunning in-home theater, but day-to-day chores? Not so much. So that's where I stepped in. Once it was clear to Dad and Casey that I'd pick up the pieces Mom left in her wake, Dad just sort of moved on. We never saw him cry over the divorce. Casey's mentioned to me more than once that he thinks it's weird we never saw Dad break down when they split, always doubting it was true love if he couldn't even shed a tear.

"Hey." Dad's voice gets deep when he wants to signal

we're on the verge of crossing the line. "We each handle our hurt in different ways. Mine was making sure life went on for you boys."

I was the one who did that for *them*, but I'm not here to make the situation worse. Besides, being so focused gave me purpose; it helped me move on. So much so that I could eventually text Mom little things like how stupid it was that our electric company's website is always down and you have to call in to pay the bill, or how the local grocery store manager must be a boob man because the number of times he has new custom sales signs for chicken breasts is bordering on a fetish.

Our texting opened the door enough that when Mom comes back for Casey's and my birthdays, it's not like we haven't spoken in months. Although her past few texts checking in on Case have started to get pretty annoying. I've been this close to snapping back: **Why don't you ask him yourself?**

Now Dad and Case look on the verge of snapping themselves. Casey sniffs and stares into his eggnog while Dad downs his drink and asks Zelda for another cocoa, but "make it a double." The way they avoid eye contact makes me question my choice to seat them next to each other. The whole point of this trip was to get Casey out of his funk, not make it worse and have Dad get all butt hurt as an extra helping of crap I'll have to clean up.

"Okay, look," I say, just as the captain comes over the

speakers with a *Ho ho ho* to say the reindeer have all been harnessed and we're ready to take flight. It takes everything in me not to roll my eyes as we push back and taxi down the runway. I've got to fake being the excited activities director to make sure we walk out of this trip happy and in the holiday spirit. "I know in the ideal world, you'd want Raquel with us."

Casey nods over and over, a desperate, dumped bobblehead. "I would."

"Sadly"—I reach across the aisle and grab his hand—"that's not going to happen. It wasn't your fault and it's not fair. But it would be even more unfair if you let this breakup completely ruin your love of Christmas. You've adored it forever, and I want to remind you of that. I promise I'll be by your side for the next twelve days, doing every last holiday thing you want to do. By the end of this vacation, you'll have all-new memories about all things Christmas. Will they replace your memories with Raquel? Of course not. But it might help, Case. If you let it."

Am I really that confident? No. Casey's only ever had one girlfriend, so I'm not entirely sure what it's going to take to get him to move on. But sometimes when you're the only person who has their shit together, you've got to give orders to get people to fall in line.

Casey's eyes well with tears; his lip trembles. "You mean it, bro?"

"Of course I do."

Casey unbuckles his seat belt and flings himself across the aisle to hug the air out of my lungs, just as the plane takes off.

Zelda is not having it, but I've got to give her credit for keeping up her holiday spirit as she scolds Case over the speakers.

"Please remain in your sleigh until Santa turns off the fasten-seat-belt sign."

# Kris

"I can't believe this is going to be your last Christmas Twelve before you graduate," Mom says, using the title for the Twelve that falls over the actual holiday, when people seem to get extra high off Christmas cheer, including our parents. She picks a piece of nonexistent fluff off my green Winter Wonderland jacket before cupping my face in her palms. "You are so handsome."

"Mom, seriously, this isn't a big deal. I'll have many more Christmas Twelves in my future. It's not like I'm moving away or anything." Especially not after I win this thing and reunite our family.

The oven timer goes off, and she shuffles over to take out her latest batch of cookies. Mom is one of the Mrs. Clauses on the island, working at the bakery. She takes her job extremely seriously, always trying out new recipes to see if they should add them to the menu.

"And good thing too," Mom continues, spatula-ing a few

gingerbread men onto a plate. "I don't know what is with all you kids hating Christmas so much." She takes out her disbelief by snapping a little baked dude in half, handing me the torso. "Try this. Blood orange and cranberry mixed into the usual recipe."

I bite into it. The cookie has that crisp snap, as always. Mom is another member of the family who really upholds the Bright reputation of kicking ass at Christmas. She's an only child from a small but mighty Italian family, but her parents passed away before I was even born. Mom says she learned all her culinary tricks from Nonna, which she's used to bake everything perfectly for the holidays, giving her creations that expert mix of spices and sweet that have the distinct flavor of Christmas.

"I definitely don't hate this, and we don't hate Christmas." I take a swig of the milk Mom pours me, ever the Mrs. Claus knowing a cookie can't be had without an ice-cold mug of it. "It's just, you know, *weird* to be obsessed with a holiday."

Thank god for social media, or else none of us would have a sense of what normal people act like. Nicky and Noelle obsess over fashion accounts, Dasher has all his athletes he admires, Rudy's got the travel vloggers he can't get enough of, a whole map pinned on his bedroom wall of the places he's going to go when he graduates. The irony, though, is that if we start our own accounts, *we* get followed by all the Holiday Heads fantasizing over our lives.

I set my profiles to private years ago, but some of the locals have huge followings showing the "magic" of Winter Wonderland, which Kringle Korp encourages. Liam, a guy who graduated in the year ahead of us, is probably the most famous Wonderer. He has like half a million followers, thanks to his footage of practicing flash mob dances and hockey training sessions. Both heavily feature his ass, and honestly, I get the hype.

"Well, I'm just thankful that you're going to stay here," Mom says. "You're too good at Christmas to leave. It's in your blood."

"The other thing that's in my blood is my gayness, but they don't seem to like that so much here, do they?" I snap.

Mom's face falls, and I instantly regret it. She is not the problem. Both she and Dad were super supportive the second I came out to them freshman year. They even went overboard, finding rainbow-patterned stockings for all three of us that Christmas, and asking maintenance Elves to change out the solid white lights decorating our company-provided gingerbread cottage with multicolored ones instead.

"Oh, honey," Mom coos, trying to bring my head to her shoulder, which is always a struggle seeing as how I'm eight inches taller than her. "Do you really feel that way? Like you can't be yourself here?" She gets serious, her mouth forming a thin line, that ever-present holiday cheer dropping out of her voice. "I don't want you to leave like Tobias."

When I don't say anything, she asks, "Is this about gay Santa again?" I can already tell by her tone that today is not going to be the day she sees the light. She says as much when she adds, "I guess I just don't fully understand your passion for this, sweetheart. You know I want to. But isn't it okay if some characters are just straight? You wouldn't love me or your dad any less because we aren't gay, right? I don't want you to be straight. Why can't we let Santa be who he is?"

I can never find an answer to this question that doesn't make me sound whiny or self-centered or—in the biggest of ironies considering where we are—like a snowflake. When the call to add a gay Santa to the Wonderland lineup was first made, the term "snowflake" was the one most used against us by the internet trolls. They thought they were *so* clever.

"It's different, Mom," I say. "I know that seems like a cop-out, but I promise you I'm going to find a way to explain it. Maybe even to Kris Kringle himself."

"Now, Kris." Mom laughs nervously. Because here's the thing about the "wonder" of Winter Wonderland: Kringle Korp makes no bones about being able to take away the life they've given us. Too many missteps, or one major foot out of line, and they won't hesitate to give you the boot if you ruin the magic of Christmas. Everyone who moved here sees the opportunity as such a gift, they would do anything to protect it, especially seeing as how Kringle prioritized hiring "good people who are just down on their luck but have never lost that Christmas cheer."

"Let's not be hasty," Mom says, trying to say it with a smile, but it comes out wonky. Then her face softens and she adds, "I love you more than anything, sweetheart."

"Love you too." The mechanical sounds of our dancing Santa in the living room make their way to the kitchen, accompanied by "Walking in a Winter Wonderland" playing over its tinny speaker. Every Wonderer's home has one. The songs good ol' Saint Nick dances to tell us what we're needed for.

"That's our cue," Mom says, rushing to the front door and grabbing her frilly red and green Mrs. Claus jacket off the coat rack.

"Yep," I say. "Christmas waits for no one."

Okay, there actually *is* something nice about the first day of every Twelve. There's this energy in the air as visitors point and grin their faces off at everything they see. It's amped by a magnitude of ten today as people freak out that they get to be here over Christmas. It's the only time of year that the energy is greater than the summer Twelves, when Holiday Heads go gaga over the fact that there's snow here all year round, even in the middle of July.

To me, snow is just another trapping that I see day in and day out, like the dozens of gingerbread cottages for guests and Wonderers, or the penguin dances in the cove on the southern tip of the island. Technically, penguins should feel exotic, since they aren't native to the Northern Hemisphere, but you can only watch one waddle so many times before you're like, "Meh." But for the thousand arriving guests, all this is magic. There's a twinkle in their eyes, a constant laugh in the air as they take it all in. Gleeful shouts of "Look over there!" and "How is this real?" and "It's Santa!" are more noticeable to me than the holiday soundtrack that plays over the Santa's Square speakers 24-7. It's truly pure joy, and even if I know how this whole sausage is made, I like being a small part of this moment. Uncle Toby always says this is his favorite part, seeing people forget about their worries and just get lost in it all. I don't know that that's necessarily the healthiest way to avoid your problems, but it is hard to stay so Scroogey when you see this many people genuinely happy.

At least there's one perk to the Race that makes me pretty happy too. Typically, the tourists we pair off with—or at least the ones I pair off with—want to kiss. Like Nathaniel, who made out with me hard and fast. The only thing I'm better at than Christmas is kissing. I love the way it lights up every single atom of my being when another person just wants to connect over lips. It's entirely on them if that leads to real feelings. For me, it's all about the physicality. Besides, I don't even think love actually exists. If I can get someone to feel it just from a perfectly planned date—one I've been on dozens of times before, I might add—then the emotion can't be real. It's just a hormonal response to external stimulus, and I happen to be an excellent stimulator.

Not to sound like a douche or anything.

I scan the crowd in Santa's Square and try to catch eyes with any guy who might be checking me out. There's only one problem: Chris. He's standing right next to me, and he's objectively hot. He's got that bed head that looks intentional, these deep brown eyes that are irresistible, light brown skin that's always blemish free, and don't even get me started on his dimples. He kissed me once freshman year because, as he put it, "How will I know I'm not into dudes if I never kiss one?" I've got to hand it to him, he really committed. From light kisses to full-on tongue, he tried it for about a solid four minutes before he gently pulled back, patted my hand, and sweetly said, "Nope. It's all ladies for me." But it was one of the greatest four minutes of my life.

All that to say, the two guys I see looking our direction could be looking at me, *or*, more likely, they're looking at Chris. I've got to move.

I take a couple steps away from him while he also scans

the crowd for a date. But the second he hears my boot hit cobblestone, Chris whips his head my way. "Hey, where are you going?"

"You're too hot!"

"Um, I'm . . . sorry?" I can tell he really means it. He's peak adorable jock, and I shouldn't snap at him.

"No, my bad, Chris. It's just, how am I going to find my match if I can't tell whether someone's trying to flirt with me or you?"

"But how am I supposed to lift you if you're clear across the square?"

"Don't worry. I'll do a few leaps once the music starts and be back before our cue."

The tourists know they're in for a big welcoming musical number thanks to all the former visitors who've posted it online. But they don't know the exact moment when it'll happen. It's the first of six holiday flash mobs we do every Twelve, switching up the holiday classic from "Walking in a Winter Wonderland" to "Welcome You to Winter Wonderland." For our part of the routine, Chris lifts me on his shoulders, and we sing "We're happy tonight" in the opening verse.

But first, boys. Sure enough, when I leave Chris behind, the guys checking "us" out were actually ogling him. Here's hoping they aren't the only two gays in this cohort.

People swarm the square, getting their first real look at Winter Wonderland. Here in town, the buildings are all deep-red wood with green and gold accents, stained-glass windows of polar bears or elves, and massive candy cane streetlamps. There's a lot to look at, and as far as I can tell, everyone's checking out the sights (or Chris) and definitely not me.

I hop onto the lip of the fountain in the center of Santa's Square to try to get a better vantage point. An outrageously tall, scruffy white guy glances my way, but as soon as we lock eyes, his wander to the side. I can't help but keep staring, though. His cheeks are puffy and tearstained, and he's got the biggest basset hound frown I've ever seen in Winter Wonderland. People are all smiles and amazement when they get here, but this guy looks like he's been told Christmas has been canceled. Who died, right?

Oh shit, maybe someone actually *did* die. I'll find out who this guy is and alert the Head Elves—the Wonderers who oversee and arrange all guest experiences—that we've got a visitor who needs some extra cheer.

The opening notes to "Welcome" play, and I jump off the fountain. I do a few leaps and skips to get to Chris just as Nicky and Noelle sing "Sleigh bells ring" to kick off the rest of the townies in our routine.

"There's my boy," Chris says as I arrive right on time, lifting me up on top of his shoulders in one fluid movement. It's pretty impressive, seeing as how I'm 190 pounds, but Chris makes it seem like I'm as light as a feather. He's got a solid linebacker build, but unfortunately we're the only school on this island, so other than low-stakes hockey games with visitors, organized sports aren't really a thing here. The guys who were checking Chris out swoon, no doubt picturing him sweeping them off their feet. Dammit, why can't they look at me like that?!

I hear Nick and Anjelica over the speakers sing "A beautiful sight," leading me and Chris to throw our arms wide and really ham it up. "We're happy toniiiiiight." It always gets a laugh, and I glance over at the tall sad sack to see him give the slightest smile. Good. So he *can* be cheered up.

As other townies from the bakers at Mrs. Claus's Masterpieces (including Mom) to our teachers (including Dad) to the North Pole nurses of the Ho-Ho (who've hopefully given Rudy something to keep him from ruining this competition) belt out the rest of the lyrics, those of us who've already sung are supposed to mingle among the crowd. We get visitors to dance along as every Wonderer joins in on the remixed lyric of "We'd like to welcome you to Winter Wonderland." This is my chance to head over to the sad guy and get him to smile a bit more.

I do a few slide steps and am next to him in no time. He glances down at me and seems surprised that I've stopped in front of him. When I make clear eye contact and sing the welcome line, he grins. He wipes a tear from his cheek and lets out a weak little chuckle. Which only makes me lean into it harder.

We take a ton of dance classes for our choreographed flash mobs. But in moments like this when we're supposed to improvise, I've found that nine times out of ten, guests prefer if you make them laugh. I always end up going full-on jokester, like now when I turn around and shake my ass. Sad Boy lets out a hearty guffaw and even mimics slapping my butt. Mission accomplished.

The number's almost over, and I'm supposed to shimmy back to the fountain, where all the townies gather to belt a final "Winter Wonderland." But as I take my first step, I see a guy who looks an awful lot like Sad Boy, only shorter and clean shaven. He's running in the little alley between the Festive Flicks movie theater and the bakery. He looks frazzled, maybe because he's missed about 95 percent of the opening flash mob. Then he slips, and that frazzled goes to full-on panic. We Elves do our best to deice the place, especially the main walkways, and the cobblestones all have heaters underneath to prevent accidents. But occasionally those heaters go on the fritz, which must have happened in the alley. Slip Boy could crash and break a bone, or barrel into the gathered townies and knock them over like bowling pins. We could have a very public disaster, putting a terrible ending on what's supposed to be a warm welcome. I've got to catch him.

I step into his path and brace myself for the impending collision, throwing my arms out to intercept this wayward visitor. We've got about two seconds to impact.

What I don't see coming is just how much he flails his hands. My plan works, though, and I'm able to wrap my arms around him so he doesn't fall, saving him and all my neighbors.

Too bad I couldn't save myself.

Because those flailing fists punch me right in the face.

# Aaron

It was *Advil PM*! I can't believe I didn't check the bottle better before packing the medicine in my pill case. If I hadn't accidentally drugged myself, I wouldn't be clocking this guy in the nose!

It's the latest in a string of disasters since popping this pill. I just about face-planted into the prime rib and mashed potatoes with hot apple pie Zelda served on the plane; after we landed, I snoozed through our reindeer-pulled carriage ride to our gingerbread cabin on Blitzen Boulevard; and when I sat on my bed to regain my composure, I woke up two hours later with drool slipping into my pillow. I promised Casey I'd be by his side for everything, and I'm already breaking my promise!

"Oh my god, I'm so sorry!" I scream directly into my victim's face, but there's no time to worry about volume control. My problem-solver instinct kicks in, and I swipe away the trickle of blood slipping down his upper lip with a bit of my shirtsleeve. "I know I've got tissues in here somewhere." I unzip my jacket pocket and reach for the travel-size pack of Kleenex waiting inside.

I pop out a tissue and rip off a chunk that I smoosh into a tiny, pellet-shaped wad and shove into this guy's nose. He winces, but it isn't until I'm gently checking to make sure the wad is good and up there that I realize I'm acting like he's my four-year-old son.

I whip my hand back into my pocket. "Sorry. Sorry. Oh god. Sorry."

The guy grins. Even though it's partially hidden by the bit of Kleenex sticking out of his nostril, I can tell it's forced.

"It's fine, really," he says, his voice a little stuffy, no doubt from the blood that *I* made fill his nasal cavities.

"No, it's not," I insist. "We should have you checked by a nurse. There's the Ho-Ho-Hospital here, right? I read about it on the website. I'll walk you. Let's go."

I move to take a step, all business, but then remember I'm still looking *up* at this guy, up from the embrace of his arms. His grip is sturdy, and I realize he didn't let go to check on his nose even after it was crunched by my fist. He's been taking care of me this whole time, and that has never happened once in my life. I'm the caretaker, not the other way around. When I sprained my ankle in tennis practice last year, I drove *myself* to urgent care.

But here this guy is, cradling me in his arms. I look into

his eyes, and that's when *it* happens. First, everything around us goes out of focus. All I can see are his dark brown irises, the olive tone of his skin, the close-crop shave of his haircut, the way his green jacket hugs his biceps. I feel the weight of his arm beneath me, how he's not even shaking one bit despite the fact that he's been holding me up all this time. I feel his long fingers splayed out on my back, proving that yes, this coat is too thin for literally zero degrees, but the warmth that blooms in my cheeks is enough to wash away any cold. When my eyes drift to his plump, pink bottom lip, bubbles burst in my gut, deep in my belly, and my heart starts to race.

Oh no. I know this feeling.

I'm getting a crush. I have to tamp this down just like the handful of others I've felt in the past. Feelings lead to heartache, i.e., the whole reason I'm on this secluded holiday island to piece my devastated brother back together.

But god, this is going to be difficult. Even though I know that forming any sort of attachment is a bad idea, it takes everything in me not to crane my neck upward to bring my mouth close to his. All those magnetic feelings Casey's talked about when you finally touch someone and your body just reacts all on its own are actually happening. Sure, I've crushed before, but I've never had physical contact with a crush until now, and . . . wow, it's wild. I've got electric tingles so strong I'm sure I could power every

Christmas light on this whole slab of land.

"Come on, let's get you back on your feet."

Casey comes in and grabs my hand, yanking me up and ending the internal fireworks as soon as they started.

Oh crap, Casey. Casey, my sad older brother who I'm here with so he can get out of his relationship funk. I can't give in to crushes when intimacy is the last thing I should be focusing on. It'd just be salt in the wound for Casey if sparks fly for me when they were involuntarily extinguished for him.

But still, I can't stop staring.

"Who knew my brother had such a right hook on him?" Casey says. "And he's not wrong. We should take you to see a nurse. Just to make sure you're okay."

"No!"

The word pops out of me so suddenly that both Casey and my rescuer jump. My cheeks flare, but I'm not entirely sure it's from embarrassment. It could very well be because my nose-punching victim is now looking directly at me, and my body doesn't know what to do under his gaze.

Casey frowns. "No?" It's the exact opposite of the problem-solver brother he knows. The exact opposite of my suggestion just seconds ago that we should go to the Ho-Ho-Hospital.

Meanwhile, this Winter Wonderland worker is looking at me like I'm the biggest prick on the planet. Which, honestly, I might be, but I know if I walk him to the hospital, I'm definitely going to end up kissing him. I'm sure of it. My mind is beeping and booping now, and all calculations know that this buzzing in my body is going to win out over my brain. Then I'd be shoving romance—or at least *heavy feelings*—right in Casey's face. How is this possible? Who am I right now? I'm supposed to be the Robot!

"It's just that I'm sure you've got other Wonderland duties, and we don't want to keep you, or, or, or . . ." Why can't I shut up? "Or get you in trouble or anything. I don't want to make it worse."

My rescuer takes out the wad of tissue from his nostril— its upper half a dark red that matches his turtleneck—and tentatively feels his nose.

"There's no more blood," I say.

The guy presses harder without even a wince. "The pain's fading, so there's that," he says. "We're all good. Welcome to Winter Wonderland."

He turns, but just before he steps away, I blurt, "Thanks."

He glances back, his thick eyebrow quirked in question. But I can't figure out how to voice just what it is I'm thankful for. For saving my ass. For making my brother laugh again, like I heard in the alleyway seconds before I slipped. For giving me that undeniable *holy shit I'm into you* feeling after he caught me in his very sturdy arms.

Since I can't figure out how to voice any of that without

sounding like a creep, I mutter, "For everything."

"Don't mention it."

"What's your name?" Casey asks. "I don't recognize you from any Wonderer social accounts."

I cringe. Way to come across like a totally obsessed holiday fanatic from the start. I mean, Casey *is* that, but he doesn't have to make it so painfully obvious.

"Kris," my rescuer/victim says. "Kris Bright."

Casey laughs that guffaw of his. "No way. I'm Casey, and this is my brother, Aaron, and our last name is Merry. Together we're Merry and Bright. Maybe we're meant to be best buds. Or it's a sign I should move here." He snaps his mouth closed, clamming up.

Oh shit. *Signs.* Signs were Raquel's thing. She was always looking for cosmic clues that she was on the right track. Or Christmas miracles. She always said those were nudges from Santa that were supposed to set her on the correct path. And I know for sure that Casey's now totally thinking about how Raquel would interpret this. Which, of course, means he wishes he could just straight up ask her. I can practically see him fall into the rabbit hole of despair.

"It just might be," Kris says, before turning on his heel and booking it out of there. He seems hurried now, and I don't blame him. It's best that he go before Casey gets extremely sad again. Or before I end up punching him for a second time, or worse, start crushing on him even harder. He walks away and, oh god, his backside looks just as good as his front.

I'm toast.

# Kris

I've lost the Race. I'm sure of it. As soon as I left the not-so-Merry brothers, there were no gays to be found. That's the problem when you get only a thousand guests at a time. Sometimes it's like an entire queer friend group traveling together, so there's a whole gaggle of gays. Other times, you get just a handful. Or there are times when it's all queer adults, and this competition is not meant to be creepy or illegal or nonconsensual in any way. The number one rule of the island is to always make a guest happy, but you can absolutely say no when it comes to your body or love life or any of that. And for the guests too. If they make it clear they're not into dating us or having a fling, you let it drop. This is all just about having good ole-fashioned flirty fun, which is definitely not something that's going to happen for me now.

To make matters worse, everyone else in the Fling Ring seems to be making headway. Nicky and Noelle have partnered up and are going on a double date with a couple guys to a gift-wrapping class. Nick, Dasher, and Chris are currently surrounded by a whole army of girls outside Festive Flicks, and you can tell at least one of the guys is going to be making out with a mainlander during tonight's showing of *Holiday in Handcuffs*. That leaves Rudy and me lagging in the rear, but that's because Rudy's been put on bedrest while I'm just . . . gay. Yet another reason why it'd be great to have a gay Santa, so that at no point could any queer person come to the island and feel like they're the only one who's a part of the LGBTQ+ family. Even if no other queer guests came to the island, they'd always have gay Santa to let them know they're not alone.

But for now, I'm stuck sulking in Santa's Square, catching the reflections of the golden statues of Santa and Mrs. Claus in the heated fountain, their smiles mocking me with aggressive straightness. The metal elves surrounding them all stare with frozen creepy grins that I douse with an angry splash.

"Shove it."

"What's got your stockings in a twist?"

Anjelica makes her way across the square, never missing a beat as she dodges visitors and walks over the cobblestones in her heels.

"Your stupid game, that's what."

"You're not supposed to frown around the guests, you

know," Anjelica says. "That's like rule number one on this island."

"Easy for you to say. You can break every rule and still have a life outside this place that doesn't hinge on your level of Christmas spirit."

But she's right. Part of always making a guest happy is to never let the magic of the holidays slip, and frowns definitely count as slipping.

Anjelica's small smile typically never falters. She gives off so much cool-girl confidence, refusing to let anyone ever see her sweat. Noelle once told me she thinks Anjelica believes expressing any kind of emotion around other people makes her weak, but I know that's not it at all. Anjelica's been trained, hounded by the paparazzi her whole life. They've followed her mom everywhere, and, by extension, Anjelica. Any look of distress, any tear, gets analyzed in the press, people thinking her life is theirs for the taking. So she doesn't drop that cool confidence. Ever. Even after the Maserati incident.

Unless it's just the two of us.

She looks over both shoulders to make sure everyone's too enamored with the North Pole vibes to eavesdrop, then takes an Hermès scarf from her bag and wipes down the edge of the fountain before sitting. When she looks at me, her smirk is gone and her eyes crease with worry.

"This is about Uncle Toby, isn't it?" she asks.

I nod. "I'm completely failing at my last shot to get his

job back. Without the Race, what am I going to do?"

Anjelica sighs. "God, I wish Daddy hadn't taken my credit card."

Anjie knows the ins and outs of the Uncle Toby situation. As soon as she heard that he wasn't picked for the open Santa spot, she vowed to call her dad right then and there and demand he call an emergency board meeting to tell them all what homophobic shits they were. That obviously went nowhere. But Anjie did gather the few other queer Wonderers at her place to rally support. When Uncle Toby arrived, he told all of us to stand down. He said if any one of us made a big deal about this—created a social media campaign, started protests, anything at all—he'd never forgive us. He didn't want to become the poster child for progress in Winter Wonderland. His whole life's goal since moving to this island genuinely was to be the best at Christmas and become Santa, letting people get lost in the fantasy of magic and generosity that the holiday figure creates. But if his face—Santa-like or not—became associated with some scandal, nobody would ever be able to get lost in that fantasy when they saw him. Even if he then got hired as the first gay Santa, people wouldn't see Santa; they'd see Tobias Bright, the gay man the company refused to hire until they eventually caved. That was his worst nightmare. Well, second worst, after not getting the Santa spot to begin with.

"You know I'd pay for a ticket for you to see my old man right now if I could," Anjelica says.

"I know." And she would too. But after her big display of debauchery, Anjelica was banished to freeze in Winter Wonderland, and her funds were frozen too. No credit card. No spending cash. Just the meager wages we get for time spent in flash mobs, or serving coffee at the café, or working the registers in Santa's Workshop. For being *Elves*. The Race is our only option, since Kris Kringle pays for a friend to fly with Anjie back home for spring break. Anjie suggested rigging the Race and getting the rest of the Fling Ring in on sending me, but I quickly squashed that idea. I truly do care for the rest of my class with all my heart, but I know how much an opportunity off the island means to them. If even one of them got upset about me getting special treatment, they could blab online, blab to their parents, tell any wrong person, and my whole plan to help my uncle could go public, exactly what Uncle Toby doesn't want. Somehow, even though Winter Wonderland is the wrongdoer, Uncle Toby could still be the one hurt the most in all this.

Anjelica stands, towering over me in her stick-thin heels. "Come on. I've got something to cheer you up."

The ride out to Anjelica's house is always a thrill. Most of us can just walk the few blocks to our family's little gingerbread cabin from anywhere in town. They're the same two-story, three-bedroom, three-bath configuration that all our visitors stay in. Anjelica's, however, is on the northern part of the island, and you can get there only by snowmobile. She uses the private lanes reserved for workers going about Wonderland business, and she takes them like we're being chased by Krampus. If my hair wasn't shaved into a tight buzz cut, it'd be whipping in the wind, like Anjelica's does right now, nearly taking my eyes out in the process.

I'm always impressed whenever I pull up to Anjie's place. It's massive. Six bedrooms, six baths, and seven thousand square feet. Essentially a gingerbread palace. It's right on the water too, which means sometimes she gets a killer view of humpbacks on their migratory swims.

Most Wonderers say having a house this grand is a perk of being the founder's daughter and can't really be considered exile. But they don't look at the whole situation. How much of a perk is it to be without any family, even if you do live on the one and only mansion on the island? It's just Anjie and her butler inside these massive gingerbread walls. Her mom stays out in New York with her dad, or goes to their chateau in France, or back home to Colombia. Winter Wonderland is too secluded for Mrs. Pérez-Kringle, and she supported moving her daughter to this island to reform Anjelica's party-girl ways. But the permanent glint in Anjie's eyes hints those ways will never entirely be gone.

Anjelica's shoes echo on the hardwood as we enter her house. It's an open floor layout, and steel-framed windows on the far side look onto the water that's beginning to ice over. A fire pit roars just outside, the flames bright against the deep dark of the night sky.

"Follow me." She clicks over to an elegant Christmas-tree-shaped bar, yanks on an ornament to open it, and pulls out a bottle of brandy. Without saying a word, she saunters to the kitchen and snags a carton of eggnog from the fridge, then two mugs from a nearby cupboard.

Anjie hoists the brandy bottle and says, "Want some?"

She knows I don't drink, but she always makes me turn her down first. "I'll pass."

Drinking just makes people seem like bigger asses than they already are. When this guy Leith told me last year he loved me (in second place for the competition by *thirteen minutes*), he was wasted. Yet another reason why I don't think love is real. Not only can glitz and glam make you feel it, but you can be fooled into thinking you have real emotions for somebody by booze. It's all so fake.

"I knew you would." She pours a couple shots in her cup, then tops it with nog before pouring the creamy yellow liquid by itself for me. She throws hers into the microwave, eyeing me with that confident smirk the entire time it heats. When it's finally ready, she passes me my mug and says, "Let's go, Bright."

She leads me outside to the Adirondack chairs lining the fire pit, covered in pristine white faux-fur throws. She gets bundled in and gazes out to the frozen ocean for a bit, where stars and the northern lights reflect off the snow-dusted ice. "I couldn't tell you this in the square in case anyone overheard, but you're not out of the Race, Kris."

Even out here, away from everybody, my stomach squirms thinking Anjelica's about to break the rules. "Anjie," I say, my tone low. "Don't cheat. You know we can't handle the fallout if the others find out."

She waves me off. "This isn't help, Kris, jeezus." She takes a swig of her eggnog, closing her eyes in pleasure.

Anjie never drinks too much. At least not here in Winter Wonderland, anyway. I haven't seen her go overboard, nowhere near a level where she might crash her snowmobile or a car. Apparently in her Maserati-crashing days, she had alcohol in her blood. You can still find the pictures online of her red and green sports car smashed against the big bull statue outside the New York Stock Exchange.

"I can't believe you drink that stuff," I say. "When partying got you stuck here to begin with." I glance back into the house. Kringle Korp paranoia always gets me. Despite how goody-two-shoes it makes me sound, I don't want to be seen as the bad kid and get our whole family kicked off the island. But Anjie's butler slash chaperone, Gerard, is always fast asleep by 9 p.m. sharp, and at 9:14, Anjie's in the clear.

"Oh, my sweet innocent little Elf." She reaches over and pats my forearm. "This is not even close to a party. It's just a simple social enjoyment among friends." She lifts her mug and takes a gulp, sighing when it goes down. "Speaking of enjoyment, there's definitely a guy here who wants to enjoy you."

I scoff. "The only queer guys I spotted were into Chris. They couldn't stop staring at him during the welcome mob. Besides, I saw the two of them holding hands today. I think they're a thing now, and I'm not about to try to break any couples up. This whole love competition may be fake, but I still have my standards."

"How noble," she says, rolling her eyes. Then her face gets all blank as she gives me a hard stare. "You really are the best of us, you know that? You actually have character. I know Daddy wishes I was more like you." She doesn't say it like it's my fault or like she's mad, but her words definitely have bite. "And I don't mean in the *Can craft the world's smoothest snowball* kind of way."

She looks back out to the ocean, and I know her thoughts are somewhere else, nowhere near the Race at all. Anjie's known for being kind of moody, which is a very uncommon trait on this merry and bright island. One moment she can be all smiles and mischievousness and fabulous outfits; the next she's inside her own head. But I don't mind. I can sit with silence. Sometimes I even prefer it. Guests hound us for things *constantly*. So if Anjie just needs to sit quietly and think for a minute, I'm more than happy to let her.

After five minutes have gone by, I finally place my hand on top of hers. She doesn't typically like people touching her, but she always lets me when it's tentative like this, bringing her back to reality and checking to see if she's okay.

"Want to talk about it?" I ask.

That wicked grin pops up again, and she meets my eye. "No, no, Dr. Bright, we're here to talk about you." She takes another swig. "And I wasn't talking about those guys who were into Chris. What makes you think there wasn't anybody else who found you *titillating?*"

"Come on, I know a flirt when I see one. I've been through . . ." I try to do the math in my head, but math was never my strong suit. I'm good at Christmas things, not academic things. "So many Twelves since we started the Race."

"Well, I think you might need to get your eyes checked, because your vision seems to be a bit rusty. I saw a little cutie who was *obsessed* with you, and he was right under your nose."

I rack my brain for anybody she could be talking about, but I come up blank. "You're talking about me, right? Kris with a *K*? The gay Kris? Kris Bright? Not the bulky himbo straight one with a *Ch*, Chris Jimenez?"

Anjelica nods. "Yes, *you.*"

"Who was he?"

"It was so obvious the way he *crushed* on you. He was crushing on you so hard, you probably *felt it.*"

She gives me eyes like, *You cannot be this stupid.* And then it hits me, almost as hard as a fist.

"The clumsy one? The guy who nearly broke my nose?"

His brother told me his name. What was it?

Aaron.

Aaron Merry.

Anjie mimes zipping her mouth shut. "I told you nothing. You asked me not to cheat, so I didn't."

What would I do without Anjelica Pérez-Kringle?

I'm still in this Race.

# Aaron

I couldn't sleep all night. Maybe part of it is that I got a full eight hours thanks to accidentally drugging myself on the way here. Or maybe, and much more likely, it's because I couldn't get my stomach to stop buzzing. I haven't been able to get my body to power down after experiencing those electric tingles brought on by Kris. I can still feel his hands on my back, can still feel the faint bit of stubble under my fingers when I shoved a wad of Kleenex up his nose.

I wince and open the refrigerator door to cool my burning cheeks. This is why crushes are so stupid and must be avoided at all costs. They make you do the dumbest things; they make your body act in weird ways outside your control. Why would I ever think the correct thing to do in that situation was to jam paper up a stranger's nostril? I'm completely over it, and I've had a crush for less than a day.

"Let's go, Aaron. Get your head in the game." I'm not

one for sports talk, even when I'm playing tennis. It all just seems a bit much, overly put on. Major emotion in general just feels totally illogical. It doesn't matter if it's love, sports pep talks, fears that get you so worked up you cry and shake. They always start to control the person experiencing the emotion, not the other way around.

I cannot become one of those people.

I tried analyzing it when I couldn't get to sleep. What about this guy in particular made my body react so strongly? I've seen guys for years who I've been attracted to. Soccer guys with great butts, a cub who's got amazing curves, boys with smiles that are just magnetic. There've been things I'm attracted to that go beyond the physical as well, whether it was confidence or jokes or their overall energy that made them captivating. But this is more than a general hotness boner in swim class. No one has ever made me actually want to make a move like Kris.

I thought about telling Casey about my instant crush on the walk home from the flash mob. I mean, he is the guy who's been trying to set me up for the past four years. But Casey shut that down so fast, Santa's sleigh would be jealous. All from one simple comment when he stared longingly (and creepily) at a couple making out under a sprig of mistletoe.

*"I'm so glad we're both single, Aaron. I don't know what I'd do if I had to watch all this holiday romance alone."*

He called me Aaron and everything. He only uses

my name when it's serious.

"What's taking you so long, bro?" Case calls from the dining room. I peek my head around the corner where Casey, Dad, and I have gingerbread houses in progress spread out on the dining room table. Bowls of candy, tubes of frosting, stacks on stacks of gingerbread. "I need sustenance to get my builder on."

"On it," I say. "Sorry." I picked up supplies from the Kringle Kafeteria to make Casey's favorite holiday lunch: stuffing sandwiches. It's your traditional table roll cut in half, piled with stuffing and turkey, and slathered in gravy with a dollop of cranberry sauce on top. Dad and Casey start cracking up when I'm about halfway through assembling the feast. Then the doorbell rings.

Once.

Twice.

Three times.

"Uh, can somebody get that?" I call.

"We've had a bit of an incident," Dad says.

*Ugh.* Don't they always. Aaron to the rescue, yet again.

On the fourth ring, I shout, "Coming!" before rounding the corner to get to the front door. Dad and Casey are covered in frosting from the waist up.

"I squeezed too hard, bro, and *PFFFT!*" Casey mimes an explosion. "Frosting splooged everywhere."

Dad's chuckling stops immediately. "Never use *splooged* as a verb again."

I point at Dad as I walk past the table. "Agreed. Never. Again."

I hustle to the front door, fling it open, and suddenly I'm face-to-face with the guy who's simultaneously the last and only person I want to see right now.

Kris.

"OH GOD!"

I slam the door shut, the jingle bells attached to the knob clanging loudly.

"Uh, everything okay over there?" Dad asks.

"Yeah, yeah," I say. "It's fine." My heart is racing. Why won't it stop racing?

This is entirely my point: I can't keep it together around him. What is he doing here anyway? I look through the peephole. He's holding a wicker gift basket with the most gorgeous bow on it. Bringing presents like the world's hottest Santa, although his forehead's furrowed in a massive scowl. Most likely from having the door slammed in his face.

"If it's fine, then why are you out of breath?" Casey asks.

"I, uh . . . I thought I saw a fox across the street."

"Cool!" Casey says, while Dad chimes in with, "There isn't any natural wildlife on this island outside of birds."

Of course Dad comes in with all the facts. It's this habit he picked up from realty. Whenever we travel anywhere new, he looks up all the tidbits he should know about the area in case he ever ends up selling a place there. Not that he could sell property on this remote Alaskan island, but it still doesn't stop him from doing his research.

"Yeah, well, must have been a visitor's ferocious-looking dog." I check through the peephole again to see Kris's hand hovering over the bell. I've got to stop him before Casey comes over and investigates, and I'm stuck acting like a middle schooler with a crush in front of my devastated brother. "Somebody left a package. Must be from the Elves or something. Maybe a welcome gift. I'll be right back."

I swing the door open again and step out onto the porch before slamming it shut behind me.

"Is that how you handle every door?" Kris asks. "Slamming it?"

I laugh way too loud and way too awkwardly. Then I realize that if I keep this volume up, Dad and Case are for sure going to hear me inside, so I drop my voice to library level before saying, "You just surprised me is all. I wasn't expecting any callers."

*Callers?* Since when do I live in the nineteenth century?

He laughs, a deep chuckle that sends vibrations up my spine. "I was actually here to drop this off." He lifts the basket. "It's for your brother. I noticed he looked a bit down yesterday, so I put together a little care package. All the most popular treats from the Christmas Confectionary are in there. A voucher for a few free movies on Santa's Streaming Service. And a gift card for a massage at the Merry Masseuse." He holds the basket out for me to take.

Every ounce of feeling pours from my bubbling stomach straight up to my heart. In just a few minutes of interaction, this guy could tell Casey was off? And he wants to help?

"That's really thoughtful of you," I say. "Especially after I punched you in the face."

He chuckles again, and a few of those crush tingles are back. "In case it got lost in the excitement of yesterday, my name's Kris. Kris Bright."

"Yeah, no, I *definitely* remember." Why did I emphasize *definitely*? "Nobody would want to give us a ship name when our last names are already perfect together, just like Casey said. Merry and Bright!" I cringe at how I've not only linked us as a couple within seconds, but gone way too sappily into the holidays. This place is rubbing off on me. "Well, thanks, Kris." I take the basket. Just before I'm about to go inside, Kris says, "If you're not busy, I'd love to show you around the island."

"You mean like a date?"

Oh, holy night, I did *not* just say that.

But Kris seems unfazed, and even smiles. "Yeah, like a date."

My hand hovers over the doorknob. Everything in me is begging to say yes, fantasies of holding hands, cozying up with cocoa, experiencing my first kiss flying through my head.

But no. This isn't a trip for any of that. This is a trip for

Casey. And it'd be the ultimate betrayal if I ditched him just like Raquel did. Especially for romance.

So without turning to look at him, I say, "Sorry, Kris." Then I slam the door in his face. Again.

I can't stop chewing my lips. I'm worried if I let them have one second on their own they'll pucker into kissy faces as I think about what it'd be like to make out with Kris. Sitting here in the Polar Pastaria with Dad and Case right across from me, it's got to be obvious. I mean, I'm gnawing at my own mouth like I haven't eaten in weeks.

"Here, need this?" Dad tosses a tube of lip balm my way. "We're not used to these cold climates. Your lips are bound to get chapped. You've always got to be prepared."

"Thanks." I laugh awkwardly and slather it across my mouth. I'm overzealous, and the entire bottom half of my face comes away slimy.

"Who has the Festive Fettuccini?" Thank god for our server, who expertly balances a tray of pasta topped with parsley and tomatoes arranged just so to look like holly.

I raise my hand. When she sets down my dish, the little garnish nestled on the noodles makes me think of mistletoe and how much kissing I wish I could have. Dad gets his order of Santa's Spaghetti Bolognese and Case has Lovers' Lasagna, a dish built for two. When he ordered it, I practically dropped my Sprite thinking he would melt down wishing Raquel were here to tackle it with him. Seeing its heaping red mass in front of him, I worry again that the size of it is going to remind him that he should be sharing the meal.

But instead he just smiles, raises his fork, and says, "Bon appétit."

Crisis averted.

A movement near the front of the restaurant catches my eye, over Casey's shoulder. It's one of the Wonderers rushing to the door and wrapping a woman in his arms. A big reunion, obviously. A worker seeing a guest he recognizes. Maybe a friend or a family member from the mainland.

When he pulls back, I get a good look at the person the Wonderer's hugging, and I choke on my fettuccini. Full-blown, can't-catch-my-breath, pasta-in-my-lungs choking.

It's Raquel.

Casey's Raquel.

Casey's Raquel, who's betrayed my brother not only by dumping him but by *kissing this guy dressed like an Elf.*

"Oh"—*cough cough*—"*shit.*"

"What was that?" Dad asks in his serious tone. He lets me get away with so much, but never cursing, even if I am about to drown by pasta.

I hold up a finger in a *just a sec* signal when I finally have enough breath to drink some water. I take extra-small, slow sips, giving myself time to think about how to approach this situation. I can't point her out. If Casey knows Raquel's here, we'll be right back to square one.

No. If Casey knows she's here and is kissing another guy, we'll be at square negative one thousand.

That's when Casey chooses to do his long-limbed giant stretch move. What is it with straight guys and having to stretch out all. The. Time? They're always extending a leg here, leaning back there, manspreading as if their lives depend on it. Watch any straight guy sitting down for only five minutes, and I guarantee you the radius of space he takes up increases with each passing second.

Casey's radius is expanding quickly. He stretches out a leg, then links his hands over his head and pushes them back. With one twitch of his neck, I know he's about to bend his head from side to side too. I've seen this routine so many times that I know the next step is him grabbing the back of his chair and twisting to try to crack his back, which means he will temporarily face the door. The door in front of which Raquel is making out with an Elf.

"CASEY!"

I'm way too loud. It gets everyone's attention, making my face blaze with heat.

"Jeezus, bro, I'm right here," Casey says, thankfully looking straight ahead, right at me.

"Yeah, um, I wanted to ask what's on the docket for tomorrow. I'm just excited, I guess. Your holiday spirit is finally starting to rub off." Cue awkward laughter.

"I thought we could take a class on decorating

ornaments," Casey says. "I kicked your ass at gingerbread houses, so I wanted to see just how far my Christmas powers can reach."

"Language," Dad says, before taking a massive bite of spaghetti.

Then it happens. The absolute worst thing, our entire vacation to make Casey snap back to himself about to fall into a holiday hellhole.

"Oh my god, Aaron? Casey?"

*Don't turn around. Don't turn around. Don't turn around.*

But it doesn't matter how hard I wish it. Casey would recognize that voice anywhere. We all would recognize that voice anywhere.

Casey whips around so fast, his back finally cracks.

"Ra*quel*?" His voice breaks when he says her name, that little squeak in his throat filled with so much emotion.

"It's me," she says, and at least she has the decency to smile sheepishly. "I heard Aaron shout your name, and when I looked over, I couldn't believe it was really you."

Great. I'm sabotaging my own plans. I glare at Raquel, wishing my stare could make her burst into flames.

"W-what are you doing here?" Casey asks. He's gone totally pale.

"Yeah, Raquel," I seethe. "*What* are you doing here?"

Raquel looks over her shoulder, back at the Elf who's now serving tables near the front of the restaurant.

"Um, my, uh . . . My boyfriend works here. On the island."

I guess Casey's suspicions that she was seeing someone from work weren't right after all.

"*Boyfriend?*" That one's Dad, and it's the only time I've heard him use his *I mean business* tone on anyone other than me or Casey. I love him for it. "That was fast."

Raquel's laugh does nothing to ease the tension. Her smile is so forced, and her eyes keep nervously darting to Casey, who cranes his neck to get a good look at his replacement.

"You're dating Liam?" he asks, in stupefied disbelief. "The most famous Wonderer on the planet?"

"We got to talking online, and, um . . ." Raquel's whole body slumps, and she takes it upon herself to sit in the one empty chair at our table. That's the thing about three-tops: there's always an open chair for an unwelcome visitor.

"Casey," Raquel says, and she even reaches out and grabs his hands.

"Whoa," I say while Dad chimes in with a "Hey now." We've been privy to just how destroyed Casey's felt the past few weeks, and now Raquel comes in thinking it's cool to *hold his hands* when *she* dumped *him*?

But Raquel's totally oblivious, blabbing on. "I know what we had was special. And I know we haven't talked since—" Raquel's eyes flash with guilt, and we all know when the last day they communicated was.

"I know it might have seemed harsh to block you on everything," she adds. "I just needed some space to be able to move on. On my own."

I can't help myself. "Move on with Liam, you mean."

Raquel finally notices the tension oozing from our side of the table like the marinara sauce oozing over the sides of Casey's lasagna. The lasagna he now stares at intently, unable to look any of us in the eye.

"I'll just go," Raquel says. When she stands, she turns to me, then Dad. "I'm sorry. I shouldn't have imposed." Then to Casey. "Really. I'm sorry."

We all watch her go, see her give a weak wave to Liam—who's in the middle of taking an order—before walking out the door.

When it finally shuts behind her, we collectively let out a breath.

"Case—" I begin at the exact same time Dad says, "Son, I know that was hard, but—" Casey jumps from the table, his chest heaving as he braces himself against the back of his chair. His eyes are wide, his nostrils flare, and is he . . . smiling?

Casey throws his fists in the air and *cheers*. Like, shouts so loud that the entire restaurant stops. Pasta dangles from forks in stunned silence while everyone takes in the guy who's whooping his ass off. We've become the yelling table. But their stunned silence turns to celebration when Casey hollers, "A round of eggnog, on me!"

That's it.

He's finally snapped.

He plops down into his seat, all smiles and exhilaration.

"Uh, who do you think is going to pay for that?" Dad asks.

Casey grimaces, then to the restaurant says, "Sorry, folks. But here's an extra helping of Christmas cheer from me to you."

Most people shrug, some laugh, and one boos. But Casey stares at us with the biggest smile on his face I've ever seen, and that's saying something. When he's not emotionally wrecked, he's a pretty smiley guy.

"Casey," Dad tries, tentative, like he's worried one wrong word will send his son over the edge again. "You okay?"

"I'm better than okay!" He snags a giant bite of lasagna on his fork and shovels it into his mouth. "I'm great!"

"You, uh—you know that was Raquel, right?" I brace for emotional impact, but Casey just nods, exuberant.

"Of course I do." He grabs another bite of lasagna. The thing about Casey is whenever he's excited, he has to eat. So based on the amount of food he's scarfing, he's really feeling this happiness. Not that I want him to be wrecked or anything, but this sudden burst of joy just doesn't make sense.

"You're okay with her seeing that young man?" Dad asks, motioning toward Liam, who's glanced our way a couple times now.

"Not in the slightest," Casey says.

"Then why are you acting this way?"

Casey grins again, a piece of parsley stuck in his teeth. "Because I'm going to win her back!"

Dad and I have the exact same reaction. *"What?"*

"Don't you see?" Casey takes in the whole room, from floor to ceiling, his smile getting creepily bigger as he soaks up the North Pole energy. "It's a Christmas *miracle*. Christmas has brought Raquel here so I can prove that I'm the best man for her, not that schmuck she's dating." He laughs. "It's so obvious. I should have seen this coming!" He looks up toward the ceiling again with a cheeky wink. "Thanks, Christmas." I guess he thinks the holiday is some sort of ever-watchful being in the sky? Like Santa? Or God?

"Casey." Dad's tone is gentle, protective. "I'm not sure this is the best idea. What if she decides Liam is the person for her?"

"That's not going to happen, Dad," Casey says, grinning at us like we're silly little kids unaware of grown-up things. "That's not how Christmas works."

When Casey gets like this, there's no stopping him. He *believes* in Christmas with his whole heart and soul. The only way out of this is to see him through it.

"Okay, so, how exactly are you going to win her back?" I ask.

Casey's halfway through his lasagna now, smashing

another bite in before saying, "Her Google calendar. You know how obsessed she is with using it. It's how she shared everything with me. Christmas parties, costume-planning sessions, ski trips. I still know her password."

Dad scowls. "I do not condone you hacking into someone else's account for your own personal gain, Casey."

"It's not hacking if someone gave you their password. I bet she hasn't even changed it."

He fishes out his phone, taps the screen a few times, and says, "Bingo! I'm in!" He frowns. "Tomorrow it just says *Liam*." He practically growls the name. "But the day after that it looks like she's . . . entering the toboggan race. Then the snowman competition the next day. With the schmuck. But I'm going to be there, and I'm going to win, and she's going to remember just how much of a holiday passion *we* shared. How when it comes to a bond over Christmas, there's no one better suited for her than me." He laughs. "Rasey will be back in full swing before you know it!" He scoots his chair back and stands up. "Gotta run! I'm carbo-loaded and ready to make a plan. See you guys back at the cottage."

With that, he books it out of the restaurant, even giving Liam a *what's up* nod. He's feeling confident. He's feeling cocky.

But I'm feeling sick.

Because I'm going to have to sabotage my brother.

*　　*　　*

**Meet me at the Globe.**

It was a curt text, but to Raquel's credit, she replied with a thumbs-up and even shared her location with me, despite the fact that we didn't really have that kind of relationship when she and Casey were together. I have a sinking suspicion that after seeing him yesterday, she might be having second thoughts about the breakup. Casey was right: she's that kind of woman, always looking for signs. With Casey hell-bent on making sure their paths cross, Raquel could assume it's Christmas telling her to choose my brother. I've got to make sure that doesn't happen, hence, meeting her at the Globe.

The Globe is one of Winter Wonderland's masterpieces. It's a glassblowing center where Elves make not only the island's world-famous ornaments, but their collectible snow globes as well. The entire building is made to look like a giant snow globe. There's a whole winter scene splayed out inside it, with life-size plastic pine trees and polar bears and penguins all covered with nontoxic synthetic snow that falls from fake clouds in the ceiling. It's one of the island's most popular attractions, so choosing to meet Raquel here should be pretty safe. If Casey sees us, I'll just say that we both randomly decided to see today's ornament-making demonstration, and I took the moment to tell Raquel that she really crushed my brother's heart.

I look at the entrance as soon as Raquel's little GPS

dot moves on top of the Globe. There she is, decked out in Wonderland-branded snow gear and earmuffs, a sprig of holly nestled in her red hair. She looks so Christmasy it makes me want to barf. Not that she shouldn't get to love the things she wants to. It's just that I know every single time he looks at her, Casey is going to fall even more in love with Raquel, and we'll get further and further from him ever becoming his own person. That's the whole reason why I have to keep them apart. Casey needs to understand how great of a person he is *on his own*. Being this codependent is unhealthy for both of them.

Raquel locks eyes with me and waves, her smile bright. I try to give her a smile back, but I'm sure it comes out more as a grimace. God, I hate being such a prick. None of this is Raquel's fault. I mean, sure, her dumping Casey was the domino that started his whole existential crisis, but that crisis is on him.

Raquel is so distracted by all the glitz and glam of the Globe that it will take her forever to get to me. She stops to gawk every time the glassblowers make molten glass billow out in bright orange bubbles before they twist and pull them into snowflakes, each one unique like their real-life inspiration. Not to mention it's like she has to touch *every single ornament* hanging from the shop's fake trees. I've got to get out of here quick, so I shove through the crowd until I'm pushed up against Raquel.

"I need you to stay away from Casey," I say.

"Wow." Raquel laughs. It's good-natured and sweet, and honestly she's too good for the world. "You sure get right to the point, don't you?"

"It's just, I'm helping him move on, and then you come in here and—"

"Wait." Raquel's brow is furrowed, eyes full of concern and hurt. "I didn't come here to ruin anybody's time. I came because I was invited. By Liam."

"No, I know, I'm not saying this is your fault," I rush to add. "Sorry. I'm just flustered seeing you here. How *are* you even here?" She and Casey always talked about going someday, but we all knew that wouldn't happen with how pricey this place is.

"Liam's aunt is letting me stay in her spare room," she says. "And she was sweet enough to pay for my flight."

That's just the segue I need. "That's great that you get to spend time with Liam. I need you to remember that *he's* the reason you came here, not Casey."

"Uh, yeah," she says with a giggle. "Of course Liam is why I'm here. Why would I forget that?"

I throw my hands up, exasperated. "Oh, come on, Raquel. We both know how you're always looking for signs. I was sure that you'd see this whole invite to the island during the exact Twelve that Casey was here, over *actual Christmas*, as some cosmic sign from the holiday gods that you and my brother are supposed to be together. Like being a couple is such a sure thing that the universe brought you together thousands of miles from home where there's nothing else to do but run into each other and remember all the Christmasy things you have in common. You honestly didn't think that?"

It isn't until I finally shut up that I realize Raquel has moved a gloved hand over her shocked mouth, her eyes wide with wonder.

"N-no," Raquel stutters. "I hadn't. But that makes so much sense. Why didn't I see it before?"

Oh. Dear. God. What have I done?

"Actually, that's not what I meant." My heart races about as fast as the words fly from my lips. "I meant the sign is that *Liam* invited you here, that you're supposed to be spending time with *Liam*, that if the universe didn't want you to be together it wouldn't have trapped you on a tiny island with *Liam*." Why am I using the word *trapped* when trying to convince her she should fall for someone else? "You see that, Raquel? Don't you? You do, right? Right?"

Raquel's eyes are bright, and she matches my desperation with breathless excitement.

"No, you're right, Aaron," she says. "The universe *is* giving me two solid men to choose from, bringing them both here so that I can gauge them side by side and discover who is truly meant for me. It's the perfect holiday rom-com set up. I've seen it so many times, but Christmas is finally making *me* the star."

Wow. Narcissistic much? But I should have seen this coming, knowing she's just as delusional about the holiday as my brother.

"By the end of this trip, I'll know which boy is for me." She grabs my hands. "Thank you, Aaron. I see it all so clearly now." She glances to the door, no longer distracted by the glassblowing displays. "I should go. See which of them Christmas brings to me first."

She practically flings my hands away before dashing out the door. Now it's two against one, Casey *and* Raquel trying to force the signs that they're meant to be.

If I'm going to stop them, I'll need reinforcements.

My body buzzes before my brain catches up.

I know just the guy.

# Kris

All anyone can talk about are the mainlanders they've paired up with. *Everyone* in my class has found somebody that they're well on their way to having fall in love with them. Even Rudy. He came across a girl who wants to be a nurse and *volunteered* to help at the Ho-Ho. While on vacation. She's a saint apparently, and she and Rudy have become smitten with each other behind their face masks.

The school day goes by with my classmates talking about what they're going to do when they win the Race, while I'm seeing my only shot to get Uncle Toby reinstated as Santa fly out the window. My last class of the day is chemistry, and we have a midterm, which feels like the universe shoving my face in failure. I've found no chemistry with anybody, *and* I'm going to bomb this test. I'll be forced to ask Dad for some epic extra credit to actually pass this exam and graduate in June.

I trudge out of the front doors at four o'clock, everyone

off to meet up with their pairings, and me off to . . . I don't know. Home, I guess?

"Hey."

My heart flies into my throat as a boy steps into the ring of light under the nearest candy cane streetlamp.

"Aaron," I breathe.

Maybe the Race isn't lost after all.

"Hey," he says again, and then awkwardly kicks his boot in the snow.

"Uh, why are you here?"

He scowls.

"Not that I'm complaining," I rush to add. "It's just, you were pretty clear yesterday that hanging out wasn't really your thing."

"Well, I—" He stops, his mouth opening and closing like a fish. After a few failed attempts at starting a sentence, his cheeks turn bright red, and he covers his face with a hand that I can tell is getting dry and chapped from the cold. It's between negative two degrees and negative seven here this time of year. Even though the Winter Wonderland–issued thermal underwear for guests and all the heated walkways prevent any life-threatening events from happening, having his hands uncovered has got to be a killer. "I'm not very good at this."

"Good at what?"

"Asking for *help*." Aaron looks like he hates the word, even sticking his tongue out a bit like it tastes bad. But as soon as I take a step toward him, his eyes get big, doe-eyed even.

I am *so* still in this.

He meets my eyes, and his lips tick up in a tiny smile. He doesn't say anything, just looks at me. It gives me time to check him out too, to notice the smattering of freckles across his nose and cheeks, the dirty blond hair he's got combed neatly to the side with a slight sheen of product. I can tell if he did nothing to style it, it'd be the same mop of hair as his brother's. His eyes are hazel, a mixture of grays and greens and soft browns, and it hits me that Aaron is cute.

Really cute.

There could be a lot worse people to be paired up with for this competition.

Here's my favorite part about the Race: the moment when you know you've found the person you're going to be making out with for the immediate future. I get this whole-body rush when I think of kissing someone new for the first time, and the images running through my head right now are all Aaron. My stomach turns, but in that way like when I hit the gas full throttle on a snowmobile. My tongue instinctively licks my lip, just the slightest, like I can already taste him. I wonder if he uses ChapStick or chews gum.

A gust of wind goes by, cooling my cheeks and making Aaron shiver.

"You're still in that flimsy jacket," I say. "It's three below zero. The island recommends goose-down coats for a reason."

Aaron shrugs. "I didn't think the cold would be so . . . cold."

"It's kind of in the name," I say and smile, all charmingly playful teasing. "You're from somewhere warm, yeah?"

He nods. "Newport Beach. Orange County, California."

"Knew it." I place my hand at his elbow, and he shivers again, only this time there's no breeze. "Let me take you to Claus Clothier. We've got to get you a jacket that actually works in this weather." I glance at his hands. "And some gloves too."

Aaron holds his hands up to the light glowing down from the candy cane above, taking in the tiny cracks forming around his knuckles. He quickly shoves his hands into his pockets.

"Lead the way," he says.

The store's only a couple blocks from here, Wonderland High being right in the center of all the madness. We join the throngs of people going about their holiday outings, Christmas music playing from the speakers hidden in every red-and-white-striped streetlamp.

"It's weird to think that you have school in the middle of what's basically the North Pole," Aaron says. "School feels too normal for this place."

"We may be the world's premier Christmas theme park,

but we're just a regular town in Alaska too. We've got the same school requirements, taxes, all that. Even an actual jail. But don't tell anybody I told you. We're not supposed to let on that we don't just run on Christmas cheer."

"It must be strange, your whole life revolving around one never-ending festivity."

One of those classes in our "normal" Winter Wonderland High experience? Visitor Relations. The school uses it as a social studies credit. We're given the ins and outs of societal views on Christmas, the importance of holiday merriment, and how to respond to comments like Aaron's.

"Honestly, I love Christmas," I say. "We all do. It's literally the most wonderful time of the year, they didn't just make that song up out of nowhere. Why wouldn't I want to be in a never-ending festivity?"

The words sound phony even to me.

Aaron scoffs. "I don't know. Just seems like if you can have something all the time, it takes away how special it is."

He's hit the nail on the head. And he's the first mainlander to ever do so. I get it. When you're shelling out thousands of dollars to come here, you don't do it because you hate Christmas. Same for the lottery winners; they signed up for it because they want on the island. Everyone else gets so caught up in the spectacle, but not Aaron, apparently.

"God, I really am a wet blanket sometimes," he says. "I

didn't mean to take a dump on your life. I'm glad you find the positive in it. Casey does that with Christmas too. He can watch holiday movies all year round and never stops feeling the joy."

I don't have the heart to tell him that people who deep-dive into Christmas usually have something they're trying to escape in real life. Some pain. That's not to say that people can't be fans of the holiday and have a healthy relationship with it. A bit of escapism, a bit of magic, a Christmas vibe that makes everyone hope humanity really is good at its core. Then there are the folks who need Christmas constantly. They need that jolt of joy or else they sink into some sort of despair. Based on the unkempt level of beard and bed head he had going on, I'd say Casey is one of the sinkers. But it seems counterintuitive to tell a guy I'm trying to get to love me that his brother has problems.

So instead I ask, "Is he the one who dragged you here?"

"Yeah. Trying to cheer him up from a funk."

See? I was right.

"Where is he now?"

"Off making plans to—"

"Well, look who it is!" Aaron stops dead in his tracks, turning around to find his brother next to the fountain in Santa's Square, looking way more chipper than he did the last time I saw him.

"H-hey, Case." Aaron glances at me, then takes a step away.

Casey's over to us in three easy strides of his long legs. "You two sure look cute together." Casey's eyes go wide. "Bro! Is it happening? Do I sense a little holiday romance?"

"That's not what's going on here." Aaron's words are so stiff, he sounds like a robot.

Casey turns to me. "I saw the way you were looking at him. Don't let my brother fool you. I swear he has a heart."

The way I was looking at him? He's misinterpreting my desperation to win the Race.

"What are you doing here?" Aaron's clearly trying to change the subject. "I thought you were taking a nap. You said the constant darkness was messing with your body."

"I *did* take a nap and had a dream about giving Raquel a snow globe with *us* in it," Casey says. "So I'm off to the Globe to make that happen."

"Is Raquel your girlfriend?" I ask.

"Ex. She broke up with me," Casey says, but with a beaming smile that's entirely unexpected when talking about getting dumped. "I'm going to win her back!"

"Good for you," I say. Aaron shoots a glare my way that could melt icicles.

"I'm off!" Casey says over his shoulder. "See you two lovebirds around. Who knows? Maybe we'll be double-dating by Christmas!"

As soon as his brother's gone, Aaron whips a very accusing finger at me.

"If this is going to work, you can't do that again," he

snaps, then turns on his heel to speed-walk to Claus Clothier.

I chase after him. "If *what* is going to work?"

"Sabotaging my brother's love life." He says it matter-of-factly before stomping through the clothing store's door without a backward glance.

He may as well have yelled it. My heart races, my palms sweat, and my eyes dart around nervously as I pray no one overheard. We can never ruin a guest's experience. If Casey wants to win Raquel back, me getting in the way of that and intentionally trying to tank his time in Winter Wonderland could be serious. I know of only one person who crossed a visitor before: Nicolas St. Nicolas. When he clapped back at a customer for snapping at him when we temporarily ran out of oat milk on the island, the Polar Patrol (our version of cops) sent Nicolas and all the St. Nicolases packing (as in the family, not the Santas). That was just for having a brief meltdown. What would happen if the Patrol discovered I went out of my way to derail a guest's love life? It goes against everything Winter Wonderland stands for. But then again, so does having a gay Santa, so what do they know about right and wrong?

I've got to learn more.

Claus Clothier is packed with all kinds of "fashions," and I use that term loosely. There're sweatshirts and hoodies featuring the Winter Wonderland logo, elf ears of every size and skin tone, kitchen aprons with terrible sayings like *Cooking Just BeClaus*, and a whole winter wardrobe section featuring the puffiest coats and thickest gloves. Aaron heads right over to that area, as he should, and it's full of others who are just as poorly dressed for this weather as he is.

Aaron grabs the pillowiest jacket he can find and tries it on. "So, are you in?"

"Aren't you trying to make this the best vacation for your brother? Don't you want Casey to be out of his funk and happy again?"

Aaron nods, a steely determination in his eyes. "Yes! Exactly. I've given this a lot of thought." He talks with his hands so emphatically that his coat swishes with every word. "I *do* want Casey to be happy. But he's based his entire personality on one person, and that person is not him. He needs to know what *he* likes, alone, not in some codependent relationship. And let's say his whole plan to win her back works? She's so determined to see nonexistent signs that there's a very real possibility she'll interpret Casey and her being here as a sign to get back together. But what if she sees a whole other sign down the road and leaves him *again*? No, I've got to rip the Band-Aid off now and get Casey to realize he's fine without her. He's *safe* without her." He whips his hand out to shake so suddenly that I flinch. "Have we got a deal?"

"I don't know, Aaron." Nausea sweeps through my gut. What if we're caught? What if I get kicked off the island

and Mom and Dad get the boot too? What if they lose their housing and health care in one fell swoop, all because of a guy I went along with in some stupid scheme before he returns to his regular life and mine blows up? Not to mention if we're kicked out, my mission to get Uncle Toby back on the island and reunite my family would go up in smoke, just like that.

"I know it's a lot to ask," Aaron says. "I'll love you forever if you do this."

There's that word. This definitely doesn't count as a declaration of love, but he's telling me point blank that he'll feel grateful to me if I go along with him. Maybe I can get him to believe that he *actually* loves me if I help out his brother, the one person he seems to truly care about. I could win the Race even while destroying a guest's time in Wonderland. I'll just have to be a little stealth to make sure no one finds out how badly I'll have to torpedo Casey's experience. That way Mom and Dad's futures here are safe, and Uncle Toby's will actually be a thing again. It's a win-win.

"Okay," I say, the best chills going down my spine as I take off my glove and shake Aaron's hand. "It's a deal."

"Great." Aaron beams. But the smile's gone in an instant as he turns around to check how the coat fits in the mirror behind him. "This should work. I've got to get going."

"Where to?"

"I'm Casey's partner in the toboggan race tomorrow,"

he says. "Raquel's entering too. I've got to stake out a spot that'll give us the bumpiest, slowest ride so we're sure to lose."

If I'm going to use this as a way to get Aaron to fall for me, I better get started.

I tap him on the shoulder, and when he turns to me, I grab Aaron's hands, gently holding them in my own. "Well, before you go out there, these will need proper covering." I lower his hands to his sides, taking extra time for the side of my palm to skim his before I grab a pair of gloves. Not big thick ones that will make his fingers useless sausages, but lined gloves that still give him the ability to use his hands for things other than just molding snowballs. I have a feeling Aaron's the kind of guy who wants to be in control always.

"And you Californians have the hardest time picking the right jacket." I motion for Aaron to follow me in front of a pinewood rack full of performance coats. These aren't big and puffy like the one he tried on. They're formfitting and deceptively thin but keep the heat surrounding your body like nobody's business. I pick one that's a neutral blue, with the small Winter Wonderland logo of a snowflake with a cursive *WW* in its center stitched in silver on the left pec. I know the blaring red or bright green of most of the store's offerings wouldn't be his thing. His brother's, sure, but not Aaron's. If I'm going to win the Race, I've got to show Aaron that I'm thinking only of him.

"Turn around," I say, holding the jacket open. Aaron removes his coat and does as I ask, letting me lead his hands through the arms of the jacket. I step behind him, as close as I can, and lead him in front of a mirror. Then I ever so gently pull the zipper up from behind, taking care to make sure it doesn't snag on his clothes. When I finally release the zipper, my hands are at the base of his neck, and his Adam's apple bobs as my fingers graze the skin there.

"What do you think?" I ask, looking at him in the mirror.

"It's nice," Aaron whispers.

I turn Aaron to face me. He's a bit shorter than I am, and when his head tilts up to look me in the eye, our noses are barely an inch apart.

"Meet me at the sledding hill at midnight. We'll plan our sabotage. Does that work?"

Aaron nods once. "Mm-hmm."

"See you then."

I walk away, looking back only when I've made it to the front door, and give Aaron a wink.

His mouth falls open, and he waves slowly, in a daze.

I've got this in the bag.

# Aaron

"What is going on with you?"

Crap. Casey sits across from me in this wrapping workshop, and he's giving me weird looks from behind a massive green and gold bow.

"What? Me? Nothing. Nothing's going on with me. W-why do you ask?"

"It's just that you've started over on that cut about fifteen times."

"Yeah." Dad nods while trying to perfect a corner of wrapping paper featuring a shirtless Santa tanning on some tropical beach. "You're the wrapping aficionado. Hell, you could teach this class if you wanted to."

He's not wrong. As soon as Mom left, I taught myself how to expertly wrap presents by watching YouTube tutorials. A picture-perfect tree complete with meticulously wrapped gifts has always been one of Casey's favorite Christmas aesthetics. Mom was pretty good at it, and I knew during our first Christmas with her gone, if Casey saw sad masses of crinkled wrapping, *he'd* become the sad mass.

But you wouldn't be able to tell that I'm such an expert based on the box in front of me. It still sits unwrapped, while Dad's nearly done and Casey just placed the finishing bow on his. It's nowhere near as good as what I could do, but at least he did it. And all without tearing up once, which is a total win. So far during gingerbread house making, caroling, Santa's Square strolling, you name it, there's been at least one moment when I find his eyes glistening with tears. When I ask him what's up, he just shrugs and gives me a look that we both know says *Raquel*. Their whole relationship was built on Christmas shit, and when it wasn't Christmas, they were preparing for Christmas, so of course there's nothing we could do here that *wouldn't* have some memory tied to her.

"Sorry to tell you this, bro, but I'm going to take your title as raddest wrapper," Casey says.

I raise a skeptical eyebrow. "Raddest?"

He shrugs. "I don't make the titles, I just take 'em."

Casey comes to my side of the table and throws an arm over my shoulder before pulling me into him, while Dad looks on at the two of us and smiles. He does that a lot. When he sees Casey and me together, he just sort of takes us in and grins. He never used to do it before Mom left, and it doesn't take a therapist to know Dad is appreciating that the three of us are still together and not leaving at the drop of a hat.

While Dad might be in the moment, my mind is far away from here. The thought of sneaking out to see Kris is making me so nervous that I can't get my wrapping right. But then the thought of not sneaking out to see him makes my stomach sink. It's wild to go a lifetime without feeling anything for anyone, and then *bam*! You get electric tingles slamming into your gut and your heart and your . . . other places, like so many snowballs.

But I can't tell Casey any of this. I know he thinks there's something between me and Kris, but if I tell him about our meetup, it'll only spur him on. He'll insist that we *both* need love by the end of this trip, and I'm trying to get his thoughts as far from Raquel as possible.

"Haha." I laugh awkwardly. "You can have it, bro." I cringe. *Bro* just sounds gross when I say it, all clunky and douche-y. It's Casey's word, not mine, which has been established between us for years, so Casey looks at me quizzically.

"The winter weather's got you all out of whack, huh?" he says. "You never did like our ski trips."

"That's right," I say, with even more awkward laughter. "I need the sun."

"We live in the sunniest place in the country, and you need *more*?" Dad asks in that parent way where they love making their kids seem unreasonable with a terrible joke and a smug smirk. It's like he thinks his cleverness deserves a parade or something.

"You know what I mean," I snap. "I need it to be hot."

"Hey now," Dad says, getting that stern tone. "It's not my fault your wrapping skills aren't so *hot* today. Don't take it out on me."

Case tugs me behind him as he throws his other arm over Dad and squeezes. "Okay, time for a Merry Mash-Up!"

It's what Casey says whenever he wants to group hug. All of us smooshed together, one big mass of Merry men. It's a little too cheesy and wholesome if you ask me, but that's totally Casey's brand, so here we are. Or I should say, that's his brand when he's *not* upset. I just wish it wasn't Raquel's presence on the island that was making him so chipper. He's falling deeper and deeper into his codependency.

Still, Dad doesn't deserve to be my emotional punching bag; he's been dealt enough psychological blows to last a lifetime. Besides, me lashing out at Dad would just be replacing one grumpy Merry with another, not to mention it'd probably end with me getting grounded.

"My bad," I say. "Sorry, Dad."

Casey squeezes us tighter. "There we go." Then he yawns loud and long, right in my ear, and his hot breath feels disgusting against the side of my face. I yank away as he says, "Man, I'm beat."

With those three words, I want to jump back in for another cheesy hug. "That." I point at him. "You know what? I'm tired too. We should head back to the house and catch some Zs."

*Catch some Zs?* What is wrong with me? I just need to act natural or else Dad and Case will know something's up.

"You don't sound tired," Dad points out, and he's not wrong at all. I'm talking a mile a minute, and why am I out of breath?

I do that thing where you think of yawning really hard to get your body to follow along. Thank god my lungs pick up on the cue and I let out a long, low yawn.

"Come on, fellas, let's head back to the cabin." My brother looks at Dad with big puppy dog eyes. They're the signature *Casey wants something* look. "I found the best set of matching pajamas for us all to wear. Can we get 'em, Dad? Please?"

That's one of Casey's go-to ways to make people feel included: matching outfits. He'd always go out of his way at Newport Beach Family Services to get matching shirts or hats or sunglasses for the foster kids so they felt like part of a group. So they felt like they had people they could turn to. It's one of those things that shows Casey's sappiness is real and heartfelt, even if he can be cringey at times.

Dad groans and rolls his eyes. "All right, let's go. But no pajamas for me. Just for you boys."

Casey grins wickedly, nudging me with an elbow. "That's what he thinks."

I lie in my bed in a brand-new set of hunter-green pajamas with snowflakes and moose—meese?—embroidered on them. They're actually onesies, which Casey thought was hysterical. There's something about clothes that create a junk bulge that he thinks is funny. It's wild to me how straight guys react to penises, or, like, need to show them off a bit, but somehow in ways that make them not "seem gay." Not that Casey's homophobic or anything, it's just that he totally falls in line with that straight guy thing of being obsessed with dicks.

But even him laughing at how awkward our pajamas are isn't enough to keep him awake. He insisted Dad take a few pictures of us, including one where we both "proudly" posed with a leg up on the coffee table before crashing, wanting to rest up to be in "peak physical condition" for the toboggan race in the morning. When I crack open my door, I can hear his snores from the next room over. It always used to piss me off how loudly he snores, but today I want to thank his tonsils for making him roar like a lion. At least I know he's out and won't notice if I'm gone. Dad will be fine too. He's fairly cool about letting me do my thing as long as I let him know where I'm at. Once Mom left, I think he thought we got cosmically slighted or something, so he pretty much has always let us do whatever we want. It was a weird reaction for him to think the right thing to do when losing a parent is to parent even less, but I'm not complaining. I sent him a text that I couldn't sleep and went for a run in case he wakes up and notices I'm gone.

I sneak down the stairs, my feet covered in extra-thick socks so I don't make any noise. I throw on my boots and coat, the one that Kris wrapped around me in the clothier in a way I haven't been able to stop thinking about since. Ready to be that close again, I fling the door open much more enthusiastically than I should.

*JINGLE JINGLE JINGLE.*

*Shit!* I forgot about the jingle bells on the front door-knob!

I freeze, listening.

Casey's snores still reverberate down the stairs.

I exhale. We're good.

I take off my coat and wrap the bells in it, trying my hardest not to make a sound. My whole body shakes with the cold as I tiptoe out the door, shut it, and let the bells fall from my jacket into the snow. We'll say some gust of wind took it—I don't know. I can't think about that now. I've got four minutes to trek across town and get to the sledding hill. I zip my coat up tight, covering my neck, and thank the Elves for deicing the sidewalks so I can run without slipping on my ass.

All of Wonderland feels like it's asleep, aside from the

scattered laughs every now and then from people going to the Naughty List, the island's only bar a handful of blocks away. When the bar door shuts and the sounds of their debauchery are cut off, though, I feel completely alone. Dashing through the snow-scattered cobblestone streets, it's almost like I'm in an enchanted village, perpetual starlight and old-world charm, my own personal fairy tale.

When I get to the edge of town and the trail winding up the sledding hill, that feeling only intensifies. Because Kris is standing on top of the hill, his face lit by the swirling greens and purples and blues of the supernatural northern lights.

"Midnight," he calls down. "Right on time."

I'd probably seem uncool if I told him I've never been late for anything in my entire life. Or maybe I'd seem unfun. At the very least, as extremely type A as I actually am. Even if I don't want this crush to go anywhere, I at least want him to think I'm attractive.

"Are you wearing a onesie?" he shouts.

So much for that.

I look down to my legs in all their green-pajama-ed glory. I shouldn't be worrying about whether he thinks I'm an analytical loser. I should be much more concerned about the reality that I am in fact wearing a onesie, and one that happens to feature a bulge. Not to say that I'm, like, *bulging* or have something down there that's massive. It's just that the very nature of penises makes it so that the fleece fabric molds around the one body part that may noticeably react next to this guy who somehow sends electricity through my being like no person ever has before. I was so freaking focused on making sure Casey fell asleep that I didn't think to change.

"Uh, yeah. Maybe I should go back and switch outfits."

"No, it's fine. As long as you're not cold. They're pretty cute."

*I am* cold, to be honest, but completely don't care after Kris calling me cute.

"Come on." Kris beckons, keeping his hand open like he plans on holding mine when I get to the top of the hill. "We can't wait all night. Your chariot awaits."

The "chariot," it turns out, is a gently rumbling, bright red snowmobile. Kris straddles it as I crest the top of the hill and make it to the machine's side, only slightly panting. Kris motions in front of him, telling me to get on. But here's the thing. I don't let other people drive me. Most are terrible at it, tailgating or texting or speeding. There may not be traffic here, but who knows if Kris is going to steer us right off a wintery cliff.

Not to mention this was not part of the plan.

"Where are we going?" I ask. "I wanted to scope out the perfect toboggan placement."

Kris nods. "I know. Trust me, I've got you covered. I know this place like the back of my hand. I thought I'd show you something more special instead."

Butterflies swarm when he looks at me with a mischievous smile I could never turn down.

"Well, then I should probably drive," I say. "I don't know how reckless you are behind the wheel. Not to brag, but my driver's-ed instructor said I was the safest driver he'd ever seen in his thirty-eight years of teaching."

Kris looks up to the sky, where a handful of small, wispy clouds drift in front of the swirling lights. A dusting of snow falls, landing on his eyelashes, and wow, why have I never noticed how gorgeous eyelashes can be before?

"I bet you haven't driven in the snow, though, right?" Kris says. "Plus, I'm assuming your driver's ed was completed in a car. This"—he revs the engine—"is a snowmobile."

The way the engine roars makes my heart race, but I think it has more to do with the guy revving it than the vehicle.

"Besides," Kris continues, "you don't know where we're going." He pats the seat in front of him again. "Hop on."

That decides it. My brain still acknowledges that I have no idea how safe of a driver Kris is, but my body buzzes with the thought of sitting in between Kris's legs.

So I do exactly as Kris asked: I literally *hop* on, landing with Kris's thighs on either side of me. It's sensation overload. The snowmobile shakes as it idles, the vibrations making my butt itch, while also feeling better in my crotch than this thing has any right to. Increasing the crotch sensory pile-on is the fact that I can feel Kris's muscular legs flexing as he sandwiches me in my seat. And like a thirsty idiot, I point them out.

"Those are some serious muscles."

Kris laughs, and it rumbles through my chest, mixing with the vibrations of the snowmobile. "We take a lot of dance classes for the flash mob routines in PE. And if not dance class, it's hockey. Both do wonders for the legs and glutes."

*I'll say.* Thankfully I keep that one internal.

Kris leans forward, his arms enveloping me as he reaches for the throttle. I didn't think it was possible, but somehow we're even closer together than when he helped me try on my coat. He smells like woodsmoke and deodorant mixed with wafts of diesel from the engine, and I swear no man has ever smelled better in the history of Earth.

"Ready?" We're so close that Kris's stubble scratches my cheek.

"Mmm." What are words again?

"Let's go."

# Kris

I didn't think this through. I knew as soon as my arms were around Aaron—keeping him warm and cocooned in my body heat—that Aaron would melt. And he did. He let his weight sink into me as I took us down the path leading to the beach.

What I didn't anticipate was just how often he would back up into me, and how his butt constantly moving against my crotch would get me so worked up. It's taking everything in me not to get a boner right now. I don't need Aaron getting scared off thinking this was all just some trick to get into his pants. Would I turn down the chance should the moment consensually arise? Hell no. But I can't rush the process. The cold wind whipping our faces is doing nothing to get my dick to chill out. I spend the remainder of the seven-minute ride thinking of the least sexy things I can.

Unwrapping tangled Christmas tree lights.

The orphans we send gifts to every year.

Grandma.

That does it.

But just barely. So when we finally arrive, I shut down the snowmobile and jump off as quickly as I can. Too quickly, I think, because Aaron looks up from the seat with a scowl.

"Are we in a hurry?" he asks.

"No, sorry." I'm way too flustered. "Just, uh, excited." In more ways than one. "To show you what I've set up."

Aaron doesn't look like he buys it entirely, but he walks over to me anyway. "Set up?"

"Yeah." I let my hand brush against Aaron's, but he doesn't pick up on my signal and grab it or swipe his pinky against mine. Even in gloves, that trick usually works with tourists, but Aaron seems too in his head. He needs to get lost in the moment. "Just because we're making plans in secret doesn't mean the setting can't be nice. Right?"

I brought us over to the western edge of the island, to the tip of a little peninsula. If you squint at the map just right, it makes the island look like it's candy cane–shaped. From this beach, you get the absolute best views of the sunset, if we had any significant sun movement over the horizon. At this time of year, the sun stays steadily below it, so the most you'll get is a bluish haze in the middle of the day for a couple hours before we're plunged into darkness. But that pure black has its perks. Like right now, when every single star blazes in the sky, bright dots of bluish-white that sparkle between the swirls of the northern lights. The best part is, on a calm night like this, all those stars and colors reflect off the ice of the Arctic Ocean. It couldn't be more magical if I tried.

Aaron will fall for me if it's the last thing I do.

"Okay, wow, this is gorgeous," he says, taking in the snow-dusted rocks of the beach and the little dirt path that leads to a couple of Adirondack chairs on either side of a fire. Already lit, thanks to Chris. That's the thing about the Race. We may all be pitted against each other, but we aren't out to tank our classmates. We want love to happen organically, not get derailed by bitter and jealous competition among Wonderers. Although selfishly, I made up an excuse for why I couldn't help Noelle and play server during a private dinner she had with the guy she's courting. Seeing these beautifully crafted homemade chairs that used to get made by Uncle Toby is a reminder that I can't play as nice as I used to if I'm ever going to get him back. I won't cheat, but I'm not going to go out of my way to spark something for my classmates either.

"It is, isn't it?" I agree. A bit of pride blooms in my chest at a first date well executed. This romantic setting always makes the boys fall hard.

"You take all your dates here, don't you?"

Maybe Aaron sees through my tactics better than I thought. He doesn't ask the question angrily, or like he's jealous or anything. It's just straight-up fact again, something Aaron seems to like the most. I have a feeling if I lie or try to talk around the truth, he'll catch on and get turned off pretty quickly.

So I just state the facts. "Yeah. It's a good view. I like to show it to people who I think would appreciate it."

"Mmm." Aaron nods and takes the chair on the left, looking out at the icy ocean with the firelight reflecting in his eyes. I take the other seat, not knowing what to say to fill the quiet. I'm usually better at this. Normally I can smile, laugh at whatever it is my date says, and the townies leap at me. They *want* to fall in love. Aaron, though . . . He's hard to read. So I just sit in silence. That way I can't unintentionally blow this thing.

"This is so weird," Aaron finally says. "I've sat and watched the ocean a million times before. But it isn't frozen. And it's always on a beach." I open my mouth to say we *are* on a beach, but Aaron keeps on going. "A *sandy* beach. Never with snow." He holds his hand out to watch a few small flakes land on his glove. "Maybe weird isn't the right word. *Special*. This is more special, somehow."

He catches my eye and gives a slight smile before we both look out to the horizon. It's easy to get hypnotized by the colors dancing there. Something surfaces too far out in the distance to see, out where the ice hasn't taken hold, huffing a breath, most likely a narwhal or beluga at this time of year. The fire in front of us crackles and flashes, little swathes of red and yellow joining the colorful reflections off the ice.

I know without a doubt this is objectively pretty. Especially when you compare it to the trash piles we burn once the tourists leave, or to the heaps of dirty snow we plow and shovel out of Santa's Square. But this scenery is so familiar and I've been here with so many potential matches that it doesn't seem as unique as Aaron makes it sound. I've been told someone loves me on this beach three times already (twice last year, once the year before that). I wish I knew from experience how special and different this moment truly is for most people.

Aaron doesn't say another word until the fire burns into embers, the dark closing in. Yet it's a comforting dark, one still filled with color thanks to the swirling patches of green above us.

"Does it ever get to be too much?" Aaron asks. "All this darkness?"

I shrug. "Not really. Alaska always balances it out. For every hour of darkness we have now, we get that much sunshine in the summer. It'll never get totally dark then, and you'll hardly see any of these stars. Just the brightest ones, and the moon for a bit, but it's all whitewashed. A sad ghost of what it's like right now. But honestly, this is my favorite time of year." I nod toward the sky, toward the millions of pinpricks of starlight blazing there beyond the aurora borealis. "It feels kind of poetic that there's only certain kinds of light you can see in the complete dark."

"Wild," Aaron says under his breath. "I think this would make me go a little insane. I need more order. I like the routine of regular day and night shifts. The concept of needing blackout curtains to sleep in the summer annoys me already."

I laugh. "Why does that not surprise me?"

Aaron cringes. "I know, right? I'm so predictable." He shakes his head, sighs, then looks away from the stars to lock eyes with me. "Do you believe in love, Kris?"

You'd think I'd want to convince him that I do, in fact, believe in love, because if he thinks I don't, this whole mission of him falling for me could be over before it really even starts. But again, something tells me if I lie, he'll see through it. It's going to push him further away. Sure, I've perfected how to seem like I'm in love, both from all the times I've done it in the Race and through hours of training in drama class. We're taught all sorts of methods to portray the emotions our guests are hoping for, namely, unbridled holiday cheer. I know I could say a line right now that would fool anyone else.

But not Aaron.

So instead, I say, "No. Love is just a trick influenced by a really good show." I motion out to the ice, reflecting the light of the galaxy. "So many visitors see this as some sign from the universe that they're meant to be with whoever is sitting next to them, right here. But what they don't know is this looks exactly the same, every night, no matter who comes to this beach. Yeah, some days there's cloud cover, but most days, it's just like this. Those same tourists think our paths were fated to cross if I wink at them during a dance routine, but I cross paths with literally thousands of guests. If I choose to spend time with any of them, or date them, or kiss them, it's because my options are limited being a gay teenager on an isolated island. It's just luck, or chance, never fate, and definitely not a destined love."

I should probably end it there. There's no need to go on, but now that Aaron's got me started, I don't want to stop. I've never been allowed to openly talk about this with a guest before. There's something exciting about doing the opposite of what Kringle Korp demands.

"And all those people who tell me they love me? They never say it again once they leave the island. They might DM a few times once they're home, text too, but once they realize I'm not coming to them and it's prohibitively expensive to come to me, the romance is over. It's not like I'm hurting about it, though, because I never loved them back. I was just trying to make their time in Winter Wonderland that much more special. But when you really think about it, it's laughable how phony it all is. So, no, I don't believe in love. Not one bit."

Aaron's eyes never leave mine. The more I talk, the more the furrow in his forehead softens. His lips part, and his eyes shine in that adoring cartoon kind of way. The way so many people have looked at me, because of all the pieces I put into place to get them to feel cartoon levels of adoration. Except this time, I did something completely different than I've done before.

I told the truth.

Aaron swallows. "Is it weird that I want to kiss you now?"

My heart skips a beat. This is working. Aaron doesn't want me to be some make-believe Kris that other guests always need me to be.

He just wants me to be myself.

It's so unbelievable that I laugh.

"Not weird at all."

# Aaron

Kris's deep chuckle makes my whole body tingle, even when I'm a yard away from him in this chair. Every single part of me explodes when he says "Not weird at all" and beckons for me to sit on his lap. I practically fly from my seat and sit sideways on his legs, his hands wrapping around me, steadying me. On some instinct I had no idea was lying in my subconscious, I wrap my hands around his neck. Within seconds our mouths are an inch apart.

I hesitate before going in.

This is it.

This is going to be my first kiss. My stomach swirls with nerves. I definitely want this. But I don't exactly know how to go about it. How parted should my lips be? Are they too chapped? Maybe I should put some ChapStick on first. How long should the kiss be? Will he think I'm a perv if I use too much tongue?

"Hey." Kris jiggles his leg a tiny bit to snap me back to

reality. "You're up here, aren't you?" He gently taps the side of my head.

I groan. "Am I that obvious?"

"You're just a thoughtful guy, that's all. You know you don't need a plan for this, right? You can just kiss me."

"Right," I say, but I still can't stop the questions that spin through my mind.

"So, are you gonna?" Kris asks after another few seconds of silence.

"Going to what?"

"Kiss me."

"I think I need you to do it fir—"

He cuts off my sentence with his lips. They're warm and wet and soft and taste so good. Like mint and hot cocoa and the tiniest bit of woodsmoke. One hand goes up to my hair, and it surprises me that I don't snap back to stop him from messing up what I meticulously styled. I'm just . . . in the moment. This moment. I let his tongue slip between my lips and gently press against mine. I let his upper lip fold over my own, my mouth his. He knows he's in control, but he doesn't take advantage of that. He's a contradiction: soft and sweet, yet firm and strong. To top it all off, his stubble scrapes against my skin, a roughness that's decidedly welcome.

After who knows how long, Kris pulls away. "So?"

"Hmm?"

He laughs. "What'd you think?"

"I have nothing to compare it to."

His eyes widen just a bit. "That was your first?"

I nod, my cheeks blazing.

"That doesn't mean you can't have an opinion," he says.

I chew my bottom lip, which is still warm from his mouth. My face tingles with the aftermath of his scruff. "I think I liked it."

He quirks an eyebrow. "You think?"

"Yeah. I can't really be sure. But you know what might help?"

Kris grins, catching on.

"Something to compare it to," I say, then lean in again.

We sit like that, kissing, mouths moving harder and softer until even the embers in the fire go black, as black as the deep, dark ocean out in the distance, but my body feels more lit up than it's ever been in my entire life.

We don't stop until a buzzing in my pocket snaps me out of the moment.

It's yet another lame meme from Mom. It says, *Wakey, wakey! Eggs and bac-y!* with a picture of her holding up a plate of eggs and bacon. I think she accidentally positioned them so her two fried eggs look like the balls to a bacon schlong.

"God, she's so cringe," I say through a laugh, showing Kris the text.

"Wow, that's . . . some good morning."

"Jeezus, how late is it?" If Mom's sending good morning

texts from Wisconsin, we've been here way longer than I thought. I spring up from Kris's lap. The cold air that breezes over my thighs makes me wish I was firmly planted back on top of him.

Kris glances at his watch. "Three in the morning. I should get you back."

"We didn't even plan any Casey sabotage," I say. *This* is why crushes are so stupid. They distract from the matter at hand. But Kris doesn't seem bothered.

"What's there to plan?" he asks with a shrug. "You tell me where to show up, and I'll improvise. It's what we do. Wonderers make plans on a dime tailored to each guest. This time it'll just be a little more . . ." He searches for the word. "Destructive."

His evil grin is so wide, even the Grinch would be jealous.

Improvisation goes against everything I believe in. Going in unprepared leads to mistakes. But in this post-kissing haze, I can't come up with any better ideas.

"All right then," I say. "At least take my number in case anything happens."

My heart pounds way more than it should as I recite the digits. I feel like I could float when he gives me his.

*Stick to the plan, Aaron.*

"Meet me tomorrow at the toboggan races," I say. "Or I guess it's today, isn't it?"

Kris nods. "Got it, Captain."

We hop onto the snowmobile, and despite how late it is, I feel more alert than I've ever been before. The feeling continues when I finally make it back into bed, Casey's snores vibrating the wall between us. Which means I lie awake for another couple hours, coming to a solid conclusion: love might not be real, but kissing sure is.

And it's great.

"WHAT HAVE I DOOOOOONE?"

My scream echoes around the snow-covered hillside as we careen down it on a "good ole-fashioned toboggan," as the Winter Wonderland Elves tried to sell it. A good ole-fashioned death trap is more like it. Activities that can result in broken bones, sprained ankles, and missing teeth are not something I would ever label *fun*. The potential injuries from tennis are bad enough, but it's a good résumé booster for colleges, so it's worth it. Killing yourself on a sled, however, is not.

Casey has his long arms wrapped around me, hanging on to the little red and white rope to steer this thing. I tried to convince him that we should bow out of the race seeing as how he's six foot eight, and while I'm just five foot nine, the toboggan was made for two people, not an average-size person and a giant. But he insisted. He said something about it being like when we were kids, going up to the mountains together. His eyes got all big and doe-eyed, so I couldn't resist. I guess if I do sprain an ankle on this thing, at least Casey will be happy.

He was even happier when it was Kris who gave us our sled, nudging me in the ribs, saying, "It's a sign! It's a sign!" If I ever hear that word again, I'm going to strangle him. But when Casey ran off to stake out our place on the starting line—as close to Raquel and Liam as he could get—Kris promised he gave us the rustiest sled around. "The skis will definitely drag," he said.

Drag, my ass. We are *flying*, Casey cackling like mad while we zoom down the hill. He's good at steering, sending us zigzagging so we don't hit anyone. But then I realize his plan all along as I see bright red hair whipping in the wind. He's steering us *toward* Raquel. I yank on the reins, jerking us hard to the left to avoid her. The only problem is that toward the left is the advanced hill, the extra-steep one, which we now barrel down to our deaths.

"MAKE IT STOP!" I yell, to which Casey replies with a glee-filled yip. It's high-pitched, reminiscent of a middle school girl, and that's one of the things I love most about my brother that I'll miss when I'm dead. We're going so fast now that I'm sure we're going to zip right down this hill until we slide all the way off the side of the island.

"CASE! CASE, I WANT OFF!"

"Put your hands up, bro!"

"NEVER!"

"Come on! Like this!"

Casey lets go of the reins, and we're free-falling. Not

that we weren't before, but it felt like we had some modicum of control with his hands on the rope. Now there's no hope.

"CASEY!"

He takes the rope again, expertly guiding us back onto the bunny hill, narrowly dodging a grandma with a toddler. We've really got speed now thanks to my little detour, and we soar across the finish line.

"The Merry brothers win!" an Elf calls over the speakers, while I shout, "FUCK!" and Casey lets out a celebratory whoop, loud and sharp in my ear.

It cuts off quickly as he realizes we aren't slowing. We are zooming past the finish line, straight for the very thick forest just beyond. The very thick *tree trunks* that we'll no doubt smash into. That's it. Lights out. Merry Christmas.

"WE'RE GOING TO DIE!"

In all my years of planning, I never expected those to be my last words, but here we are.

Casey yanks on the rope with all his might. The weight of two full-grown dudes, one of whom is a Mega Person, makes the entire sled tip backward, end over end. We roll off at top speed, limbs everywhere, legs bumping into knees, feet hitting shins, jarringly cold snow finding its way down the collar of my jacket and inside my gloves.

We finally, *finally*, roll to a stop. Casey's right boot is smooshed up against my cheek, my mouth is full of snow, and I think I've got a pine bough or two stuck in my hair.

But at least we aren't smashed against a tree. I wiggle my limbs, and nothing seems hurt.

"Casey, you okay? Anything broken?"

He doesn't say a word. For one beat. Two.

"Casey?" I get onto my knees, ignoring the sensation of ice-cold water trickling down my back as the snow melts under my shirt. "Casey!" I shake him, and he finally takes a huge breath before letting out his giant guffaw.

"*HAAAA!*"

When Casey thinks something is seriously funny, he laughs so hard that no sound comes out at all. Then it builds in his chest until it finally comes out in one great big honk.

"Did you—haha—hear—hahahaha—yourself?" He kicks his legs in the air, completely losing it. "That was—hahaha—great, bro! Ooooh!" He clutches a hand to his chest. "I can't breathe! I can't breathe!"

I chuck a snowball at him. "I'm glad to know you find my very real fear amusing."

"Better than amusing." Casey finally sits up, snow cascading down his moppy hair. "We won!"

He pulls me into a smothering hug.

Casey's genuinely smiling again. It's so good to see him more himself, but I hate that he's directing that smile right over at Raquel, who's got her eyes locked on my brother as her new boyfriend runs over to help.

"Are you all right?" Liam asks, the Wonderland version

134

of a superhero. His white skin glows under the sledding hill lights, his jaw is chiseled, his voice is deep and reassuring, and he's already assessing me for bruises.

"Yeah, yeah," I mutter. "Just great."

As Liam turns his inspection on Casey, it's clear the Wonderer doesn't know who my brother is. No spark of recognition, no jealous pride. Not like the way Casey's chest puffs out with each passing second. So Raquel hasn't told Liam that Casey's her ex.

"Oh, I'm all right, all right," Casey says, glaring daggers at Liam's outstretched hand. He doesn't take it, instead launching himself from the ground and throwing his fists in the air in victory. The crowd goes wild, cheering and whistling.

"Good to see you're okay, man," Liam says, then with a smile he heads back to Raquel's side. They walk away, but not before Raquel gives Casey one last look over her shoulder.

"Hail the conquering heroes!" the announcer shouts. "A free starlight cruise for the Merry brothers!"

"Did you hear that, bro?" Casey whips his head my way, his neck giving a loud *crack*. "Okay, yeah, that hurt. I'm gonna need to have this kink rubbed out at the Merry Masseuse." He reaches down and pulls me to my feet. "Did you see the way Raquel was looking at me?"

"I sure did."

"The plan is working."

"That's great, Case." But it isn't.

Casey nods toward the crowd, where a couple waiting Elves have first-place ribbons for us. "Let's celebrate!"

"You go join them," I say, grabbing the toboggan. "I'm going to return this, then I'll catch up."

"Righto, bro!" Casey takes off, his long legs flinging up buckets of snow.

I stomp over to the Sled Shack and slam the toboggan on the counter. "So much for dragging! This thing was supposed to be *slow*."

Kris points a gloved hand toward my brother. "That guy should be a Wonderer. He's got Christmas in his blood. I haven't seen sledding skills like that since . . . well, since me."

"If we're really going to make this plan work, we're going to have to play dirty."

Kris smirks. "Dirty, huh?"

The way his eyes flit to my lips makes my heart slam against my chest. I know I should have some witty comeback that shuts him up. I know I should move on and focus on the plan.

But that stupid smirk is making my brain go haywire.

"Y-yeah," I breathe, biting down on my bottom lip.

Could I *be* more obvious?

Kris grabs my toboggan and hangs it up with the rest along the wall. "There. All the sleds are returned." He walks from behind the counter and steps beside me. "Want to get out of here?"

I can only nod.

He grabs my hand and leads me into the woods. I didn't want to crash against these trunks before, but I don't mind being pushed against them now.

And while Casey gets lost in the victor's celebration, I get lost in Kris's kiss.

# Kris

I've kissed dozens of guys. I'm not sure exactly how many, but I've found somebody to pair up with almost every Twelve since ninth grade minus the ones where no gay teens come in. That's two-ish guys a month, with one month off for summer break and the two-week vacation in the spring. So that's twenty-one a year, and we've been doing this for the better part of three years. Even on the years when someone's told they're loved early, or in spring semester when the Race is on hiatus, I'll still pair up, because what can I say? I like to make out.

So I've kissed dozens of people. I don't know if that's a lot of guys in the wider world, but on Winter Wonderland, we're all at about the same number of kissing partners, give or take a few. At least for my class. It must be a side effect of the Race, because all the other classes tend to pair off with each other in terms of dating. The town's baffled we don't follow suit, a mystery to them, but we've kept the Race under wraps all these years. Honestly, since most of us will stay on the island, we'll probably all eventually end up together, minus yours truly thanks to the lack of gays my age. What I'm trying to say is, I have a lot of experience when it comes to making out. But no one's come close to kissing as good as Aaron.

I haven't been able to stop thinking about him since I had him pressed up against a pine tree yesterday. We could only make out for about five minutes before he had to go, making sure Casey didn't chase after Raquel once the post-toboggan revelry died down. For the first time I found myself disappointed *not* to spend time with a guest. Usually, hanging with the person we hope falls for us feels like a job. It can be exciting because there's a prize at the end, but it's definitely not relaxing. When Aaron and I kissed on that beach, and then again in the forest, I kind of forgot the competition. Which is totally stupid and can't happen again. I've got to make sure Aaron's actually falling for me, which entails more than making out. That way I can get that audience with Kris Kringle and convince him that he made a mistake letting Uncle Toby go.

"Uh, hello, you in there?" Anjelica snaps her red-manicured fingers in front of my face.

"Wait, what?" I shake my head. "Sorry."

"I was telling you about the time I got hit on by a Grammy-nominated boy band member, and you *zone out*? I know it's not because my story was boring, so what is it?"

"It's nothing. Nothing."

The dance teacher and choreographer for our town-wide numbers barks in our earbuds. "Places everybody!" It's our cue to scatter throughout Santa's Square and blend in before we grace the mainlanders with our music and magic. This time it's "Frosty the Snowman," the intro flash mob to the snow sculpture competition. When the song ends, we'll lead guests to a clearing just south of town that is positively heaping with snow.

Anjelica and I are partnered up on this one for the line "And a button nose," where we lean into our roles of a doting couple. She takes a big gold button and places it smack in the middle of my face, and we laugh and laugh.

It's so lame.

"Just watch where you put those gigantic feet this time," Anjie says as we hit our mark in front of the stained-glass windows of the Workshop. Uncle Toby always used to burst through its front door to belt about Frosty's coal eyes. "Last Twelve I almost broke a heel tripping over them."

"You know I can't help the size of my—"

Whatever I'm about to say, it doesn't matter, because there's Aaron. Standing on the edge of the fountain and scanning the crowd.

"Seriously?" Anjelica scoffs. "You're zoning out again?" She follows my line of sight. When she sees Aaron, her whole face shifts. She *knows*. "Ooh. Okay. I see."

"What? What? What?" Why am I repeating myself? "You see nothing."

"Yeah, right, and that boy band member *didn't* try to get a handful of my butt before I kicked his creepy ass in the shin." Anjie puts a hand to her mouth in mock horror. "Maybe I've created monsters." She eyes me up and down like I might go feral on her at any moment.

"What are you being so dramatic about now?"

"It's just that you seem to have forgotten what it's like to have an actual crush. You're getting all googly-eyed over here, but you're so caught up in the Race that you can't even tell when you have real feelings for your mark." Anjelica shakes her head. "It's my fault, really. I never should have put our class up to it. I'm Dr. Frankenstein, and you're all my deranged little creations that have forgotten how to love. Except no, Frankenstein's monster did want love, actually. You're all worse than a being made up entirely of corpse parts. Think about that."

"Love doesn't exist, Anjelica, and you know it." I've got to admit, my body does feel like I've had a five-shot dirty cocoa when I look at Aaron. But it's not from real feelings, despite how much Anjie wants to turn this into some holiday rom-com.

Anjelica waves me off. "All I'm saying is, it's not like it would be a *bad* thing if you had real feelings someday. But probably not with your Race pairing since, you know, he's leaving the island when this Twelve is over."

I'm too distracted to pay attention to Anjie. When Aaron finds me in the crowd, he beams, literally jumping from the fountain to jog my way.

Anjie watches him heading straight for us. "Speaking of googly-eyed."

She cackles but is cut off by the opening notes of "Frosty." Aaron's instantly caught up in the motion of all us Wonderers leaping and dancing through the square. He keeps his eyes on me the whole time, though, despite a few of the Elves from the Confectionary pulling him into an impromptu conga line.

At the end of the number, Santa—played by Noelle's dad, Roger, who's one of the Black Santas we've got on the island—tells everyone to follow him to the Snowman Stretch, the big clearing where we host the snow sculpture competition. Everyone hustles out of the square, Anjelica included, but not before giving me an *I told you so* look as Aaron and I fight against the stream of people to find each other.

"You ready?" Aaron asks, out of breath. He grabs my hand so he can't get pulled away by the crowd. Even through our gloves I can feel a sort of electricity on contact. "We've got to find some way to completely destroy Casey's sculpture without being too obvious. After yesterday's race, Raquel can't have another data point telling her Christmas is Casey's thing. She needs to see that the holiday runs in *Liam's* blood and choose him."

"Wait." I plant my feet, stopping Aaron's forward momentum. "*Liam?* As in the most famous Wonderer, Liam Campbell?"

He's Kringle Korp's favorite resident thanks to all the positive buzz his ass gets on social media. He's also one of the few Wonderland High alums who doesn't have a Christmas-related moniker. If Aaron had said the names Nick or Carol or *Kris*, or listed off any reindeer, I'd need last names to clarify. Liam, however, is easy. He graduated last year and has always been a nice guy. I wouldn't say we're close by any means, but we've shared classes, competed on hockey teams together, all the typical islander stuff.

"Raquel needs to choose Liam?" I ask. "Like for a holiday fling, right?" I saw them sledding together, but I guess I didn't think anything of it. Townies do activities with guests all the time. It's what we're *supposed* to do.

Aaron shakes his head. "Nope. They're full-on dating, apparently. Met online, and now they're together."

My stomach squirms knowing Liam's now a pawn in our scheme. I am trying to help him get the girl, because Casey and Raquel are not Aaron's end goal, but this complicates things.

Movement out of the corner of my eye catches my attention. It's a wave of Mrs. Clauses pouring out of the bakery, ready to give fresh-baked cookies to the snow sculpture competitors and audience. Sure enough, Mom is in the group, and she gives me a wave.

"Hi, sweetie!" she calls. "I'll save you a sweet treat!" With a wink, she's off with the pack of Santa Wives, and I'm here with my stomach turning like I've drunk a glass of spoiled milk.

It's not just Liam whose fate will be determined by how successful Aaron and I are. Mom and Dad too. Because if I'm caught ruining Casey's experience, this could be the end of the Bright family's stay in Winter Wonderland. Mom's dream bakery job, my parents' secure housing and health care gone, just like that.

Aaron gently shakes my shoulder. "Kris, you okay?"

"Yeah," I grunt. Crap. That wasn't convincing at all. I clear my throat and give him my best Wonderer smile. "Totally. My mind is just full of all kinds of ideas on how we can do this. Listen, you go on ahead without me. We've got to be incognito, right? I can't just blatantly sabotage a guest's sculpture without it being too obvious. I'll only be a few minutes behind you, and then we can meet in the forest. I'll be in the trees closest to you and your brother."

Aaron grins mischievously. "You totally get me. Thinking through the details. See you there."

He dashes off without a backward glance, excitement practically dripping off him as he gets caught in the crowd headed to the competition. Meanwhile my nerves are on edge as my mind whirls with ideas how *not* to get caught with so many people around.

*Bzz bzz bzz.*

My coat vibrates as a text comes through the phone in my pocket. I don't hesitate to pull it out. It could be a command from the Head Elves, and if you ignore their texts, your name's written on the Naughty List. And I don't mean the bar. Three times on that thing with minor infractions, and you're out.

But the message isn't from any Wonderer. Well, not a current one at least. It's from Uncle Toby, a picture of him in a Santa outfit. He's beaming from ear to ear, his rosy cheeks pushed about as high as I've ever seen them.

**Check me out! Finally wearing the red coat! I can't begin to tell you how amazing it is to watch kids' faces light up when they see me in this. Wish you could see it in person. How's the Christmas Twelve going? Love you, Uncle Toby**

That spoiled-milk feeling is burned away by fiery indignation. Uncle Toby's Santa suit is nothing compared to what he'd be wearing here. His mall-issued costume is dull, the red faded, the buttons more matte than shiny— it's all wrong. Uncle Toby should be *our* Santa.

I shove my phone back into my pocket. If I don't help Aaron, there goes any shot of him falling for me, and of me winning the Race. Without that personal audience with Kringle, there's no way I'll be able to remind our founder of his spirit of generosity he seems to have lost to the board.

I've got to get my head in the game.

It's time to melt some snow.

# Aaron

The path to get to the Snowman Stretch is actually pretty magical. The trees are towering and snow-covered, candy cane lampposts glow along the trail, and there are fountains and statues and benches along the way for you to take in the enchanted forest vibes. When you come into the clearing, snow billows down from clouds that glow slightly orange thanks to Winter Wonderland's joyful light. It's extremely romantic. It really would be the perfect setting for Casey to win back the love of his life. But instead, it's just going to have to serve as a whimsical locale for making his dreams crash and burn.

"Okay, there she is," Casey says, whispering to me even though Raquel and Liam are all the way across the clearing. They wear matching snowsuits, red and white with patterns of log cabins, pine trees, and snowflakes. They are objectively adorable and should be spokesmodels for whatever company made their outfits. If Casey were seeing this in a picture back home, it'd break him. Now, though, seeing them in person lights this fire inside him that I know won't stop billowing until Liam is out of the picture.

"So, the rules say we can make any kind of sculpture we want," Casey explains. "And all these chumps are sure to go the easy route and make a snowman. But Merrys aren't chumps, are they?"

He stares at me expectantly, like a very hoorah cliché sports coach or something, and I try to match his energy with a "No, sir?" It comes out like a question, but Casey's on board.

"That's right, we aren't. We're going to go all in and make something that really stands out. Santa's sleigh. Pulled by Rudolph."

He says it like it's the simplest thing in the world, but I have my doubts. "We're going to make an entire sleigh and a reindeer in an hour?"

"Of course we are. Raquel always said she thought the idea of Santa's sleigh was the most romantic thing in the world. Cozied up together while you sail through the sky, feeling like you could touch the stars."

He looks up, even though it's too cloudy for any stars to shine through. It reminds me of how otherworldly it was to see all those stars on the beach with Kris. It was an objectively romantic moment, and I almost feel bad it was wasted on me. I've decided that while he's been giving me all sorts of feelings, this is just going to be a brief fling. And since Kris doesn't believe in love either, it works for both of us.

Thank god Casey hasn't taken Raquel to that beach. She for sure would have fallen for him right then and there. Just like she might if Casey's successful, taking the snow sleigh as a sign they should be the ones cozied up in Santa's magic vehicle of choice.

But thankfully, Casey dreams big. His idea sounds fairly complicated, and there's no way we're going to get a good-looking and functional sleigh built in sixty minutes. Not functional in that it could actually move, but you know, sittable. Maybe Casey will make sabotaging this way easier than I thought.

Casey gives orders like a drill sergeant. "Okay, I'll get to work on building the sleigh itself, and you grab the accoutrements we're going to need." He waves his hand with a flourish when he says *accoutrements*. "Start with sticks for antlers."

"Got it." I hustle over to the trees while Casey gets to work heaping shovelfuls of snow, one on top of the other.

My work here should be pretty simple. I just won't show up with any sticks, or I'll find puny ones that don't look at all like antlers. But knowing Casey, he's going to come looking for himself if I don't have anything that fits his vision. This is where Kris comes in.

As soon as I'm hidden by the trees, I start looking for

my Wonderer. Oh god, I did not just call him *my Wonderer*. One, that's creepily possessive. Two, all we've done is make out. I cannot go all Casey and put way more attachment into Kris than either of us wants.

Anyway, Kris said he'd lie in wait here, hidden by the forest. "Kris? Kris, where are y—"

A snowball hits me square in the chest. "Keep it down! All of Winter Wonderland is going to know we're working together if you keep yelling my name."

Kris pops out from behind a tree, a dark green beanie on his head. It's the pièce de résistance on his head-to-toe camouflage gear.

"You had time to change?"

Kris shrugs. "I'm trying to be incognito."

Why is it that whenever someone wants to blend in, their outfit makes them stick out like a sore thumb?

"What's the plan?" Kris asks.

"I need you to gather sticks. And hide them."

Kris looks over both shoulders, scanning the woods. There are literally hundreds—probably thousands—of fallen branches out here away from the groomed paths. "Uh, hide them? *All* of them?"

He's got a good point. "Just do what you can. I'll help. The longer it takes me to get back, the better, right?"

We get to it, gathering sticks and branches and tossing them as far back from the clearing as possible. It's surprisingly hard work, bending down over and over again just to toss branches another ten to twenty feet, depending on how good our aim is between the trees. As time goes on, it becomes clear that this is a losing battle. All Casey will have to do is run deeper into the woods to find decent makeshift antlers. It'll cost him an extra thirty seconds, max.

But the time isn't entirely wasted. Kris's face gets pink with effort the more he works. He takes off his jacket, so I can see the deep green Henley he's got on and just how wonderfully it hugs his biceps.

After a solid minute of me staring, Kris finally notices. "Something got your attention?" We both know he's caught on to being my eye candy.

I give him one last up-down before saying, "No, nothing," but I have to hide my face so he can't see this unstoppable grin. All I want to do is kiss him, but there're sculptures to ruin. I've got to *focus*. "I should get going. Casey will be suspicious if I'm gone too long. Just keep doing this."

Kris throws his hands up. "There's got to be more I can do than unsuccessfully hiding fallen branches."

"I don't know, just *improvise*," I say, bending down and grabbing two tiny twigs that would be the sorriest excuse for antlers anyone's ever seen. "That's what you do, isn't it? What would really make Casey lose?"

I dash off before I can get his answer, but I hear sticks snapping and branches swaying, like they're being plowed through. Hopefully that means Kris is off on a mission that will actually be productive.

By the time I get back to Casey, I've been gone for sixteen minutes. But wow, what a difference those minutes can make. Casey's already created a huge block of snow. Three sturdy sleigh sides stand tall and perfectly straight. On the fourth, he's hacking away with his shovel, creating the beginnings of a seat.

"You're, like, actually really good at this," I say.

Casey doesn't look up, just responds between panted breaths. "Of course I am. You didn't think I wasted all that time on the mountain doing nothing, did you?"

I mean, I kind of did. I thought whenever he and Raquel went on ski trips, all they did was post up in their room in matching pajamas and have sex. But based on the smooth seat that's now very in focus, Casey honed some serious skills.

When the seat's complete, he throws his shovel down and beckons for me to come closer. "Show me what you found for antlers, bro."

I proudly hold up the little toothpicks.

"That's all you got?" Casey asks.

"Uh-huh."

"In an entire forest full of trees?" I knew he wouldn't buy this, but I need to try to convince him either way.

"Yeah. They really groom the place. Must be for visitor safety, you know? Winter Wonderland wouldn't want guests wandering through the woods only to trip and impale themselves on some massive spruce spear." *Spruce spear?* I'd roll my eyes at myself if I could. Instead, I give Casey big *I'm sorry* eyes to hopefully make him believe I'm not bullshitting.

"You're probably right," he says. "I'll figure something out. In the meantime, go and make four long snow tubes, would you? I'll use them as Rudolph's legs."

"Reindeer legs. Got it." Here's where I can really slow the process down. I'll make the four most misshapen limbs anybody's ever seen, and Casey will have to spend so much time backtracking to fix my mistakes that there's no way he'll be able to pull out a win.

I scan the trees as I half-heartedly pack snow, looking for Kris. I don't see him anywhere. I hope he hasn't totally given up on helping me; he seemed anxious in the square.

Another twenty minutes go by before Casey's hovering over me, blocking out the light of the golden bulbs strung through the trees.

"What are those?" He points to the four weird blobs surrounding me, the closest of which I'm adding little mounds of snow to like it's ground beef and I'm molding a meat loaf.

"Legs!" I say, all oozy enthusiasm. "Can't you tell?"

Casey scowls at them for a second before he cracks up. "Those are terrible, bro!" But he doesn't seem upset about it in the slightest. "I should have known these artsy competitions weren't really your thing. If this was a snow spreadsheets comp, I know I could count on you, but this?" He's all smiles while he shakes his head. Then he drops to his knees, snow pillowing out around his legs. "Mind if I take over?"

I motion for him to have at it, and Casey gets to work. He picks up each of my weird snow masses, cuts them in half lengthwise, and smooths them out by rubbing them between his gloved hands like if he swirled them fast enough, he could start a fire.

While he gets to cleaning up my mess, I take in the sleigh. My heart instantly falls into my butt. This sculpture is *good*. The sleigh sides are now curved, their ends curlicued as if they're made from carved wood. It's so clear what it is, while looking around at some of the other creations leaves me wondering what the hell these guests are trying to make. Like with the next group over, I can't tell if it's a penguin or some sort of fanged demon. Casey's begs to be ridden with its perfectly smooth seat that two people could totally cozy up on.

I scan the rest of the entries, and Casey was right: most are doing snowmen. My brother has a serious chance of winning this. When I do a full 360 of his sculpture, I find that he's even included a little license plate with *RASEY* written in snow letters. If any sleigh could win her back, it's this one.

"Ten minutes to go, contestants!" Santa calls from the

middle of the clearing. Casey has somehow molded an entire reindeer and is just now putting finishing touches on its face. It's not lifelike by any means, but it's definitely cartoonish, and you can tell without a doubt that it's supposed to be Rudolph. Casey even pulls a red ornament out of his pocket to place on the little sleigh puller's nose. Somebody came prepared. Short of just kicking it all down, I can't think of any way to sabotage his artwork. And while stumbling on top of Rudy might make me succeed, the look of hope and pride in Casey's eyes is too much for me to go through with it.

Casey notices me taking in his handiwork and pulls me into his side. "I know. It's pretty great, right? Last thing I'll need—and please don't take this the wrong way, bro—are some different sticks for the antlers. I appreciate you helping, but those things are too tiny. I know the Claymation Rudolph has little nubs for antlers when he's young, but we need grown Rudolph, *ripped* Rudolph. Gotta remind Raquel that I'm the man for her, not some stupid kid she met when I was a sixth-grade boy."

With that, he and his lanky limbs go lumbering through the woods. Just as he exits, Kris trudges down the path into the Snowman Strech holding a giant, bulky stainless-steel coffee percolator.

"Casey already seems pretty amped up," I say. "I don't think he's going to need the caffeine."

Kris has a gleam in his eyes. "This isn't full of coffee."

He pulls off the lid and steam billows out. "I told the Elves back in the cafeteria that I wanted to take some cocoa to the snow-sculpting participants." He puts the lid back and sets the percolator down, right between Rudolph and the sleigh. "Get to it."

"To what?"

"To dumping the piping-hot liquid all over Casey's sculpture. I would do it, but if anyone sees me, I could get in trouble. Guests are forgiven everything."

"Right." I swallow, picturing Casey so full of pride again. I already feel guilty, but this is for my brother's own good. I look to Kris, trying to soak up the determination that's set in his eyes. I can do this. I can improvise.

"Oh, wow," I say, and I know my voice is too loud and my enthusiasm sounds too forced. "Hot chocolate!"

I barrel toward the percolator. "Oh no. I'm slipping." Living up to my nickname, my tone is much too robotic. But even still, I trip myself and stumble, then fling my leg back and smack it against the stainless-steel container. The lid flips off, and steam puffs into the sky like a column of smoke. Hot cocoa pours over the side of Casey's sleigh, instantly melting the snow with a hiss. The seat gets wobbly before it collapses in on itself. Splatter even hits part of Rudolph's ass, making his butt pockmarked with the brown liquid. We were able to undo in five seconds what Casey made in fifty-five minutes.

Heavy footsteps crash through the snow as Casey

makes it back from the woods. "Hey, look what I found." His voice drops the instant he sees the aftermath of the great cocoa catastrophe. The gigantic, perfectly antler-reminiscent branches he has raised over his head droop to the ground, leaving trails in the snow as Casey trudges over to what was formerly his sleigh. "What happened?"

His eyes well with tears as he glances between me, Kris, and the percolator on the ground. He hardly looks at the sleigh, occasionally glancing at it but only for milliseconds at a time. I can tell if he really gave the mess a nice long look, it'd push him over the edge.

"I-I slipped," I stutter. "I am so, so sorry. Kris was bringing cocoa to the sculptors, and I must have hit some ice, because one moment I was walking to get a cup, and the next moment I was tripping straight toward the container and—and . . ." I motion to the decimated sleigh.

Casey wipes at his eyes quickly. "Are you all right?" He grabs my shoulders and holds me at arm's length, looking me up and down. "That cocoa seems like it was pretty hot. Were you burned?" He looks over his shoulder to Kris. "How 'bout you? Any get on you? You okay?"

I want to barf. This was all a setup, and Casey's first instinct is to make sure that we weren't hurt. I am a terrible, terrible brother.

"Yeah, no, Case, we're fine." I can't even look him in the eye when I say it. "I'm just sorry about your sculpture." I'm not acting anymore. I am sorry about it, yet I've got to remain firm that this is the right thing to do. This pain is what Casey needs to finally become an independent person. This backstabbing is ultimately going to be character-building.

"That's time!" Santa calls. "The judges will now score your creations. The winner gets a one-night stay in the Santa Suite!"

Everyone *oohs* and *aahs* at the possibility of getting to stay in the most luxe room in all of Winter Wonderland, perched on the top of the Workshop and overlooking the entire idyllic town. Kris perks up too, eyes on Santa and his helpers starting to head our way.

"Well, I'd better go get some more of this for the other guests," Kris says, snagging the percolator and lid from the ground. "So sorry about your sculpture."

"It's fine," Casey says. "It wasn't your fault."

Kris quickly locks eyes with me, gives a wink, and then bolts back into the woods before the judges arrive. He definitely doesn't seem off anymore. He seems so sure of everything, a man on a mission. Meanwhile, I feel about two seconds away from confessing the entire thing to Casey and begging for forgiveness. This trip was supposed to be about boosting him up, yet here I am bringing his spirits way down.

"Oh no no no," Santa says when he and two Elves survey the crime scene. "What happened here?"

"It was supposed to be your sleigh," Casey mutters.

"Then . . . cocoa accident."

"It happens to the best of us," one of the Elves says.

"But!" The other reaches down and takes a handful of cocoa-drenched snow and shoves it into their mouth. "Delicious!"

"Ten points for deliciousness, my boy!" Santa calls, and that at least puts a smile on Casey's face. "For sculpting, however, I think we'll have to mark this as incomplete." He's just about to move on when he spots Rudolph. "But wait! What's this?"

Santa and the Elves hover over the snow reindeer. "This is one of the best Rudolph creations I've ever seen. What do you say, Elves? I think we could judge this reindeer separately from the sleigh, don't you?"

"Certainly," one says, while the other chimes in with, "Of course!"

Casey lights up like a Christmas tree. "Really? Oh, wait!" He grabs his majestic antler branches and plops them onto Rudolph's head. "There. Now he's complete."

*Of course*, right when Santa leans in for closer inspection, the back half of Rudolph collapses to the ground. Those cocoa pockmarks compromised the integrity of Casey's construction.

"Well." Santa doesn't seem to have words after that. He just shrugs and moves on to the next group and their fanged penguin demon.

"Casey, I'm so sorry," I say.

"Don't worry about it, bro." He sounds completely defeated. "You didn't mean to do it."

He had to say that, didn't he? He just had to add the one thing that could rip my heart in two.

Casey looks across the clearing to where Raquel and Liam stand by their very generic snowman. But they're laughing, throwing snowballs at each other, Liam hamming it up and taking a bite out of their snowman's carrot nose. He even videos it, evidence of their adorableness sure to go to his hundreds of thousands of followers in no time.

"Do you think she saw it?" Casey asks. "Before it all came crashing down?"

He looks at me with hope in his eyes. He needs her to have seen it. He needs her approval.

And that's when my guilt vanishes, faster than I melted his sleigh. Casey's attachment to her makes him weak. He *shouldn't* need Raquel's approval, but here he is desperate for it. He can't see that he made the most epic snow sculpture out of the dozens of people participating. He can't see his own talent without getting Raquel to sign off on it first. I'm doing the right thing by getting him used to not having Raquel around. I'm making him a better person. A stronger person.

I put a consoling hand on his shoulder, which always feels weird since he's so much taller than me. "I don't think so, Case. But I saw it. And you know what?"

Casey looks at me, his cheeks red from what I wish was the cold, but from what I know is holding back tears. "What?"

"Your sculpture was amazing."

"But—"

"There's no 'but,' Casey. You hear me? No 'but.'"

"Yeah, okay." But Casey can't stop himself from looking back at Raquel. That's the "but" I have to worry about.

Thankfully, Raquel doesn't look over once. She's completely in her moment with Liam. Anybody watching would think she's clearly moved on.

Yet it's too early to think I've got this in the bag. Knowing Raquel, a new sign could pop up at any moment, leading her back to Casey.

I've got one week left to make sure she officially leaves my brother behind.

# Kris

My body buzzes. Really truly buzzes. This is like the feeling of making out but magnified. I've never done that kind of thing before. Knowingly and willingly fucked up a guest's experience. At first, my mind couldn't get over the destruction we caused, especially considering that I'm literally the best at everything on this island thanks to Uncle Toby's teachings. That's not to be braggy or whatever, it's the truth. I've sculpted so many snow statues that I could've used my talents to craft something that would have made Casey's entry stand out. Not that he needed much help, to be honest. He'd do well living and working on a Christmas-themed island. But instead, we went full Grinch on his skills, and you know what?

It felt good.

I know that makes me sound terrible. But I've spent over eighteen years on this island, and it's always fake smiles and dance routines and the "magic" of Christmas.

Just this once it was great to do something that would label me a certified Scrooge. Only, I guess it's not just this once, is it? I've got to keep doing this until Aaron says we're good to go. Until he hopefully falls for me by messing with his brother. In any normal situation, I'd say starting a relationship this way—by destroying someone's dreams—is all kinds of toxic, but Aaron will be gone in one more week. Nobody will be hurt. Well, nobody except for Casey, but Aaron says it's to make his brother stronger, so it really can't be bad, right? I'm not the kind of guy who would take pleasure in another person's suffering.

At least, I don't think I am.

"That. Went. Perfectly!" Aaron plops right next to me in the golden bleachers surrounding the ice-skating rink. He sounds just as excited as I feel, so really, I shouldn't be worried about anything. This is just two people following through on a plan, not ruining someone's life. Then he leans over and kisses me on the cheek.

Aaron snaps away as soon as he realizes what he's done. "Oh god. That was all kinds of sappy. Making out is one thing, but kissing you on the cheek? Pretend I didn't do that."

"Will do," I say with a chuckle, but inside my heart soars. He's totally falling for me.

Aaron hurriedly laces up a pair of rented skates. He said to meet here because there's always a steady stream of visitors, so if Casey or their dad happens to spot the two of us together, Aaron can just explain it away as coincidence as opposed to the two of us looking like we're conspiring.

"Your acting skills were brilliant," I say. "A little rocky at first, but then you leaned into that apology to Casey. He totally fell for it. Great work."

"Thanks. But one melted sleigh isn't going to get the job done. Casey was planning all night to make up for it."

"So what can we tank next?"

Aaron looks over both shoulders. "Come on. Let's skate in case anyone's listening."

"Who would be listening to us?"

Aaron shrugs. "I don't know. Maybe it's just the whole Santa thing making me paranoid. 'He sees you when you're sleeping. He knows when you're awake.' We're too easily overheard on these risers. But on the ice, people will be too focused on not falling to care what we're saying. I'll skate a couple feet ahead of you when I give you the rundown."

Wow. Nobody can say this guy doesn't think of everything. "All right, James Bond. Lead the way."

Aaron takes one step down the bleachers and instantly loses his footing. I snatch him by the elbow before he smashes his nose on the unforgiving metal. He looks up into my eyes, chest heaving. "Th-thanks."

"You've probably never been in skates before, huh?"

He shakes his head.

"Can I at least walk you down to the ice? I promise we can go back to being incognito once I make sure you don't break anything."

"Mmm."

I'm beginning to learn that Aaron talks a lot in hums. He lets me lead as I steady him down the steps. For me, ice skates feel like a second set of feet. In fact, the skating flash mob will be tomorrow.

"Okay, the next step," Aaron says as soon as he hits the rink, but then he quickly stops short. His arms windmill to catch his balance. "Whoaaaaaa!" He sounds like a comically scary ghost as he teeters and wobbles, hinging back and forth at the waist to stay upright.

I know firsthand what damage those flailing fists can do, so I duck and weave at just the right time to pull up behind him and place steadying hands on his hips. He sucks in a breath when I make contact, but then he places one of his frantic hands on top of mine. He doesn't pull them away, so I think this suddenly intimate moment is okay by him.

Bingo. This is without a doubt one of the most romantic positions we could be in on the entire island. And Aaron's into it.

Time to up the flirting.

"Are you sure this was the best choice for a meet-up location?" I ask. "Because you seem to be having a lot of trouble."

Aaron squeezes my fingers. "No. No. This is good."

"I'm sure it is."

"Don't be so pleased with yourself. If I wasn't positive

I'd fall on my ass if I looked over my shoulder, you'd see that I'm totally rolling my eyes at you right now."

"Oh, is that how it is? I can just let go then." I lift my hands, and he instantly starts to lose his footing.

"No, don't!" he shouts. My hands fly back to his sides, and we're good again. "Just a little bit longer."

"I'm here for as long as you need."

Aaron actually sighs, the sound mingling with the *swish* of dozens of blades on the ice. Then he clears his throat and even shakes his head a little, like he's trying to knock himself back into his senses. "Anyway," he says, "I've been thinking. Casey can't see you on our next mission. If he catches on that you're present every time his plans to impress Raquel go wrong, he's going to know something's up. He's a pretty optimistic guy, but he's not stupid. I mean, he can instantly tell if one of the kids he works with is off. He's perceptive."

"Behind the scenes from here on out," I say. "Got it." Which should be very easy. We're sent on missions to make guests' stays extra special every Twelve. Kringle Korp wants the magic to happen without them always seeing us. That way visitors truly do believe it's the spirit of Christmas at work. Not to mention staying in the shadows will keep any witnesses to a minimum, so I won't be found out in my Casey sabotage and kicked off the island.

"Well, you say that now, but based on your schedule tomorrow, it might not be so easy to stay incognito."

Aaron keeps his head pointed forward while he says it, but I can feel him tense up.

"What did you have in mind?"

"The skating flash mob? Casey plans on cruising right up to Raquel during it to profess his love. He's been studying Wonderland videos on social media and thinks he can get the choreography down. Raquel will think it's a Christmas signal yet again, and Casey will be one step closer to winning her back. We've got to stop him. Actually, *you've* got to stop him."

"When the whole town is gathered?"

Aaron nods.

"Including a huge chunk of the other townies who could witness me messing with a guest's experience?"

"Yep."

"And if we're caught, not only will your brother know that you're deliberately trying to tank his love life, but I would most likely lose my job?"

Aaron finally looks over his shoulder. "Oh god. I didn't even think of that. I know you said yesterday you could get in trouble, but they'd actually fire you?"

Crap. I should have kept that to myself. I can see the wheels turning in Aaron's mind. If he cuts me out of the plan, he'll have no time to hang out and fall for me while he continues the Casey corruption. So I wave him off. "No, no. It's fine. I've thought this through. I'm in this."

Aaron's silent for a bit, staring straight ahead as we

circle the rink. I didn't notice it before, but he's synced up the movement of his skates with mine. I also didn't notice just how close my hands are to his butt, and how well his snow pants fit the form of his body. What I really want to ask Aaron is when in his plans has he made time for us to make out again? Because there's always time for that, right?

Aaron takes my hand from his waist, snapping me out of my horny thoughts. His forehead is furrowed, the usual position it's in, like he's always calculating how to be a step ahead of everyone else. Only this time, there's something else there. Not just obsessive planning. This time there's worry.

He's steady on his skates as he pulls me up with him so that we're side by side.

"Wait. I need to know the truth. You could lose your job if you're caught?"

Yet again, I can tell that Aaron will know if I'm lying. So worrying that he might pull the plug if I confess that there are actually pretty strict rules on the happiest island on Earth doesn't matter. Aaron's a planner. I guess I can just tell it to him like it is and hope that he comes up with a solution that works for both of us—and keeps him falling for me.

"It's possible," I say. "Townies have to keep the spirit of Christmas alive at all costs. Sometimes that cost is our place in Winter Wonderland if we fuck with the joy."

"All along I thought the only thing that could go wrong is Casey finding out and hating me forever. I didn't realize that your life could go up in flames too."

The thought of getting me and my whole family kicked out of Wonderland does still make my stomach turn. But something's changed after the Casey cocoa incident. Now when I picture figuring out some way to mess up tomorrow's flash mob, I'm not so much nervous as amped up. I want more of that buzzing. Like, I think I now know what people mean when they say they feel like a kid on Christmas Eve, a feeling you don't really get when every day is Christmas where you live. It's like a big present is waiting for me. Something unknown and adventurous in the not-so-distant future. All my life it's just been to make Christmas happen for the mainlanders, no matter what they ask or what time of year it is. But here, Aaron is giving me permission to do the exact opposite. Well, not permission exactly, since he could do nothing to stop the Polar Patrol from getting rid of the entire Bright family if we're caught. But he's the first guest to ask me to mess shit up. And I like it. A lot.

"Kris," Aaron says, pinching my coat between his forefinger and thumb, holding on to me as we slide across the ice. "Seriously, I don't want to mess up your life. I can think of something else. Some other way to distract Casey that you don't have to be involved in. I'm sorry I let this get so fa—"

"No," I say, the word coming out way too loudly. I don't want this to end. I want to see how much I can push this, how naughty I can be without getting caught by the powers that be. "Don't worry about me. Honestly." Especially if sticking it to Kringle means getting one step closer to bringing Uncle Toby back.

That buzzing starts in the center of my gut again. It fuels me on when I tug Aaron into me, my feet instinctually leading us on the ice while I press my lips to Aaron's. I'll seal the deal with a kiss. We pull away after only a few seconds, but the scowl that was furrowing Aaron's forehead is finally gone. Smile lines take over wrinkle duty.

I can't stop my own grin either.

Aaron kisses me again, quickly, softly, but when he pulls back, I know he wants more.

His eyes darken. He looks almost . . .

Hungry.

# Aaron

I don't even know I've stopped skating until Kris drifts in front of me, skating backward. I didn't know we were holding hands until he's far enough ahead of me that our arms are pulled taut. Then Kris flicks his wrist, and I'm sliding toward him. He wraps an arm around my waist and in one fluid motion pulls me into him while he flips forward. It makes my stomach dip like I'm taking the plunge on a roller coaster.

"Can we do more of that?" I blurt. "Kiss?" Why can I only sound like a desperate horny tween? But at least I'm honest. I want what we had back at that beach, and in the woods behind that sled shack. I was so focused on ruining Casey's snow sculpture yesterday that the other very important mission of getting as much kissing in as possible before I leave Wonderland went by the wayside.

But not anymore.

Kris bites his bottom lip as he nods, flipping back

around to skate backward as he faces me. Somehow he just knows where he's going, how not to run into people so he can keep staring at my mouth as we make our way to the exit. I don't stumble once, just succumb to his lead, and when my feet hit the padded floor surrounding the rink, there's no tripping. I guess I'm sure on my feet when my body knows making out is just around the corner.

"Take those off," Kris says, pointing to my skates. We plop down onto the bleachers with a metallic clang and race to untie them. Kris's are off in seconds, three quick movements with his hands and the laces are unknotted and skates whipped from his feet. It makes me wonder what else he can do with his hands. Meanwhile, mine are all fumbly. My anticipation makes me literally shake so that I'm unable to loosen the knot in one, let alone both skates.

Kris chuckles, and I swear I feel it through the risers. It vibrates the metal through my padded snow pants and makes my butt light up like a Christmas tree.

*My butt light up like a Christmas tree?*

What is Winter Wonderland doing to me?

Really the question should be *What is Kris doing to me?*, because when he lifts my left leg in the air and rests it on his knee, my entire body glows from within. My left skate is off in no time, the right soon to follow. At the exact same moment, we realize that my feet are now propped on his legs. When our eyes lock, Kris slides his left arm until it's under my knees, his right behind my back, ready to lift me. "May I?" he asks.

I'm breathless. I don't know what words are anymore.

I can only nod. I've never nodded harder in my life. So hard, it makes my neck crack.

He stands with no hesitation, and my arms fly around his neck. Our faces are inches apart. It would be so easy to lean forward and kiss him, which is what my entire body is screaming to do, but there are too many people nearby.

"Go," I say, and even I can hear the wanting in my voice.

Kris grins that wicked grin and says, "Shoes first." He's off to the rental kiosk, our skates draped over his shoulder, me in his arms, and holy hell, how did I get from *I don't do love* to literally being carried in someone's arms so fast?

Way too soon, Kris is setting me down next to the counter to return our skates. As my feet touch the ground, Kris gives me this look, and I know he's going to be all over me as soon as he can. It's wild to be so relationship inexperienced but to have some sort of animal instinct picking up on Kris's feelings. Those phantom tingles that have lingered ever since we kissed on the beach prick around my lips again. I want so badly for them not to be phantom anymore.

The Elf attendant is way too jolly and way too slow in getting our boots back, chatting Kris up. I have half a mind to just run through the snow in my socks, pulling Kris behind me and popping into the nearest gingerbread cabin to suck face. The frostbite would be worth it.

"Any day now, right?" Kris says as soon as the Elf leaves to grab our shoes. He's just as eager as I am. Knowing that someone wants to be alone with me as much as I want to be alone with him sends a fire through my belly. I've never felt this before. After seventeen years of insisting I'm fine all by myself, it's like every single atom of my being wants to make up for lost time.

The Elf appears with the cheesiest grin on her face. "Here you g—"

I don't let her finish. "Thanks!" I literally jam my feet into my boots and run until we're outside the garland-wrapped fence that borders the skating rink. Now that we're here, I have no idea where to go. I look left. I look right. Everywhere is packed with tourists, and we're not about to go back to my place and get caught by one of the Merry men. Casey would be insufferable.

Kris catches up to me, out of breath. Did I get so wrapped up in making out with a guy that I actually left said guy in the dust to find a place for us to be together? Talk about terrible planning.

"Whoa there," Kris says, grabbing my gloved hand with his.

"Sorry. I just . . ." How do I say I'm ready to smash my face against his without sounding pervy? So instead I ask, "Where?"

Kris knows what I mean.

He nods to the left. "Follow me."

He leads me down the cobblestone street, past the Confectionary, the Molar Express, and Claus Claws Nail Studio. I haven't been this far down Main Street. We go all the way to where the street ends in a golden gate twice as tall as I am. Kris doesn't hesitate to open it, pulling me behind him in a rush. Beyond the gate is just a snowy path, the snow compacted by dozens of pairs of boots, mismatched footprints dotting it in a chaotic pattern. It seems like a high-traffic place, not necessarily somewhere we could make out. Right now, however, it's deserted.

At my confused look, Kris says, "Elf trail. We use these to stay behind the scenes when we need to make Christmas magic happen."

"Magic, huh?" I scoff. "You know you don't have to keep up the ruse with me. This place takes epic planning and lots of skill to run smoothly. We don't have to pretend there's some other force at play here. It takes away from all that you do. *You* make this happen. The Wonderers. You're not magic; you're hardworking."

Kris's mouth falls open slightly, giving me the perfect view of the tongue that I wish was pressed against mine. Kris leans back, like he really wants to take all of me in. "Who even are you?" he breathes.

I shrug as heat rushes to my cheeks. "Aaron Merry. High-strung, thinks of everything, has a plan A, B, C, and D, and that's just for the insignificant crap like what I'll cook for dinner if the grocery store is out of ingredients. Don't even get me started on what my plans look like for the serious stuff. That's how I can tell how much precision has gone into this place." I cringe. I'm going on way too long about this. "Sexy, right?"

Kris laces his fingers through mine, only it's sort of halfway because our fingers are too thick in our gloves. But still, he pulls me close. "You have no idea."

He leads me toward a nondescript gingerbread cottage about fifty feet down the Elf path. It's indistinguishable from the other cottages that line the worker trail. They're not as big or nearly as ornate as the homes guests stay in, but still fit the vibe of the whole island. The only difference between the cottages on the path is a golden number nailed to each of their doors. In the background, I can hear people laughing, and the muffled soundtrack of Christmas music mixing with the *swish* of ice skates. We've gone in a sort of half circle. We're back behind the Frozen Pond, which isn't a pond at all, but the name for the idyllic little skating rink.

Kris lets go of my hand to pop off his right glove so he can enter a four-digit code into the electronic keypad of Cottage 5. A tinkling of jingle bells sounds as the door accepts his code and swings open, which is cute and all, but I have more pressing concerns.

"Your access code is one-one-one-one? Anybody could

guess that!" Part of planning is trying to foresee threats, and that password leaves Kris open to too many people hacking his stuff.

"You were peeking?"

My blush comes back in full force. "I'm not trying to steal your identity or anything. It's just this reflex I have so I can tell people when they've chosen terrible codes."

"I'm teasing," Kris says, and god why does it make my whole body squirm in the best way when he looks at me like that? "We each get our own passcode on the island. That's my birthday. November eleventh. Other people use their birthdays all the time. It seems sort of unfair that I don't get to use that trick just because the day I was born is an easily guessed four-digit code." He pauses a beat. "You know what? I should have put it in backward. That would throw them."

"But that's just one-one-o—"

Kris cuts me off by yanking me behind him into the cottage. "I know, Aaron. It was a joke."

I'm a freaking idiot. "Right. Right."

"You're always in your head," Kris says.

"You're not wrong."

"I think it's time we get you out of it."

"Here?" The inside of this cottage doesn't appear nearly as North Pole–ish as the outside. It's packed with winter sporting goods. Ice skates sit on metal racks, some gleaming with that brand-new, never-before-used shine, some in what look like states of repair, their laces undone or red and green fabric peeled back or blades detached. Row after row of hockey sticks hang on the wall, golden baskets full of pucks underneath. Anything you could need for an ice-related activity is all right here.

"Oh, I'm sorry," Kris says. "I thought you wanted some place secluded. Plus, if any Wonderer comes inside, I can just say that I was bandaging up your ankle after a skating fall." He points to a cubby full of ace bandages, then opens a mini-fridge underneath that's jammed with frozen ice packs. "There'd even be video footage to prove we were at the rink if a worker wanted to fact-check our whereabouts, which they wouldn't, because *who could lie at Christmas?* But if you prefer we do this somewhere more out in the open . . ." He motions to the door, like *After you.*

He really thought of everything.

That's my kind of guy.

I want him so bad.

Right. Now.

I push Kris into the metal rack behind him. A few pairs of skates fall to the floor, but neither of us cares. My mouth flies to his, lips and tongues pressing together. His stubble burns my cheeks, but it feels so good, a much-needed warmth after all this cold. I yank off my gloves so I can run my hands over his buzz cut, the short hairs sending pinpricks of electricity through my palms.

In no time, he places his hands under my butt and lifts me. This is approximately eight million times better than being carried in his arms, and that was my favorite thing that's happened to me in my entire life. He turns us around and sits me down on top of the nearest shelf. The toe of a skate pokes into my left butt cheek, but I couldn't care freaking less. Kris cups the back of my head, keeping my face tilted up to him as he kisses me over and over and over again.

I don't know how my lips could be numb and still feel every single movement of Kris's mouth at the same time. Seconds later, maybe hours, he pulls back, his own mouth redder than a poinsettia.

Jeezus, I hate that I'm thinking in Christmas similes. But if this place brought me to Kris, it's worth it.

His chest heaves as he stands over me, and my heart flutters thinking of what it would be like for him to lay his entire weight on top of my body.

I know I'd like it. And without thinking, I let out a moan, low and longing.

Kris laughs, a brief out-of-breath huff, before tilting my head to the side and kissing along my jawbone. He dots kisses lower and lower, trailing down my neck. Each point of contact is a firework, a true gift.

Why, why, why have I never done this before?

"I take it back," I say, compelled to speak by each burst of energy when his lips make their way down to my collarbone.

Kris stops, his mouth hovering over my skin, one eyebrow quirked in question.

"What I said before," I whisper. "I was wrong. You are magic."

# Kris

"Okay, Wonderers. Half-point check in." The Fling Ring has lingered after class, scooting our desks close to each other to catch up on our Race progress. Anjelica stares us down like the cliché coach in a sports movie where it's halftime and we're definitely losing. Her eyes linger on mine for just the briefest second. She knows as well as I do how much hinges on me winning this thing. If anyone else is close, I'm screwed. "Where are we at? Who's getting someone to fall in love with them?"

You can tell who's feeling hopeful and who's not by the instant reactions. Noelle, Chris, Dasher, and Rudy—of all people—perk up. I can practically see the images running through their heads of what their lives could be like on the mainland if they win this thing and convince Kringle to hire them for the new Wonderland location.

"Get this," says Rudy, who now doesn't sound like he's near death's door in the slightest. "The day you Scrooges banished me to the Ho-Ho was the day you set me up to win. Me and my nurse have seen each other every day since. I'm no doctor, but I'm diagnosing this girl with love."

We all groan while Noelle reaches across her desk to flick Rudy in the back of his head. "That was terrible," she says.

Rudy begrudgingly rubs the point of impact. "Was it, or are you just jealous?"

"Not jealous in the least," Noelle says, leaning back, all confidence. "My guy's asked me over to his cottage tonight. *To meet the parents.*"

Nick throws his hands up in desperation. "Shit. That's it. We've all lost it."

He's not wrong. Both times he was dropped the L-bomb was on the same night he met his mark's family.

"I've got this in the bag." Noelle holds her hand out to high-five Nicky, but Nicky just crosses hers. They're each other's self-described bestie, but Nicky is by far the most competitive of the bunch.

Anjelica leans against the teacher's desk, the unofficial advisor of our twisted little club. "Dasher? Chris? What about you guys? You seemed fairly pleased before Noelle pulled into the lead."

"My mark gifted me an ornament," Dasher says, a confident smirk lifting his russet brown cheeks.

Nick looks unimpressed. "So what? We're all given gifts at one point or another."

He's got a point. Most guests go overboard buying themselves Winter Wonderland goods. When they realize their haul can't all fit into their suitcases and shipping from a remote island in Alaska is astronomically expensive, they tend to give Wonderers their least favorite items as "tips." Honestly, I'd prefer cash. With money I could at least save up to visit Uncle Toby on the mainland. That's the thing about having housing and health care provided. The company keeps wages pretty stagnant at minimum wage, and when you're paying prices for food and other goods that have extra costs because of said difficulties sending things to faraway places, you don't tend to have a lot left over for trips or college or anything considered a luxury.

"But get this," Dasher adds. "The ornament *had our names on it.*" That gets us all riled up. Chris shouts, "My man!" while Nicky slinks deeper into her seat and Anjelica shoots an apologetic glance my way. Noelle gets her determined *bring it on* face.

"Okay, okay, you've had your fun, but listen to this," Chris says, leaning so far forward in his desk that he nearly tips over. "I'm going on a date with my girl." He pauses dramatically, looking each of us in the eye, wanting us to beg for more details. But we're stubborn in the Fling Ring; we're not going to take the bait. "*She* set the date up," he finally finishes. "A private excursion. Whale watching."

"That could go either way, dude," Dasher says. "Whale watching gets booked every Twelve."

"But for just *two people?*" Chris is all confidence. "*And* I checked the Elf schedule, and she's booked a private chef too. Special notes include wanting a *candlelit dinner.*"

Anjelica scoffs. "Poor girl doesn't get how winter works in Alaska. Who needs candles when you've got the aurora borealis to do all the work?" Of course, that instantly makes me think of Aaron. How he looked under the stars, how the greens and purples flashing in the sky reflected in his eyes. How he tasted when he kissed me, like peppermint bark and cherry ChapStick. "But I'll give you this, Chris, she sounds smitten."

Chris leans back again, crossing his arms behind his head. He nods to Noelle. "The Race is on. By tomorrow, I think one of us will have crossed the finish line."

"Well, to make it easier, I'm out." Nick stands from his desk. He's suddenly all smug and aloof. "I just don't think it's fair to win again. Somebody else should get the trip."

"Oh yeah, I'm sure that's the reason." Nicky rolls her eyes, and an evil grin replaces her scowl. "And not at all the fact that the *three girls you were seeing* figured out your game and dumped you together."

Nick's white cheeks go redder than Santa's suit. At least he has the integrity not to deny it.

"Don't feel too bad, Nick," Anjelica says. "I hear two of the girls are dating now. So at least you're the cause of someone else's meet-cute."

"You got too desperate, bud, come on," Chris adds in

his lovable himbo way. The very reason most of us don't date people simultaneously is because this is one small island. It's too easy for your multiple partners to see you with somebody else. Nothing stops romance dead in its tracks like jealousy.

Nick deflates a little at Chris's sincerity. "Yeah, you're right. What was I thinking?"

"It's okay, Nick." Noelle gets up and puts a consoling hand on his shoulder. "Sometimes champions get desperate defending their title. The title that *I'm* going to take."

With that, she leaves, the rest of the crew following close behind. Everyone seems fine. The competitive fire is more of a fun thing, not something we get butt hurt about if we lose. Well, except Nicky, who straight up sulks. And I guess except for me too, because I can see my chances of earning Uncle Toby's place back slipping between my fingers like too-wet snow.

I try to seem unbothered, getting up with the rest of the group so as not to draw anyone's attention that I'm acting funny. But I hang back and gently put my hand on Anjelica's forearm so she knows to slow down and let the rest of the Fling Ring take off. She raises an eyebrow but doesn't question me out loud. It's one of the reasons I like her so much. You'd think because of her party-girl reputation or her extremely rich-girl life she might be out of touch with the needs of other people, but that's the furthest thing from the truth. She's not gushy about emotions and all that, but she knows how to show up.

"I know it's not looking great," Anjelica says when the group is gone. "And you're probably convinced you're not going to win." See? She doesn't miss anything. "But you're not out of the Race yet."

Aaron hasn't given any of the telltale signs that he's close to the L-word. Not like the others have. Sure, I can tell he gets worked up around me, but Aaron has said himself he's an independent guy. It'd be stupid to think he'd throw aside seventeen years of habit and fall in love with me in twelve days. But there's no way I'm going to give up now when I've got only days left to avenge Uncle Toby. I've got no other romantic options on this island, and it'd be dumb for me to try to find someone new so late in the game.

But after hearing how close Noelle and Chris and even Rudy are, I'd be lying if I said I think there's any way in Krampus's hell that I'll end up being the victor. That doesn't mean I'm going to stop spending time with Aaron or give up on trying to take the lead. Noelle and Chris could fuck this all up, and then maybe I'll pull ahead. Besides, there are perks to spending time with Aaron. Like yesterday in the skating shed. And that time on the beach. Or in the woods. I could always go for a little more of that.

"I'm preparing myself for the worst," I say. "But I'm giving it my best shot."

"That's what I like to hear." She squeezes my arm in

sympathy. "Fuck those Wonderland assholes who wouldn't just give Toby the job in the first place. Fuck Dad too, quite honestly." After Kringle said the decision was the board's to make, she straight up asked her dad if he'd just sit down with me and talk, but his "schedule wouldn't allow it." So now we're forced to play this stupid love game in order for me to get inside his house and spring the conversation on him. With my classmates so close, it's going to take a—I can't believe I'm about to say this—real Christmas miracle for me to win.

I sigh. "All this hinges on Aaron now."

Anjelica stops short, the hallway eerily quiet without the clack of her heels on the hardwood floor. "He has a name, huh?"

Oh shit. She's right. Usually, we just refer to whoever we've paired off with as the "guy" or "girl," our "mark," "partner," or "pair." They don't get names when we're talking about them with the Fling Ring, because they'll be gone before we know it. There's no point wasting brain space in remembering their names, so why share them with each other? That I just told Anjelica Aaron's real name makes my insides squirm.

"You like him. I'll say it again: be careful." Anjelica has this really annoying habit of hardly ever phrasing anything as a question. She just *knows*, and it's kind of unsettling that she can see into me so well right now.

"I do not like him," I say, making her blow a raspberry.

"No, seriously, I'm not that stupid. He's leaving the island in, like, a week. I'd be an idiot to get attached. But he is different from other visitors, I'll give you that."

"And that difference made you fall for him." There she goes, stating it again.

"Nooo, that made me *interested* in getting to know him, nothing more. He's immune to this place. He's not so obsessed with Christmas that he can't see what's in front of him. He sees what goes into making Winter Wonderland work. Even if he doesn't have the specifics down, he can at least guess what it takes to keep this place running instead of just assuming Santa taps his nose and makes it all come true."

Anjelica nods. "I get it. He validates you. He knows you're an actual human being."

"Sure. Maybe. But I think he noticed all that stuff more because he's so caught up in his head, not because he's necessarily paying attention to me. He plans everything. I've never met anyone more type A than him."

"Sounds like a barrel of laughs," Anjelica deadpans. "A guy you could really get into some trouble with." She rolls her eyes, thinking that's the furthest thing from the truth. What she doesn't know is that Aaron's plans really could mess up my entire life. I haven't even told her how we're tanking Casey's chances at wooing Raquel. I thought the fewer people who know, the less likely we'll be found out. But Anjie's my *best friend*. I've become hooked on the danger of it all, doing this forbidden act of messing up Christmas for a guest, and she's probably the one person on this island who might understand that.

"Did it ever feel good?" I ask. "Sneaking out? Doing all the things your parents didn't want you to?"

We've made it to the front door now, and Anjelica stops mid-reach into her green and red Birkin, her hands hovering over the gloves inside. Her eyes drift, lost in thought, a small smirk creeping up her cherry-red lips.

"Of course it did," she says. "Why else would I keep all those clippings?"

Anjelica once showed me the album she keeps of all the internet articles written about her: "Kringle Heiress Attends Jingle Ball." "Anjelica Kringle Rumored to Have Dated Three of Five Boy Band Members." "Kringle Kid Hooked on Spirits? (And Not the Christmas Kind)." Each article was accompanied by a picture, from Anjelica walking a red carpet, to Anjelica making out with an up-and-coming rock star, to Anjelica leaning back and laughing at a party when she was in New York City over the summer.

Her favorites were the ones written about the crash. The Fling Ring flocked over those online when we learned Anjelica was going to move to the island. Our parents used them as warnings for how dangerous life on the mainland could be and to prove a point that we've got it good growing up away from barbaric civilization. All the pictures featured a red and green Maserati crushed against the stock market bull in New York. They were accompanied by even more headlines with terrible wordplay: "Kringle's Christmas Crash." "The Plight before Christmas." "Heiress's Holiday Headache."

I know she's picturing every last article right now. She doesn't seem remorseful or embarrassed. She seems wistful. Nostalgic for those times when she was an out-of-control fourteen-year-old and a paparazzo's dream.

"It felt *great*," Anjie says. "Every last bit of press. Every last bit of attention. Growing up, it was always 'Christmas above all else.' 'Be good for Santa.' 'Be charitable for others.' But I was never asked what felt good to me. It's not that I didn't want to help people out or didn't enjoy seeing kids' faces when Mom and Dad and I would bring gifts for them. I love watching Dad change a family's life by giving them down payments for their first home for the holidays. It's just, my parents spend so much time asking other people what they want that I think they forget to ever ask what I want."

I've never pressed Anjie to tell me why she crashed that car, not even when she first showed me her article album. I didn't want to open an old wound if she didn't want to talk about it. Car crashes are traumatic, I assume, since the only cars on the island are Kringle Korp owned, and those have a governor that limits the speed to five miles per hour. But honestly, I don't think I would have understood what

Anjie's saying now if I'd asked about her motivations any sooner. I used to feel pretty connected to my parents, but all that changed after Uncle Toby left. They see his departure as a choice, while I see it as the last-ditch option he had to preserve a shred of dignity. That they couldn't see how unfair it all was just made me feel brainwashed. And now they never talk about the circumstances surrounding his exit unless I bring it up. It's like they just can't comprehend any reality that challenges their perception of Winter Wonderland. Before, I would have thought with her New York penthouses and designer life, Anjie and her family would be the furthest thing from mine. But now I think we have a lot more in common than I ever realized.

"I don't need a therapist to see that my actions were all stereotypical daddy issues," Anjelica continues. "Mommy issues too. I felt ignored, so I went to the parties, still do when I get my breaks off the island. When Dad is forced to pay attention to me, even if it is to punish me, it makes me feel like I have a little bit of control over my own life for once. Not having to answer to *Christmas*. To a fucking holiday. I have to answer only to me and the good time *I* want to have. Is that so bad?"

I shake my head without even really thinking about it. Maybe I don't feel the same amount of pressure as Anjie because I'm not the next in line for the whole Kringle dynasty, but I have been under the thumb of Christmas my entire life thanks to Mom and Dad's decision to move here. Even if I am starting to see them in a different light, my parents chose this path. If my actions got them kicked out of Wonderland, I'd feel terrible.

"What if somebody had gotten hurt?" I ask. "What if your good time ruined someone else's?"

Anjelica perks up. "Ah, that's the fun part. Putting the puzzle together. Making mischief in a way you know wouldn't hurt another soul. I crashed that Maserati at two in the morning when the Exchange was deserted. I waited to drink that mini of vodka until after I crashed my car so that I could genuinely make sure the coast was clear. At parties, I never push any drinks on anybody else, and all my relationships are entirely consensual. So as long as everyone involved knows about the consequences, as long as you don't let anyone else be the collateral damage of your decisions, why not live a little?"

That's just the thing, isn't it? There's no need to worry about consequences, because the worst isn't going to happen. Not with Aaron planning everything, just like Anjelica did. Any damage isn't really damage, is it? It's Aaron making life better for Casey. All I've got to do is stick to his plan, I'll get to snub Christmas spirit for once in my life, and Aaron will go back home with a stronger brother who's better off alone. And since I helped put his brother's life back together, maybe, *just* maybe, Aaron will say he loves me. It's a win-win.

"Why are you asking me all this?" Anjelica stops midway

through pushing open the school's front door. "Wait. Is my sweet little Krissy breaking *rules*?" Her eyes go wide with exaggerated worry. "The horror!"

"Keep your voice down," I snap, nodding toward the Wonderers just outside, mingling with guests, doing what Kringle Korp wants them to do by making the best Christmas ever. But in a hushed voice, I tell Anjie how Aaron and I have been doing the exact opposite, even throwing in the few times we've made out too. She cackles along the entire time.

"This is too good," she says when I've finished. "Oh, Kris, I'm so proud of you!"

"Thanks." I haven't felt this grateful for praise since Uncle Toby left. When he'd tell me I was doing a good job at holiday activities, it meant something. He was the best, and I wanted to follow in his footsteps. *Want* to, if he ever comes back. But now anytime someone says they appreciate my holiday skills, it just feels like an extra jab. I wouldn't have those skills in the first place if it wasn't for my uncle who got kicked out.

But Anjie's pride? Her pure excitement that I'm sticking it to Wonderland boosts me up in a way I haven't felt in months.

Yet as we walk toward Festive Flicks, where I'm due for ticket duty, Anjelica's smile falters.

My heart skyrockets into my throat. "What's wrong?" I can't have her tell me to stop, not when this feels so good.

"It's just . . ." She reaches out a neon-green-manicured hand to grab my arm. The Grinch's diabolical yellow eyes glare up at me from her pointer and middle finger. "I don't want you to get hurt."

I wave her off. "Don't worry. I've thought about the consequences. Just like you said."

"Have you? Because I've never heard you talk about a guy like this before, Kris. Not in all the years of the Race. But now Aaron's got you like this."

"Like what?"

Anjie gives me serious side-eye. "You just lit up when I said his name! You're smiling like half the idiots who come to this island!"

I smack a hand to my face, and sure enough, she's right. I'm grinning from ear to ear. Like one of those deliriously happy, totally grotesque Holiday Heads.

Oh shit.

I *am* falling for him.

Things just got complicated.

# Aaron

My heart bumps outside the skating rink for an entirely different reason than it did yesterday. It's not from being close to Kris and his tingle-inducing charm. It's from needing this sabotage to go smoothly without Casey realizing anything is off.

Once again, the Frozen Pond is packed. Families laugh and slide and stumble in a way that makes me wonder whether holiday movies really are all that cheesy, or if they're just true to life. Everyone here looks impossibly happy. It's unsettling that they all depend on the trappings of Christmas to get them like this. Just like it's unsettling that Casey relies solely on Raquel to determine his happiness. When you think about it, that's a lot of pressure on her. She didn't ask to be the reason Casey gets up in the morning, or for him to create his whole life's plan around her when they met in sixth grade. I definitely don't wish heartbreak on my brother or anything, but still, I think I kind of get why Raquel left. So not only am I saving Casey, but I'm saving Raquel too.

The flash mob begins at 6:30 p.m. I tried telling Casey it's 7:30, but he called the trusty Elves to fact-check me, and they told him the actual start time. The one day Casey doesn't just trust my scheduling abilities and double-checks all the details himself. Normally, I'd be impressed that someone else went the extra mile for a change, but jeezus, did he have to start now?

I know it's because in his heart of hearts, Casey thinks this is the right thing to do. But I know in mine that it isn't, so it's a war of wills. And the way I'm going to win that war is by trapping my brother in the storage cottage behind the rink. After an hour of making out in the space, it hit me that it could be the perfect prison to "accidentally" lock Casey inside. I've just got to convince him that's where he should wait before making his entrance in the flash mob.

I glance at my phone: 6:14. I told Casey to meet me here fifteen minutes early. Right as my clock flips to 6:15, he strolls up. I think I really am starting to rub off on him. This is the most punctual he's ever been in his life.

Casey looks the most *him* since the breakup. He's clean-shaven, and he's got his Christmas attire going in full swing. Under his open puffy Winter Wonderland coat he's got a red knitted sweater over ironed black pants, a nice red plaid scarf covering his neck. I know that sweater was given to him by Raquel two Christmases ago. It's one of his prized possessions, not only because it's from the love of his life, but because it fits just right. It's hard for him to find clothes when he's a million feet tall with limbs the length of a blue spruce.

He's probably thinking the outfit is going to tug at her heart. But she's not even going to see it, because Casey's not going to be here.

"Wait, bro, you know what I'm doing right now?" Casey squints dramatically, then places his hand above his eyes like he's shielding them from the nonexistent sun while he looks from left to right.

Is he really going to ask such an obvious question? "Uh, looking for a spot to surprise Raquel?"

"That's right," Casey says as his mouth splits into an enormous grin. "I'm *casing* the joint!" He silently shakes until he honks his signature laugh. "Get it? Because my name is Casey!"

He's so cringey, but in the sweetest most endearing way. No wonder all those kids love him at the family agency. He truly is perfectly suited to work with them. I want to laugh along with him, but knowing that I'm about to end his good mood stops me from really being able to get in the spirit. I can only give a half-hearted chuckle. "Good one, Case."

"Case the joint," Casey mutters again. "Man, that's funny. This has got to be a good omen for things to come.

Raquel will remember we used to laugh like this when I declare my love for her."

Game time.

"You're right," I say. "But she can't see it coming. She'll get here any minute, and if she sees you, you'll lose that element of surprise. She'll know something's up."

Casey nods along. "Mm-hmm, mm-hmm. I see what you're saying." He scans the area in earnest now, no more hamming it up, taking in every inch of the Frozen Pond illuminated by stadium lights and the multicolored glow of Christmas bulbs strung throughout the village. "Where's a good spot to hide?"

"So, I was thinking you could declare your love at the top of the bleachers," I say, pointing a gloved hand at the golden seats where parents watch their kids on the rink, and where couples adorably tie each other's skates. Just like yesterday when Kris helped me with mine before carrying me out of here. "But you can't hide under them, because the side's wide open. If Raquel looks to her right even once when at the skate rental, your cover is blown."

Casey scowls. "Then where?"

"Well, I did a little *casing* of my own." Casey lights up at that, and I feel a stab in my heart. "There's the perfect spot around the back. Let me show you."

With that, I lead him to his doom. We hustle past the fence surrounding the Frozen Pond, then down the cobblestone main street until I get to the golden gate that leads to the Elf trail.

"The sign says *Elves Only*, bro." Casey looks over his shoulder nervously, but everyone is too immersed in their own holiday dream to care what we're doing. Kris assured me this spot would be empty this close to the flash mob. The townies participating are all gathered with the choreographer, but we've only got a couple minutes.

Casey hesitates, wasting our precious time. He may not be an expert planner like I am, but he is a pretty big rule follower. He's a true believer that Santa's always watching.

"Hey, we're totally okay, Case." I grab his arm and gently tug until he follows along. I didn't want to drop details of Kris's involvement, but it feels like that information might be the only thing that could possibly get my brother to move. "I cleared this with a Wonderer. That guy you know, the one who danced with you that first night. The, er, the one who brought the cocoa before I spilled it on your snow sculpture. He felt so bad that he pulled some strings to make sure we're in the clear to go back here."

"Kris!"

"Yeah," I say. "Kris. Kris with a *K*."

Warmth pools low in my belly when I say his name, and I would roll my eyes at myself if I could.

"So you've been spending more time with him, huh?" Casey elbows me, raising his eyebrows like he thinks he's made some monumental discovery. If only he knew.

"Don't get distracted. You've got a mission, remember?" I stop outside Cottage 5 and input Kris's code: 1111. November 11. I wonder what Kris likes to do for his birthday. He's had every one of them here in Winter Wonderland. It must be hard for him to experience any sort of surprise. He's stuck on this island, so how would he see new things or have an adventure? There are new people here all the time, sure, but they come to Winter Wonderland for their own reasons, not to enrich Kris's life in any way. They're depending on him to cater to them, not the other way around.

"I'm hiding out in a storage shed?" Casey asks.

*Come on, Aaron, focus.* Enough about Kris already. Kris, who's in that group of townies waiting to flash mob, thoughtful Kris who has put everything into place to make sure that Casey misses the performance and his chance to convince Raquel to give their relationship another shot.

"It's perfect, Case. There's no way Raquel would come back here."

"What about Liam?" Casey asks in a rush, his words almost jumbling together. "What if he's with her and is a better skater and then everything I've tried to do to show Raquel that Christmas is in *our* blood is knocked aside because it's obviously way more in his than mine?"

He looks so vulnerable, his eyes practically glistening with earnestness. It's the same look so many classmates have given me, needing help moving on from an ex or desperately seeking a solution when the ASB or tennis team or Winter Formal preppers are in a pinch. This is when I shine. When I show I've thought of every possible hiccup and that you can always count on the reliable robot that is Aaron Merry.

"Don't worry, Case. He won't be there. Liam is on Globe duty. He's selling trinkets there tonight, so he won't be anywhere near this place." It's a lie. A total lie. Liam will be at the Frozen Pond, all right, and I'll do whatever I can to make sure Raquel has a front-row seat to his famous ass.

And maybe I'll catch a glimpse of Kris's.

*Focus!*

Casey sighs. "Phew."

"All you've got to do is wait here, and I'll be back in no time." I reach for the door, but just before I push it open to head back outside, Casey puts his hand on my shoulder.

"You're not waiting with me?" he asks.

"Who else is going to be able to give you the signal? I'll be at the rink and text you when the flash mob starts. Then you come out. I'll be sure there's a clear path to skate next to Raquel so no one can ruin this moment."

"What if Raquel sees you?"

"She won't. I'm not the one with the giant genes, remember? I'll blend in with the crowd. I've got this." I swallow guiltily, but hopefully Casey's too distracted to really notice.

"You really are the best, bro." He pulls me in for a hug. I push him away way too quickly. He's got to stop with all this sincerity. It's making it harder for me to see this plan through.

"I gotta go so we don't miss your big shot." I'm out the door and slamming it behind me before Casey can do anything else that will make me second-guess myself. Outside, I lean against the door, my chest heaving, breathing like I've run a marathon. Backstabbing your brother to make him a better person is a real workout.

"You can do this, Aaron," I whisper. I dash around to the side of the cottage and kick aside a pile of snow. "Voilà." Underneath is a string of Christmas lights, planted by Kris. The spool has a bright red sticker with the Kringle logo on its side, *100 feet* written in golden cursive underneath. That will be plenty to trap Casey.

All I've got to do is tie one end of these lights around the doorknob, then lead the other end to the back of the shack, where I'll tie it to a heating pipe. Casey can try all he likes, but nothing will beat my knots. It's a trick I learned going to some of Dad's showings in Newport Beach. We'd cruise around the waterways to check out properties on Balboa Island, and when Dad went inside houses with clients, I tied up the boat. Nothing could make my knots budge, and I'm certain Casey won't be able to either.

I get to work, hearing Casey practice his speech to Raquel the whole time. "I've always loved you"; "There's

no me without you"; "We're like Santa's milk and cookies: meant to be together." So many cheesy lines make it
through the small window cracked open near the roof. It
turns my stomach to hear him, and not just because his
words are sickeningly sweet. I race to finish the last knot
on the pipe, then book it back to the skating rink.

6:29.

It feels like the entire town is here, either skating or in
the risers, knowing the dance is about to start. I catch
sight of Raquel on the bottom bleacher, just as she finishes lacing her skates. She's alone, like I knew she would
be since Liam will be with the rest of the Wonderers. This
little detail going as planned puts me at ease, always com-
forted when my research pays off.

I feel an itch in the back of my skull, that sensation
when you know someone is watching you. It's not Raquel,
who's wobbling by herself as she hobbles to the ice. Her
eyes scan the crowd, ready to catch any sign of when the
routine will start. I'm sure she wants to be in the thick of
it and feel as much of this Christmas magic as closely as
she can.

I cock my head to the side and see Kris looking right
at me, his lips quirked in a closed-mouth smile. Kris was
checking me out, confirmed by his sheepish, caught-in-
the-act look when our eyes lock. He gives a light wave,
but you'd think he waved a magic wand based on the way
my whole body reacts. My heart slams against my chest,

my stomach somersaults, and there's definitely movement beneath my snow pants as I think about Kris's lips traveling down my jaw to my neck.

Music blares over the rink's speakers, snapping me out of my daze. The opening notes of "All I Want for Christmas Is You" play, and everyone loses their shit. A mass of Wonderers swish onto the ice and mix with the mainlanders, who gape at them all with the cheesiest smiles on their faces. I'm sure Casey can hear the song through that tiny cracked open window, but I shoot him a text so he's not suspicious that I never sent him a message to get moving.

**It's starting! Come out now! I've got eyes on Raquel.**

God, this actually would be the best moment for Casey to announce his love for his girlfriend. This is their song, the one they each have programmed as ringers for the other. Raquel would *definitely* read that as some kind of sign. But it's better with Casey locked away where he can't make a fool of himself. Besides, Casey's plan would have failed even if I hadn't trapped him, because there's no way I'd be able to clear a path to his ex on the ice. Tourists circle the rink while the townies do jumps and skate backward, twirl, and flip. It's executed without a single mistake, every Wonderer gauging just where a visitor might be so there're no accidents. Not to mention they pull guests in with them every time Mariah sings the title lyrics, making it seem like all they've ever wanted was for each specific tourist to be there with them in that moment.

It's expertly choreographed, and I can't stop staring at Kris's bulging butt every time he does a little turn. I want to cup my hands right over those cheeks and feel the muscle there myself. I want Kris's stubble to scrape against my skin as his tongue finds mine. I want his—

*BZZZ BZZZ BZZZ.*

My phone vibrates incessantly, piling onto my already buzzing skin.

I've got loads of texts from Casey.

**BRO!**

**THE DOOR IS STUCK!**

😨😰😨😰

**THIS IS AN EMERGENCY!**

👱👱👱👱

**COME GET ME!**

"Sorry, Case." I pocket my phone. Here's where I'll have to tell Casey that I got caught up in the flash mob of it all, that I tried to push my way through the Wonderers and tourists, but it was just too much to make it in time. It's not entirely a lie either. The crowd gets thicker as the song plays on and people push beside me at the railing framing the rink. Plus, it'll take a lot more than some texts to make me stop drooling after Kris and counting how many times he winks at me as he skates on by.

Crushes are weird. Or flings. Or whatever we'd call this thing that has a very clear ending in less than a week. It's like a spell or something—Casey and Raquel would definitely call it magic, ugh—because I find myself hanging on to the railing, leaning forward as far as I can so I never miss a second of Kris. We're nearing the big climax of the song, Mariah about ready to belt her long-winded, high-pitched "Youuuuuuuuu!" We all know that something big is going to happen when she lets that note go. There's bound to be an epic move by the Wonderers to punctuate Mariah's legendary talent.

The crowd is so excited that everyone's silent. We've collectively held our breath to see what the townies are going to do. But in our silence, another sound mingles with Mariah's voice, just as she hits her iconic note.

Huffs. Like, big bold bursts of air. Then there're grunts. Maybe moans?

That doesn't seem right.

Very few people are looking at the skaters anymore. Everyone's looking behind me, their faces shifting from pure delight to confusion to horror.

This cannot be good.

I turn around and see reindeer. Lots and lots of reindeer.

Caught in the middle, awkwardly stretched between two of the horny beasts, is Casey. His torso bounces on one while his long legs flop against the back of the other, hanging on for rein-dear life as the herd gallops toward the skating rink.

That's when the audience finally catches on.

"STAMPEDE!"

# Kris

We know something's up as soon as everyone turns around. People usually have their eyes locked on us throughout the entire routine. Here in the middle of the rink, with the speakers blaring Mariah right at us, we can't hear or see what the tourists do. I give a confused look to Chris just as I flip forward from having skated backward the last few beats of the song.

I follow the crowd's perplexed looks right as someone on the ground yells, "STAMPEDE!"

All hell breaks loose.

Mainlanders jump from the bleachers, and guests slip and fall on their butts as they attempt to skate away. I try to find Aaron, but he's been swept up in the mass of people as they run in the opposite direction of the reindeer. It looks like at least half the herd got loose. That's twenty-four reindeer galloping in wide-eyed terror toward the hundreds of visitors trying their hardest to get away. But one specific visitor won't be able to get away no matter how hard he tries: Casey. He's somehow perched between two of the reindeer, his limbs flinging every which way in their mad dash.

We've got to get him out of there.

The only islanders who can calm the reindeer are the Santas. That's part of the reason they're chosen for the gig (and yet another talent Uncle Toby has). Not only do they have the general cheer and all-around jovial features of the man with the bag, but they know how to handle reindeer. Most importantly, they know how to get 'em to chill the fuck out in moments like this. Normally, they're just working with one at a time, calming them when they're freaked out by a nervous kid's energy. But with half a herd? The Santas are going to have to pull out all the stops.

"Noelle!" I skate over to where she's helping an elderly couple shuffle away from the mayhem. "Call your dad. He can help."

Noelle looks at me like an idiot without letting go of the old man she guides by the elbow. "You don't think I already did that the second I saw those Dashers dashing the hardest they've ever dashed in their whole damn—" Her eyes go wide, realizing she just cursed in front of guests. Giving an apologetic smile to the couple, she says, "Darned lives?"

I should have known she already had it covered.

"Don't worry about us, deary," the old woman chimes

in. "The way I see it, this whole evening has gone to shit."

As if on cue, the nearest reindeer lets out a giant turd. It hits the snow with a steamy plop.

"Her thoughts exactly," Noelle says.

Fortunately, the reindeer stop their stampede just on the other side of the rink railing, so we won't have to deal with them injuring themselves on the ice. They weren't so frantic that they thought it was a good idea to jump the fencing, but they huff and paw at the ground nervously. Casey has slid to the ground, and the reindeer seem okay to let him be for the time being. A few Elves try to approach, but the reindeer grunt and tilt their heads down, clearly ready to skewer Santa's helpers.

I still can't find Aaron in the crowd. There's too much commotion, too many people racing to the top of the bleachers, farthest from the herd. Wonderers try to lead all the tourists away from the Frozen Pond, but the exit's blocked by the animals that get more antsy anytime someone gets close. Their grunts and huffs are louder, one nearly full-on roaring when Casey gets to his feet. Even his wildly tall body looks small next to the massive antlers of these sleigh pullers. Casey stares at the sharp points, then ever so slowly raises his hands, his palms out in an *I come in peace* gesture.

"Easy, Comet," he says, then turns to one that shuffles up behind him. "It's okay, Cupid."

First, he's getting their names wrong. Second, they'd

beg to differ that anything about this situation is okay. More reindeer crowd around him, eyeing Casey warily, groaning in warning. I'm pretty sure we're seconds away from having a Casey kebab on our hands.

That's when he decides to make it worse.

"RAQUEL!"

I don't think he could yell louder if he tried.

"CASEY!" A redhead stands on the topmost riser, cupping her hands over her mouth to yell at Aaron's brother. "GET OUT OF THERE!"

"I DID THIS FOR YOU!" Casey shouts.

"YOU UNLEASHED A HORDE OF ANGRY REINDEER?"

That pisses off the crowd, and shouts rain down on Casey for messing up the skating flash mob. This is not at all coming across how Casey hoped.

"NO, NOT THAT PART!"

Casey's too focused on Raquel to notice that all his screaming is aggravating the reindeer even more. The closest four surround him, heads down, horns pointed straight at his chest. Apparently, they don't give a shit about grand declarations of love.

"Casey!" I call, trying to get his attention, but he's laser focused on his ex.

"RAQUEL," he shouts. "I LO—"

"SANTAS! ASSEMBLE!"

Noelle's dad, Roger, leads the pack of eight Santas.

Actually, the *sack* of Santas, because that's the collective noun for any group of the jolly guys. They each puff their chests proudly, bulging red velvet bags slung over their shoulders. Suddenly it's Marvel meets Christmas in Winter Wonderland.

The Santas fan out around the herd, and luckily for Casey, the reindeer pick up on the presence of their favorite men. Their heads slowly lift, their huffing slows, and most saunter over to their preferred Saint Nick.

"There's a good girl," Roger says, patting the head of the reindeer that nuzzles him. "That's my Blitzen baby." He reaches into his sack and pulls out clumps of feed, a mix of grains and oats that they go bananas over. The other Santas follow suit, and soon they're leading the reindeer away with handfuls of food.

As they round the corner, there's silence in the crowd before a little kid says loudly, "Wait. There are *eight* Santas. Why don't I get eight presents?"

That's all it takes to ease the tension. People laugh, others cheer, their whistles and claps creating a tidal wave of noise that fortunately doesn't get the herd even more riled up. They've got the Santa Squad now, with the gift of chowing down to keep the reindeer distracted. I want to be happy for the job well done. Instead, I can't help but think of how much Uncle Toby would have loved to be a part of the group that saved the day. He would have told this story so many times. I can practically hear his deep laugh as he describes Casey bouncing around among the herd.

Speaking of Aaron's brother, he's nowhere to be found. But as the sea of Hoboken Holiday Hos—a bachelorette party that travels in a pack with matching T-shirts—leaves, I spot Aaron sprinting toward me. My heart skips a beat.

Fuck. I really *do* feel something whenever I look at him. I can't help but notice his adorable freckles on his cold-pink nose, his gorgeous hazel eyes, his meticulously styled dirty blond hair, only—wait. It's not in place like it usually is. In fact, he seems nothing like the perfectly planned, I've-got-this-all-covered guy that he usually is. He's disheveled, those beautiful eyes wide with worry, looking weirdly similar to the reindeer in full panic mode.

"Kris!" He runs into my arms, but this is not a romantic embrace, and clearly not a time to celebrate sabotaging Casey's skating scheme. He barely even registers that our faces are so close, we could kiss. Instead he points over my shoulder and says through panicked breaths, "We have—to stop—him."

Casey makes a beeline for Raquel. She's not up in the bleachers anymore. Now she's on the ground, making her way along the edge of the rink. She stares at Casey the whole time, a soft smile on her lips.

"You think she wants to hear him out?" I ask.

Aaron looks like he might throw up. "Yes! Their stupid obsession with this holiday will make them think this was some huge spectacle that Christmas made just for them. I can already hear Raquel saying those reindeer brought Casey back into her life."

"Where's Liam?"

"How am I supposed to know?!" Aaron shouts. "He was with her a second ago!"

Aaron scans the crowd again, but there are too many bodies to spot my fellow Wonderer.

"Not to worry, folks," a pleasantly authoritative voice calls through the dispersing crowd. A group of four green-suited adults strolls through the tourists, smiles on their faces that read confidence, assuredness, safety. The Polar Patrol has arrived.

"Those reindeer were just looking for a holiday feast," they continue. "But rest assured this will never happen again."

The Patrol is trained to use cliché superhero sound bites like that. They're technically police, since this is a real functioning town, after all. But the board thinks calling them that could dampen the mood, christening them the Polar Patrol for the cutesy factor. Cutesy or not, they won't hesitate to lock up anybody who breaks a law, public drunkenness especially. I once saw a patrolman tackle a tipsy tourist for peeing in the snow outside the penguin pen. The guy was literally caught with his pants around his ankles.

That's when it all clicks. There is a way out of this, but I don't know how much Aaron's going to like it.

"How do you feel about your brother going to jail?"

"Is that like real jail or the Christmas equivalent of Disney jail?"

"We are a real Alaskan town, but things are more loosey-goosey here. No charges will be placed against him unless he did something actually illegal. It's more that he'll just go in for questioning." I motion toward the Polar Patrol as they talk with my classmates, trying to get to the bottom of the mayhem.

Aaron glances back at his brother. Casey's made it through most of the crowd, only a couple yards away from Raquel. It's now or never.

Aaron locks eyes with me and nods once. "Do it."

"Officer!" I call, jogging over to the nearest Patrol member. "I saw the whole thing." My hand whips out, pointing at Casey seconds before he reaches Raquel. "*He* let the reindeer out."

# Aaron

"Honestly, Casey, I never thought I'd see you escorted home by cops."

Dad is pissed.

"The *Polar Patrol*," Casey corrects. "It doesn't really count."

"It counts!" Dad snaps. "If you weren't a sophomore in college, I'd ground you."

"I wasn't even charged with anything," Casey says. "It was all an accident."

Apparently, when I locked Casey in that storage shed, I didn't really think through how desperately he'd try to get out. According to his statement, Casey went into the storage cottage to hide before surprising Raquel, and the door *somehow* got jammed. When he heard Mariah Carey's voice in the distance, he knew he had to get out of the shed or else his entire shot at wooing his ex would be ruined. So he found that little window near the ceiling and squeezed through it, only he didn't account for the slippery landing. He fell to the ground and slid on top of a snow blower that he somehow switched on in the collision. It got away from him, ramming open the door of the reindeer stable just across the lane. The loud noise of the engine scared a few of the animals, they stampeded, and Casey got caught up in the herd in the process. He had no control over where they went. It was entirely coincidence that the reindeer galloped directly for the one location Raquel was in.

This led to me getting questioned about whether anything seemed funny with the door when I left Casey in Cottage 5. Obviously I said nothing about using my expert knotting skills to trap my brother inside. Of course, like Santa, someone's always watching in Winter Wonderland, but thank god for Kris. Knowing everything about the island as he does, he covered the cameras that watch over that little Elf trail with a few strategically placed snowballs just before go time. As luck would have it, when Kris went back to make sure there was no evidence of Casey being trapped inside the storage shed, he found the string of lights I used trampled by dozens of hooves. Apparently it got caught in the stampede too. Originally, I was going to go back and untie it in the commotion after the skating flash mob, but the herd took care of that.

It was all a series of coincidences that are worthy of a ridiculous made-for-streaming holiday movie. I'll never stop thanking the universe for making those incidents happen in just a way that's kept our meddling in the dark. Good thing too, because footage of the stampede went viral. Mom even sent me a custom meme of Casey flopping between reindeer after she checked to make sure we were okay. But in the end, Casey didn't get in trouble, and no one got hurt. We made it out of this one, and Casey's reunion with Raquel was totally ruined.

All thanks to Kris's quick thinking. The Polar Patrol to the rescue.

"Casey, wipe that smirk off your face right now." Dad points a threatening finger at my brother, but even the danger of Pissed Dad can't get Casey to take him seriously. My stomach sinks. If Casey's in a good mood, maybe this day wasn't a success after all. Well, for me, at least.

"Why are you smiling anyway?" I ask, trying to sound nonchalant and not nearly as invested in Casey's answer as I actually am.

"Because it worked." Casey beams. "Despite all that went wrong and almost getting skewered by a whole sleigh full of reindeer, it worked!" Casey fishes his phone from his pocket and shows me a text from Raquel.

**You really went through all that for me?**

And his reply, already hearted by his ex:

**Of course, Quel. I'd go to the ends of the earth for you. Join me for a starlight cruise?**

I don't think she's going to be his ex for long.

*　　*　　*

Kris is working this morning in the Penguin Plaza, a complete marine habitat for imported penguins to lounge around and escape the dog-eat-dog world in Antarctica. Or is it polar-bear-eat-penguin? Maybe orca-eat-penguin? Either way, it's hard out here for a penguin. But Kringle created a nice viewing platform with cozy little benches and blankets so visitors can watch Elves toss fish to the birds. Cute penguins for us, free food for the penguins.

Except that means I have to pace up and down this deck waiting for Kris to get off work while Casey is for sure figuring out his next steps with Raquel. After an attempted Merry Mash-Up group hug did nothing to chill Dad out, Dad insisted he go on Casey's toboggan race victory starlight cruise to keep an eye on my brother. The same starlight cruise Casey asked Raquel to. Casey fought back hard, but Dad said if he didn't do it, he'd tell Raquel that Casey had access to her Google calendar, and then she'd know none of their meetings were chance coincidences. So much for Dad being lenient with us. I guess that reindeer debacle really freaked him out, and thank god it did.

So Raquel was booted from the boat excursion, but I know as soon as they return to the island, Casey will meet up with Raquel. I faked a stomachache so I could skip the cruise and figure out what to do next. Only four more days until I don't have to meddle anymore. If only I could just tell Raquel what Casey's up to, but no. If word got back to my brother, he'd never forgive me.

Kris saunters over, and my stomach twists for real. It's not an ache. It's the best loop-de-loop feeling that only intensifies the closer he gets. But then, oh god. A *smell* intensifies too, one that turns my stomach in the *worst* way.

I slam my hands over my nose. "What *is* that?"

Kris scowls. "Excuse you. The penguins gotta eat." He holds up his red and green dish gloves that are covered in a glistening yellowish-gray goo. "Polar cod. The penguins love them. If you think this smell is bad, just be thankful I didn't bring over the bucket." He points to the railing, where a red bucket has *Penguin Treats* written on it in golden cursive.

"Leave it to Kringle to try to make the worst-smelling substance on Earth seem sweet," I say.

Kris pulls off his gloves and flicks them over his shoulder. They land perfectly on the rim of the fish bucket.

"Holy shit," I breathe. "How did you do that?"

"You get pretty good aim when you've been feeding penguins for half your life," he says. "You get pretty good at doing everything here when you do the same thing every two weeks, over and over and over." He crosses his arms, and instead of looking cocky at that weirdly sexy move, he looks pissed. "You work your whole life to be the best at everything, and it's still not enough."

I hold my hands up in a *whoa, slow down* gesture. "Hey, I'm sorry. I didn't mean anything by it."

Kris takes a few steps away, not looking back. "I know. It's just a bit of a sore spot."

I don't close the distance between us in case he wants this moment to himself. Well, as to himself as he can be with guests just a few yards away and multitudes of penguins watching from the other side of the railing.

"Feeling a little underappreciated?" I ask.

Kris sighs, defeated. "Not me. My uncle Toby. It's too early to tell when the shoe will drop and Kringle Korp will decide to inform me that I'm the next Bright who's not good enough."

"They did that to your uncle?"

Kris's eyes dart to the guests going gaga over the penguins. He takes a step closer, so close I can see the individual whiskers of his stubble. "Yeah. He moved here the same time my parents did, proved his love of Christmas, showed how good he was at making snowmen, wrapping presents, knowing even the most obscure holiday songs. He was the best woodworker in the whole Workshop too. They still have some of his creations for sale. But none of that mattered. Decades of prepping himself to one day be cast as a Wonderland Santa, and when he finally auditioned, despite being the best, he wasn't chosen. He wanted to be out, the first gay Santa. The powers that be didn't like that."

"Why not?" I'm way too loud. Kris places a (thankfully un-fish-gloved) hand over my mouth. At the exasperated looks of some nearby visitors, Kris adds a hurried "Sorry, folks."

He lowers his hand, and I instantly miss the warmth there. Even if he was just trying to shut me up, I want him to touch my face.

"I wish I could tell you why not," Kris says. "But why have gay people been excluded from so many things? Ignorance, lack of understanding, outright hate. Just because we're on a secluded little island doesn't mean the outside world can't touch us. It influences what goes on in every single inch of these forty square miles. I'm able to be openly out, but still."

"You think they really don't want you here?"

Kris shrugs, then starts pacing in a small, slow back-and-forth. "No. Yes. Maybe a little of both. The island has been great to me, and I've never had an issue with any Wonderer before. And we *warmly welcome* LGBTQ+ guests, at least according to all the press releases. They acknowledge the importance of Santa representation across races, as they should, but why they can't see it for queerness is beyond me."

I can tell this really hurts him, but it seems like a problem that could easily be fixed. "Why don't you leave?" I ask. "I know you can't take off right this minute, but when you graduate, I mean. There're all kinds of gay holiday celebrations in Los Angeles, New York, any major city, really. There's a place for you on the mainland."

Kris sighs again, and this time I can tell he's gone from defeated to exasperated. "It's not important." He won't look at me. His shoulders tense up. I think he's on the verge of getting angry. With me.

I put a tentative hand on Kris's forearm. "Hey. I promise I'm trying to understand. You can tell me anything."

Kris stares at my hand while he chews his bottom lip. Seeing it pillow out makes me want to lean in and kiss him. Not in that hungry way we've done in the past. In a way that lets him know I'm here and will be whenever he wants to talk.

At least, for the next four days.

"You're serious, aren't you?" Kris finally asks.

"Of course I am. Why wouldn't I be?" This is what I'm good at, solving people's problems. I am the Robot, after all. "I just like to get down to business."

"You're the man with the plan, reindeer stampedes and all."

"Okay, that totally wasn't my fault."

Kris laughs, and I could listen to that sound for hours. It's deep and boisterous and not unlike how I'd imagine young Santa would sound. Maybe it's been trained into him to make guests always think of the jolliest guy on the planet. But honestly? I don't think it's forced. It's natural. All him. It makes me want to know him more. "Anyway, I really was serious before. You can tell me anything. If you want to."

Kris pulls my hand from his arm and leads me off the viewing platform. A twentysomething girl snuggled up with who I'm assuming is her boyfriend says not so quietly, "Finally. His frantic pacing was really ruining the mood."

"What?" I snap. "The smell of rotting seafood wasn't?" Although, to be fair, I could smell it only when Kris had his slimed gloves near me.

Kris squeezes my arm, shutting me up. "Sorry about that, ma'am," he says to the woman, all smiles. "I'll be sure to comp your cocoa. Have a merry evening." As we step away, Kris chuckles that low, chest-vibrating laugh. "That's what I like about you."

"That I can't keep my thoughts to myself?"

"That you're not swept away by all this." He motions to the Christmas trappings around us. The red railings marking the path to the Penguin Plaza are wrapped with green garland. The bar is stocked with candy-cane-striped mugs, while an Elf serves up drinks with an *all is right in the world and nothing could ever be wrong* smile plastered on his face. "You see how fake it all is. How forced."

"It's just that no person could ever be as happy as holiday cheer would like you to think," I say. "Look at Casey. He's so jolly, it's delusional. The world throws him one curveball, and he crumbles. He was never truly happy, even before Raquel broke up with him. He was codependent and foolish and naïve."

"But you've made a plan to change that for him," Kris says. "I get it. You're setting him up for a life without Christmas. For a life of *reality*. Sometimes I wish I could have that too."

"You can," I try again. "Just leave. Maybe join your uncle Toby, wherever he is."

Kris leads us to the edge of the Plaza. We're away from the cozied couples, the sound of penguin calls and softly playing holiday tunes covering our conversation, so we don't disturb any romantic vibes.

"You don't just leave Winter Wonderland," he says. "We have it too good here. Housing, health care, guaranteed jobs unless we somehow ruin the magic of Christmas. Leaving all this behind would be so stupid. To what, go to school somewhere and hope there's not some economic crisis so I can get a job? And then what? I'm worried about rent and insurance and car payments?"

"But I mean . . ." I pause, wanting to pick just the right words. I don't want to sound insensitive. "That's what everybody does."

"Exactly!" Kris throws his hands in the air. "What Kringle has given us is a real gift. How terrible would it make me look if I said I don't want it? When my parents applied to come here, they were on the verge of totally collapsing. And then Kringle gave them their jobs, and it truly did feel like a Christmas miracle to them. What would it say to them if I didn't want it? Besides, even if I chose to leave, I don't have the money. My wage wouldn't even scratch the surface of rent or tuition or whatever the hell I decide to do if I go to the mainland. Not when all this is guaranteed. Look at my uncle's life."

Kris grabs his phone and opens an album of a guy who looks a hell of a lot like Santa. But instead, he's in jeans and a puffer coat, smiling in front of an apartment building. A flick of his finger and there's Toby again, this time sitting on a red throne in a cheesy North Pole mall display. "Uncle Toby is out there, in the real world, and he's only a mall Santa," Kris says. "He has roommates as a forty-seven-year-old man! It's too risky to leave."

As someone who plans for everything, I get not wanting to take a risk. I think through every situation to make sure I can get whatever outcome is most desirable to me. Weighing everything he's said, I get why Kris thinks Winter Wonderland is the best option for him. I'd probably choose it too if I were in his shoes.

"The most confusing part is I don't even think I want to leave," Kris adds. "Uncle Toby definitely didn't. He just wanted to feel as welcome here as everybody else. It's why he was so hell-bent on proving he was good at Christmas, why after I came out he wanted me to do the same. But maybe that will never be enough. Maybe *I'll* never be enough." He looks out to the ocean, like maybe if he tried hard enough, he could see past the frozen ice, over the dark waters, all the way to his uncle's apartment. "Sorry to dump that on you. It's been a weird day. Uncle Toby sent me this."

He flips through his phone again, pulling up a new picture. It's Uncle Toby with his arms around another man who's just as bearlike as he is.

"Uncle Toby's been dating this guy for the past three months apparently. We talk about everything, but he waited to bring up *Jared* until he knew their relationship would stick. They're *boyfriends*." He says the word with disgust. Or maybe . . . hurt.

"And you're not happy about that?" I can tell this goes beyond our general disbelief in love.

"If he's dating someone now, maybe he won't ever come back." Kris shoves his phone into his pocket so hard I hear a seam rip. "Anyway. I'm done bringing the mood down. What about you? What are you going to do when you graduate?"

If he needs a distraction, I can give him that. Besides, I've had this plan for ages. The answer's right on the tip of my tongue. "I applied to UC Irvine, plus a couple SoCal fallback schools. I want to stay close to home, so I can keep track of Case and Dad. I'll major in business, then go to law school and become a divorce lawyer."

"God, you really don't believe in love, do you?" Why does Kris look so horrified?

"What?" I shrug. "It seems the surest bet. Almost seven

hundred thousand couples get divorced each year. It happened to my parents, and it'll happen to millions more. Besides, I'm kind of known around school for helping people get over exes. They call me the Robot, since I can detach emotion from almost anything."

"Well, Robot, if for some reason divorce doesn't work out, estate law could be a good fallback," Kris adds. "People will always die too."

"You know what, I actually hadn't thought of that." That's a first. I'm the one who thinks of everything.

"Excuse me? Excuse me!" A man across the platform waves his hand and snaps in Kris's direction. "We need service over here! Service!"

Kris plasters on a smile, and it's more than halfway believable. But up close, I can see how the smile doesn't quite reach his eyes, how it pains him to give this guy the time of day.

"Be right there, sir," Kris calls cheerfully.

"Didn't your shift just end?" I ask.

"Yeah, but we can never say no to a guest. Even when we're off the clock."

Kris hurries away. You wouldn't tell by the way he laughs and jokes with the uptight prick that Kris has mixed feelings about being here.

Maybe I can help with that. Maybe, in four days, I'll be able to get more than just my brother's life on track.

An intense sucking sound comes from my left, the kind

of sound that sets your whole body on edge. The hairs on the back of my neck stand on end. I turn, looking for the source of that awful noise, only to find a couple sucking face. Hard. They're locked on each other's lips like their lives depend on it, their kisses so loud it's got to be intentional. I know I'm relatively new to it all, but in the hours Kris and I made out, we never made *that* sound. Like, you do not have to set your mouth on Dyson-worthy suction levels to effectively kiss. They're trying to make their love *a show*. But the other couples couldn't care less. They're all snuggled under blankets in little pods, their faces lit by gentle flames in the fire pits at their feet. The dark ocean off in the distance with the adorable penguin here and there on the icy shore sweetens the already idyllic scene.

It's so romantic.

And that's when the string of Christmas lights goes on in my head.

Romance.

Raquel came to the island specifically to build romance with Liam. She didn't even know Casey would be here.

A plan starts forming in my mind, an avalanche of ideas building momentum.

I just hope it's strong enough to wipe Casey from Raquel's heart.

# Kris

I guess now we're going from romance saboteurs to straight-up matchmakers. Aaron wants to create the perfect romantic rendezvous for Raquel, but with Liam instead of his brother. I couldn't stop myself from picturing me and Aaron going on the date that he described. He had to shake me out of my daydream too many times. It's not that the settings or details were that different from anything I've seen before. It's just that I've never *wanted* to seriously date someone before. I think that's why I word vomited everything that's bothering me to Aaron. I *don't* tell guests my problems, yet here I am, unintentionally spilling my guts, making myself vulnerable.

What is wrong with me?

I've got to get my head in the game, which leads me to Santa's Workshop. It's exactly what you'd expect, an entire woodworking store dedicated to making the most intricate, handmade toys. Our puzzle makers win awards every year for their craftsmanship, we release a new holiday doll annually, and the train sets feel like they could literally transport you to another world. I've avoided this place for the last six months at all costs, switching shifts with people if I'm asked to work the registers or anything. Coming in here reminds me too much of Uncle Toby and all the times I watched him make those legendary toys. But if I'm going to get any shot of seeing him on the island again, I've got to brave the space. And I've got to push through the doubt that he's making too many connections on the mainland. What's one guy he's known for three months versus *me*, who he's known for eighteen years? If he has the opportunity, I know Uncle Toby will come back.

Liam's shift is just about to end. He's not a woodworker himself. That's a whole apprenticeship program that has really strict guidelines and a rigorous application process. It's one of the few jobs the island will source out if no homegrown Wonderer is up to the woodworking Elves' snuff, which apparently no one was, since a job opening was posted on the WW site the week after Uncle Toby left. Liam's just cleanup crew. Logging onto the Wonderland Wide Web showed me Liam will have night shifts here for the rest of the week. Shifts that I'll be taking, hopefully. I'll pull double duty working the Claus Café before classes and in the Workshop after to make Aaron's plan succeed.

The smell of fresh-cut wood bombards my nostrils the moment I step through the door. I used to love that smell, and it would always linger on Uncle Toby's clothes. My heart clenches, thinking about how much I miss him, wishing I didn't have to win this stupid Race in order to maybe save my uncle's future.

I shake my head, trying to dislodge the thoughts. I can't let this get to me. I've got to be in the right mood to convince Liam I'm not just BSing when I approach him out of nowhere.

I spot him in the back, in full Winter Wonderland uniform. His red vest is unzipped over a green turtleneck, and even from here I can see just how pink his usually even-toned cheeks are from exertion. He's got a long broom in his hands, pushing it forcefully to get wood shavings into a consistently running vent. This is the one place where the Wonderer work outfit is way too hot, even in the winter when it's negative degrees out. It's stuffy in this place, and lugging that giant broom around doesn't help. I'm banking on Liam hating it to make this plan work.

I walk through the aisles lined with wooden toys, then nod at Maggie, the new head woodworker now that Uncle Toby's gone. She somehow winks at me behind her goggles without ever taking her eyes off the pine she pushes through a table saw. While guests aren't allowed to walk among the saw stations, they're fully visible to the public so they can see Elves in action. Wonderers, however, get to come and go as they please.

I make it to Liam just as he props his broom against the wall and leans way back. His spine cracks in three pops.

"Hey, Liam, what's up?" I try to sound nonchalant, but I think I'm already blowing it. I have butterflies in my stomach, and it hits me that I'm actually nervous this won't work out. I don't want to disappoint Aaron.

Liam straightens up, his face indifferent. It's not that we're not friends, but it's not that we are either. There're almost two thousand of us islanders, and while we all know each other, it's not like we're best friends forever. Especially the kids; when we're not working and doing events for guests, we mostly just stick with the people from our class.

"Hey, man," Liam replies. We're so not in each other's circle that he doesn't even realize I'm here to talk to him. He gets back to sweeping, and after the most awkward thirty seconds of my life, he peeks over his shoulder. "Oh, uh. Did you want something?"

"Yep." I laugh awkwardly. "Um, I heard that your girlfriend is here to visit you."

Liam's face instantly lights up. "Yeah, she is!" He stops sweeping and leans against the long broom handle. "Raquel's the best. She—" He stops and scowls. "Wait, who told you that?"

I wave him off in what I hope comes across as very easy breezy. "Aw, you know, man, this place is so small, word

233

gets around." Why do I sound so aggressively straight?

But Liam doesn't seem to care. If anything, he's more comfortable, nodding and smiling again. "I didn't even post about her coming because I just wanted this relationship for me, you know? But everyone's up each other's ass in Wonderland, huh?"

Eloquent.

"Yeah. Definitely," I say. "Which is why I'm here actually." I feel like I'm catching my stride now, getting into character. I stand up taller. "You deserve to have some time to yourself. We're all cooped up on this island, and you're the first person to start a real relationship with a mainlander in, like, forever. You deserve to enjoy that before she has to go back. I thought I could take your shifts for the rest of this Twelve while she's still here."

Liam's eyes widen in surprise. "Wow, man. You'd do that?"

I nod. "If I can't have some action, at least a fellow townie can, right?"

"I gotta tell you, I thought I might never have a relationship again. Dating girls from the island feels like dating your sister."

"I bet." I wouldn't know. The other gay Wonderers are all older.

"And then all those girls who slide into my DMs treat me like a game," Liam says. "They wait for me to respond, then just ghost. But Raquel's different. She's special. She actually asked about me instead of only commenting on my ass. I mean, I know it's good, but I'm more than just a nice pair of glutes. But with Raquel, we connected. She got to the heart of why she loves Christmas, and it was really special. She gets it."

Liam is of the Wonderer variety who truly does love the holiday. He came here when he was a toddler, and maybe it was those few years after birth on the mainland that made him different, but he doesn't seem to have the same disregard for Christmas that most of us born here do.

"You think she'd move here?" I ask.

Liam's eyes get all whimsical. "Man, that would be the dream."

"Well, let's make it happen."

Liam cocks his head to the side. "What do you mean?"

"Let's get her to see how great you are and how magical it is here. Let's set up the ultimate date. If it goes well enough, she just might stay."

What better way to ensure that Raquel and Casey don't get back together than her moving to an island far, far away from Southern California? Plus, it would be the cherry on top if this whole plan brought Liam to the love of his life. That's got to cancel out any bad vibes from tanking Casey's relationship, right?

"I wish," Liam says. "Moving here is a pretty big deal.

I've kind of accepted the fact that we're going to be long distance."

I can't let him give up on this so easily. "How will you know if you don't try?"

"What could even convince her to move?" he asks. "How could I make a date so good that she'd completely change her life for me?"

"I think I know someone who can help."

# Aaron

"So here are all the things I know about Raquel," I say. I take my binder out of my backpack, flipping to the very last section that I've dedicated to this plan. I stayed up way too late last night putting this list together, which is why I've met Kris in the Claus Café. I ordered the biggest chai tea I could find, spiked with six shots of espresso. To avoid the possibility of Casey finding us and potentially overseeing this plan to sabotage his love life, Kris arranged for us to be able to talk this out in the café's break room after his shift. Our knees bump up against each other underneath the little wooden table, and I'm not entirely against it. At all.

"Let's make sure as many of these are included in the date as possible."

*Bump bump bump.*

Kris reads down the list. There's something that makes

my heart burst with warmth hearing his deep voice say all the things I put so much energy into planning. "Reindeer, hot chocolate, Santa (still believes in)." Kris looks up, skeptical. "Wait, she's twenty years old and still thinks Santa is real?"

I nod. "You bet. She has this belief that Santa is really more like God. A cosmic being who's keeping points on how good you are and docks you down any time you screw up."

"How does she account for the Santas here, or mall Santas?"

"She thinks it's like a priest thing. She knows those Santas aren't the *real* Santa. More like his representatives."

Kris scoffs. "Holiday Heads are really good at maintaining their delusion."

"Holiday Heads?"

"Those people who are so obsessed with Christmas that they'll do anything to force the cheer of it all. Your brother's one of them."

I've never heard a term that more accurately describes him. "Definitely." But that also makes me kind of sad. He's so much more than his obsession with the holiday. He's kindhearted, generous, wants to make sure all those kids he works with really are provided for. When you think about it, he's more like the idea of Santa than anyone I know. I can already see his future helping kids out in social programs or adoption agencies, bringing families together.

*If* he realizes that those qualities define him, not his relationship with Raquel.

"Christmas is her religion, got it." Kris continues down the list. "Christmas cheer, Tiny Tim, Muppet Christmas movies (thinks there should be more of), finding ways naughty could be interpreted as nice (refer to *Alpha Phi Naughty and Nice*–themed party pics), tinsel—"

"Wait!" I stand up so hard my knee bashes against the table. "Shit shit shit." I hop around the room, losing my balance and falling back onto a beanbag-size sack of marshmallows.

Kris gets to his feet smoothly, expertly maneuvering in the cramped room. It's got to be all that dance training that's got him so aware of his body and surroundings.

His thick fingers reach down, offering to pull me up. I take his hand and he lifts, the force of his pull bringing me straight to his chest. Without missing a beat, he catches me, holding me against him. The throbbing in my knee doesn't even compare to the beating in my chest.

Kris looks at me expectantly. It's been so long since the last time we were able to kiss. If we have only three more days until I go back home, I've got to take advantage of this while I can. So I lean forward and press my lips against his. Tension eases from Kris's broad shoulders. He runs his hands down my back, stopping at my waist to lift me up and set me on the table.

I will never get over being lifted like that.

Kris tilts my face up to his and kisses me softly, slowly, more tenderly than ever before. He gives a contented sigh, one I've heard too many times. Casey's done the same thing when he gets swept up in his feelings.

I snap back. "We should focus." I wipe my mouth, reapply ChapStick, do anything but look Kris in the eye. "You know. On the plan." I clear my throat, take a deep breath. I need to let my body slow down and stop thinking about Kris's firm chest, his big hands, those perfect, pillowy pink lips.

"R-right," Kris mutters. "The plan." His shoulders tense up all over again.

"Raquel has this belief in a cosmic, karmic Santa, right?" I say, going into robot mode so I can ignore the dejected look on Kris's face. "Is there a way we could set up an experience where Santa tells her Liam is the right choice?"

Kris nods, pulling out a chair and sitting. It'd be so easy for me to plop down into his lap and get back to kissing.

*Not now, Aaron!*

"Yeah, I think we can make that work," Kris says. "We've got enough reindeer in town that there are always some to spare. Same with the Santas."

I get the familiar buzz of pieces starting to come together. We've got this.

Kris starts thumbing through the other tabs in my binder. The ones marked *Bills* and *Home Repair* and *Casey* and *Dad*. Those last two are filled with dentist and doctor numbers and when each of their last checkups were. Dad's on high-blood-pressure meds, and if it wasn't for me keeping track, he'd forget to grab his refills. The last thing we need is for Dad to have a heart attack.

"What are all these?" Kris asks.

I point at myself. "He's a planner, remember?"

"Yeah, but . . ." Kris's forehead furrows. He scans my list of utility companies with notes on when our last payments were. Everything's always on time. "These seem like things your parents should work out."

"Parent," I say, not really knowing that's what's going to pop out of my mouth until it does. "We live with Dad. Mom mostly just communicates in memes."

"That's right," Kris says with a grimace. I know we're both picturing that bacon dick she sent. "She sounds like the complete opposite of my mom. I'm lucky if I can go a day without some long-winded reminder of how *great* this place is." He cringes. "Sorry. *Lucky* was the wrong choice of words. I don't mean to be insensitive."

I shrug. "It is what it is. Mom left eight years ago, and I sort of filled in the gaps."

"As a fourth grader?"

Kris's look is disbelief, surprise, and sympathy verging on condescension.

"I don't need you to feel sorry for me."

"Shit, I'm doing it again." Kris takes a deep breath and runs a hand over his close-cropped hair. "I'm really messing this up. I didn't mean anything by it. I just . . ." He flicks the corner of my binder. "I don't think this should be your responsibility."

"Somebody had to pick up the slack. Numbers are way too much for Casey. Dad's hustling out the door every chance he gets to sell a house and make sure there's money to keep our lives going. I was the only person who had the time and ability to do it."

"I get that," Kris says, tentative. "Your family is lucky to have you." He chews his cheek, and I can tell he wants to ask more. Most people do when they find out your mom willfully left her kids behind.

"You can ask the question if you want."

He blushes, caught in the act. "What question?"

"You want to know where Mom went and why."

Kris nods. "Guilty."

"She was tired of her life. She was over Southern California and couldn't see herself with us anymore. It wasn't for a man or anything, like most people think. It was for her. And we were holding her back apparently. She left to go work on a cranberry bog in Wisconsin."

Kris gasps. "A *cranberry bog*? She wants to do that for the rest of her life?"

"Yep. She hasn't complained about it once. So I guess it was the right choice for her."

Kris gets quiet, but this time he's got a *look*. It's not the *I feel sorry for you* look or the *I want to make sure I don't hurt your feelings again* face. It's more . . . angry?

"What?"

"I don't know." Kris waves himself off. "It's nothing. Too negative."

"Is it negativity, or is it truth? Don't go all Wonderer on me. Toxic positivity is a thing too, you know. It's how my brother got where he is in the first place."

Kris's mouth drops open just a bit, his features relaxing. "You're really something, you know that?"

My palms get sweaty, my stomach burns, my heart picks up the pace. I like it when Kris looks at me like this. "Say it," I breathe. "Say what you're holding back."

Kris licks his lips, squares his shoulders. I recognize the movements; I've done them so many times before. They're the same movements I do before I give classmates my take as the Robot, giving them the real truths they need to move on from their exes. "Your mom sounds an awful lot like some of the people who moved here when Kringle put the call out for workers," Kris says. "Most of the people who moved here, honestly. They were escaping something, needing to find an environment where they could forget all their problems and never have to deal with them. A place where they were maybe even encouraged to never deal with them.

"But if they ever went off the island, their problems would be waiting right where they left them. They're not real people anymore; they're Elves who've totally forgotten what's made them human. It's one of the reasons Uncle Toby had to leave. They didn't see his humanity, or the humanity of the entire LGBTQ+ community. They only saw *Christmas*. It's like Kringle Korp thinks they can just erase the fact that queer people exist by not putting us in their Christmas lore. The company's soulless, and your mom sounds a lot like that." Kris takes in a sharp breath. "Not to judge her or anything, but . . . doesn't it make you mad? That you have to pick up her slack?"

I'm speechless. It's not that I can't handle someone talking that way about my mom. He's not wrong. She did up and leave, and rather than work through what was making her so unhappy at home, she just decided to go. But here in this cramped little break room, Kris is the first person to put a word to it that I didn't know I needed to hear. She leaves and communicates only with memes. What else do you call that but *soulless*?

Kris cringes. "Crap, I've gone too far, huh? It's really none of my business. Sorry I—"

"No," I say. "I think you nailed it. You asked if I'm mad, but . . ." I shrug. "I'm not. What's the point of getting upset about it? She'd still be gone. Besides, it's been eight years now, and if I didn't take care of everybody else, who would? We'd just be stuck in a spiral of emotions, and then nothing would ever get done."

"It sounds like a lot of responsibility for one person," Kris says.

"You should be a psychologist, you know that?"

Kris frowns. "Probably not going to happen. Wonderland's already got one, and I don't imagine they'll be leaving anytime soon. It's not like I could go to school to train for the job anyway. That's got to be one of those professions with the biggest load of student debt."

"It's wild how so many career paths set you up for thousands of dollars of loans, huh?"

"Hundreds of thousands, even," Kris says.

"You've looked into it?"

Kris shrugs. "Not psychology, but college in general. And only for about a minute. I saw that price tag and was out of there."

"What does your college counselor say?"

"My what?"

"You know, the person who tells you what options you have for life after you graduate. Colleges, scholarships, trade schools, that sort of thing."

Kris looks at me like I just told him Santa wasn't real. Or more like the Kringle crew told him that there will never, ever be a gay Santa, no matter how hard he tries.

"Yeah, we definitely don't have that," he says. "We have WWWP, that's it." At my confused scowl, he clarifies. "Winter Wonderland Work Placement. It's where they put us in jobs we're most suited for. The majority of us just get placed as a general Elf, meaning we can fill in anywhere that has retail, food service, or cleaning duties.

Some of us get specialty apprenticeships, like glassblowers or toymakers, but that's rare. I might be able to do those, though. I'm pretty good at Christmas. Not that you'd be able to tell based on how much you ask me to sabotage."

"What about the jobs on the island that require professional training or certifications?" I ask. "Nurses. Teachers. That sort of thing."

"Most were brought here when this place first opened. If they leave, any gaps that can't be filled by a Wonderer have been recruited by Kringle Korp. Just a handful here and there in all the time we've been open."

"So they really just try to keep you here your whole life? Stuck in the mold they want you to fit in?"

Kris's eyes darken, his shoulders hunch, and his whole mood shifts. "Yeah, that mold part is key. They don't try to keep you if you're not their picture-perfect ideal of a Wonderer."

Like his uncle Toby.

"I can't believe they just let him go like that," I say. "When he was the best at Christmas on the whole island, it seems pretty shortsighted."

Kris scoffs. "They never try to stop us from leaving if we want to. It wouldn't make them look good to trap us here. But just once I wish they would have fought harder for him to stay. I wish they wouldn't have put him in that position to pick his life or his integrity."

"That's a terrible choice," I say. "It's not fair." I tap my boot against his thigh, a little *I see you* nudge.

This isn't like any of the problems I've had to solve before. Usually it's just me telling a classmate how their ex was a chump and giving a whole list of reasons why they shouldn't be together. Or creating an epic spreadsheet about how with just a couple bake sales, a car wash, and a donation drive, the ASB would have all the funds they need for prom. But this? This is a multibillion-dollar corporation that kicked out an innocent guy who truly loved what Kringle had built. How does one high school senior go up against that?

"I'd do anything to see Uncle Toby again," Kris says, so quiet it almost gets lost to the hush of the heater.

I don't know that I can plan a way out of this for Kris.

But I'm sure as hell going to try.

# Kris

"What do you need the reindeer for?" Nicky asks, her eyebrow arched so high it doesn't seem humanly possible.

"It's for a date," I say.

"For the Race?" she asks. She tries to hide her competitiveness, but that's a skill she doesn't have. Besides, her workspace would give her away. She's got magazine cutouts of big cities plastered all over her desk, no doubt dreaming up the life she could have if she wins and gets Anjie's dad to give her a job in this rumored second Wonderland.

Another day has gone by, and still no love professed to the Fling Ring. It's really baffling, honestly, that it's taken so long, especially considering the private charters and meet-the-parents outings that have already happened. But it's also created this urgency, this electricity in the air that there's still a chance for all of us.

We have a standing rule that nobody can sabotage

another person's shot at getting a mainlander to fall in love with them. You can, however, still say no to helping, and Nicky clearly doesn't want to do anything that could potentially help someone else win. But hers is the only help I need. As the daughter of the lead reindeer handler and vet, Nicky's been given reindeer-scheduling duties. It's her responsibility to assign Santa's antlered buddies to various events or private excursions like the one I'm trying to plan.

"Uh, not really," I say. "It's for a date for Liam."

Nicky scowls, cocking her head to the side. "What? Why?"

"A visitor has asked him out," I say, which isn't that much of a lie. Raquel is a visitor. "And she wants reindeer. We can't say no to a guest, right?"

That cardinal rule gets Nicky's fingers to fly across her keyboard.

"You need them tonight?" Nicky asks, clicking through each of the reindeer's Google calendars. From all the blocks of red, I can tell these suckers are booked and busy.

"Yes."

"I can't get you a full sleigh," she says, referring to all eight of Santa's reindeer. She *click click clicks* between schedules for what feels like an unreasonably long time.

"I'll take whatever I can get."

"Two. I've got two for you. Cupid One and Cupid Six." She looks up, waiting for me to confirm. If ever there was a time I would start believing in signs, this is it. Only

Cupids are available? That has to mean something, right? Hopefully it's a sign that we will be making love happen for Raquel and Liam.

"Perfect," I say, putting my hand out for Nicky to shake. She just raises an eyebrow at it before blocking off the Cupids' schedule.

"How's your Race going?" she asks, flipping her long black hair over her shoulder in a failed attempt to seem disinterested.

"Eh," I say, which makes her completely perk up. "I'm not so sure."

"But you're spending a lot of time with that guy, right? I've seen you two around. I'm surprised you haven't won yet, to be honest. Your mark looks totally in love."

My heart skips a beat, and not just because of the Race. *Shit.*

"Well, good luck," Nicky says, but we both know she doesn't mean it.

I turn on my heel, somehow feeling lighter *and* heavier after Nicky's words. Aaron looks in love? That should *not* make me so hopeful. Yeah, maybe that means I'm still in this thing and could win that audience with Anjelica's dad. But I know this floatiness in my chest is about more than that. And it *shouldn't* be. Aaron's leaving in three days, when he'll forget about me like everybody else. Besides, he doesn't even believe in attachment.

But then again, I didn't think romantic love was ever

real, yet here I am developing an honest-to-god *crush*. Anjie was freaking *right*.

Nothing good can come of this, even if I want it to.

My phone rings, the company-required "Winter Wonderland" notes floating up from my pocket. My heart jumps thinking it could be Aaron, but when I read the name on the screen it's the one person who might be able to give me answers right now.

"Uncle Toby!" I practically shout as soon as I pick up.

He chuckles that deep Santa chuckle. "Hey, Kristopher. I wasn't sure you'd pick up. I haven't heard from you after that text."

He's right. I never responded after he sent me the picture of him and Jared.

"You have a boyfriend," I say, trying to use those acting abilities to sound enthusiastic.

But Uncle Toby has those same abilities. He sees right through me. "Come on, Kris."

He saves my real name for when he's serious. I don't want to shit all over his happiness, but now that he's called, I don't want to keep the truth from him either. If I hold back from him, maybe that's all it will take for us to become the next family pairing that communicates with each other only in weird memes. I don't want my relationship with Uncle Toby to sink to that.

"I'm worried you're setting up a life on the mainland," I say, cringing at how selfish that sounds. "I know that seems awful. But . . . I need you to come back."

"Oh, Kris. We both know that's not going to happen."

"But it could!" I can't tell him about my plan to win the Race and talk to Kringle one-on-one. He specifically asked for me not to make a big deal about this, but what he doesn't know won't hurt him. If anything, I could make this better. For both of us.

"Kris, you have to stop thinking like that." His tone becomes all business, no more joy. It's like he's about to tell me I'm getting coal for Christmas. "You have to accept the reality of our situation. I live *here* now, in Chicago, and I have to move forward. I can't keep living my life stuck in the past."

"But what if you could be here?" I insist.

"Kris—"

"No, just hear me out. Hypothetically, if you could be here again, would you? Would you come back?"

He sighs, angry. "This isn't right, Kris. I don't want to get your hopes up."

"Would you come back if you could?"

"In this hypothetical situation, do I get to be Santa? On my terms?"

I nod hard, even though he can't see me. "Yes. You could even bring Jared." I'll say anything to get him on board.

"Then I'd come back in a heartbeat." He sounds defeated. Like he thinks that situation will never happen.

But I'm *this close* to winning, if what Nicky says is true.

This close to making sure Uncle Toby and I don't become like Aaron and his mom, separated by states and growing further and further apart. I've just got to make Liam's date tonight go off without a hitch. Because at the end of it, if Raquel chooses Liam over Casey, Aaron might choose to finally fall and say he loves me.

My heart races with the thought, because for the first time, I picture saying it too. What if I told him I loved him back, *and meant it*?

It wouldn't matter, would it? Whether or not Aaron falls for me, whether or not I feel it too, there's nothing either of us can do about it. He'll still leave, and I'll have become attached for nothing.

Which is even more reason to get Uncle Toby here. He could help me through it.

"Kristopher," Uncle Toby says, his tone gentler now. "What's all this about? Why are you so upset?"

His question reminds me of all the times he gave me advice. Over hot cocoa, in gift-wrapping classes, when he was showing me how to use the saws in the Workshop. He listened to all my worries when I came out and what that would mean on an island with such a small queer community. How I worried there wasn't really a place for us here, even though I had everything provided for me. Even though no Wonderer ever said a hateful word to me. But he got it, from experience, always speaking to me with kindness and hope for our future, not just as literal family members, but queer family on the island.

It's the reminder I need to know that I can tell him the *real* truth.

"Because I'm worried I'm developing actual feelings," I answer. "For the first time. With a guest who's going to go back home in a few days. I'm worried that's going to hurt in a way I've never been hurt before. And I'm freaked out that if I hurt that much when knowing a guy for only a week and a half, how much will it hurt you to leave someone you've been dating for months? Especially when you haven't even been able to date for years, and I know how much romance means to you. Maybe you'll never come back, even if you have the opportunity to, and I don't know what would be worse. Me asking you to leave love behind or you never returning to Winter Wonderland."

Uncle Toby waits a few seconds to make sure I have nothing left to say before giving a soft chuckle. "So you've been keeping that bottled up, haven't you?"

I laugh despite myself. "It's really more that I didn't know I felt all that until right this minute. It had to get out."

"Kris, there are two things I need to remind you of: First, I'm a grown man. Second, I can weather any storm that life throws my way. Of course I love having your support, but you don't need to worry about me."

"But what Kringle Korp did to you was so unfair!" The words are louder than I mean them to be, and I look over my shoulder to make sure no Wonderers overheard.

"I know, Kris. But sometimes that's life."

I scoff. "Yep. You can't stop Christmas, huh?"

"No, you can't. Just like you can't stop your feelings. About my leaving, about *the rules*, but more importantly, about love. If you truly have feelings for someone, you should always tell them. Maybe life circumstances make it that you can't be together, but I know for sure *not* telling him will be so much worse than keeping it to yourself. You'll always regret it."

There's something in the way he says the words that hints at a story. "You're speaking from experience?"

Uncle Toby sighs. "Sure am, Kristopher. But I sacrificed that love life for my future in Wonderland. Which now turns out to be nonexistent. I don't want you to do the same."

He makes it sound so easy. But if I tell Aaron how I'm feeling, it will disqualify me from the Race. Leading statements—or flat-out telling a guest you love them so they'll say it back—are forbidden. There will go my one shot at convincing Kringle to give Uncle Toby that Santa job he's always dreamed of. Uncle Toby just said himself he'd still come back if his terms were met.

"Thanks, Uncle Toby. You've given me a lot to think about."

"I love you, Kristopher. Whether or not I'm in Winter Wonderland, that's never going to change."

"I know. Talk to you soon, okay?"

"Talk soon."

I hang up, but I still want to *see* him soon too.

I won't give up that dream just yet.

# Aaron

I can't say that any of my plans have ever turned me into a creepy stalker before, but that all changes today. How else am I going to make sure that Raquel's date goes smoothly, that Santa tells her Liam is the man for her, and that she moves on with her life without my brother? I've positioned myself perfectly behind a big red mailbox marked *Letters for Santa*. It's so bulky that it covers my entire body when I squat behind it. The placement of this box couldn't be better. When I peek around it, I have the perfect view of Raquel's cottage across the street. With my binoculars, I'll be able to ensure the night unfolds exactly as it should.

I pat my chest to make sure for the millionth time that the gift I made for Kris is still tucked into my jacket's deep inside pocket. It's there, like I knew it would be, but giving it to him will have to wait until after this evening is executed flawlessly.

I glance at my watch: 7:30. The date should start any—

*Jingle jingle jingle jingle.*

The sound of dozens of jingle bells means everything's about to begin. I glance down the street to see two reindeer pulling a white carriage with plush maroon benches. A Wonderer steers and does a pretty good Santa impression when he *Whoooooooas* the sleigh pullers to a stop outside Raquel's place. The Elf hops down and skips over to the door.

Wow. These people really commit to the bit.

The Elf rings the bell, and even from my stakeout point I can hear "Jingle Bells" play inside Raquel's cottage. The door opens just seconds later. She was ready. Kris made sure Liam sent her an anonymous card telling her to be set to go at 7:30 sharp for a special surprise. Her makeup is flawless, her hair done in expert curls—she even has a sprig of mistletoe perched in them. She looks amazing and truly in the holiday spirit. I know Casey would love it. It's a shame—but not—that he won't get to see her like this.

"RAQUEL!"

My binoculars fall from my fingers, clanging against the mailbox.

But Raquel's too distracted to hear my clumsiness.

Because her eyes are locked on my freaking brother.

Casey sprints up the street, waving his hands as if screaming his head off wasn't enough to grab Raquel's attention.

What the hell is he doing here? Dad was supposed to

keep him occupied! Dad doubled down on keeping Casey away from Raquel after my brother couldn't shut up about her the entire starlight cruise. According to Dad, it was so bad that he's worried Case will get up to something much worse than the reindeer debacle. If even Dad's calling out Casey's desperation, I know I've been right in trying to sabotage my brother all along.

But that's not going to pan out if Casey has his way.

Raquel steps onto the porch, and her eyes go wide when she sees him. Her face splits into a big grin, and holy crap, this isn't going to plan at all.

Casey bursts up the front pathway of Raquel's cottage and sweeps her into a hug when he makes it to her side.

"You did this?" Raquel asks.

"Did what?"

Raquel laughs like Casey is being coy. She doesn't catch on that he really doesn't know why there's a reindeer-pulled carriage in front of her place.

"Should we go?" Raquel asks, pointing toward the carriage, and realization dawns on my brother's face. He has such a one-track mind for Raquel that he honestly didn't notice the hooved beasts and giant wheeled vehicle on the side of the street. Forget DEFCON. This is DESPERATECON 1.

Raquel turns to the Elf expectantly, who I'm hoping beyond hope knows he's supposed to have only one rider and refuses to take Casey along with them. But instead, the Elf just bows low and sweeps his hand wide.

"Your chariot awaits," the Elf says, and fuck, this is going terribly. The carriage is supposed to take Raquel *to Liam*. What's going to happen when Casey and Liam come face-to-face?

It's a Christmas catastrophe.

I don't have any time to make a plan B, because before I know it, Casey and Raquel are snuggled up in the carriage and taking off down the street.

"Shit shit shit shit shit!"

I follow right behind, thankful for the size of the carriage. Its back is so tall and wide that Raquel and Casey would have to literally lean over the edge to see me behind them. They're probably so stupidly lost in each other's eyes right now that there's no way they'd look back.

We make it to the end of the street in no time, reaching the road that leads out to the island's forested wilderness. There are no more residential streets crisscrossing this road's path, and with the way free, the driver picks up the pace. The reindeer head into a clop, their jingle bells jingling aggressively, and they quickly pull away. It's not like they're going anywhere near the speed of a car, but listen, tennis hasn't prepared me to run ten to twelve miles an hour for a prolonged distance. Short bursts of speed, sure, but not this everlasting sprint.

The space between me and the carriage gets greater and greater. They take one of the lane's winding curves, and I've lost them.

"Shit!" It's all I can say apparently.

I've got to catch up to them, fast.

*Beep beep.*

I glance over my shoulder to find the most beautiful sight: Kris straddling a snowmobile. Memories of being wedged between his legs make me squirm, but there's no time to give in to that now.

"How did you know I'd need you?" I ask.

Kris waves the question away. "I know how fast those reindeer can go. I thought you would have learned that too seeing as how you witnessed a stampede."

God, I love a boy who has solutions.

"What about Liam's shift? Don't you have to cover it?"

"Twenty-minute break. I'll be able to get back just in time if you stop yakking." Kris pats the seat in front of him. "Hop on."

I don't need telling twice. I bound over to him and jump in between his legs.

Kris revs the engine before yelling, "Hold on!"

We race forward even faster than that night headed to the beach. A scream bursts from my throat, and my hands fly to Kris's thighs. I'm almost too caught up in holding on for dear life to notice once again how muscular and perfect they are.

Almost.

Kris laughs, squeezing his legs harder on either side of me, wedging me there. We leave the road entirely to race over freshly powdered snow, up and over hills, hidden by trees. Our way is lit by the singular headlight and what little moonlight makes it through the canopy. Kris never skips a beat, sending the snowmobile through trees like he's been this way a million times before, despite there being no path whatsoever.

In what feels like seconds, we slow to a stop. Kris nods toward a faint glow beyond the forest. "That's Santa's Seat," he says. "Text me when you're done." He leans forward and kisses my cheek. "Good luck."

My skin tingles where his lips touch my skin, my whole body vibrating for reasons other than the idling snow-mobile beneath us.

Kris squeezes his thighs on either side of me. "You've got to go, or I'm going to be late for work. I do not need any angry Elves reaming me out for missing a shift."

"Right!" I jolt from the seat, and Kris drives off with a rev of the engine. I stare after his retreating brake lights, wishing he could be here for this. This whole night would've been impossible without him.

I creep to the edge of the trees, and I've got to admit, the location for this date would have been perfect if Casey hadn't ruined everything. Santa's Seat is the world's most breathtaking setting for pictures with the big guy. It's entirely outdoors, with a massive ice throne placed under an altar full of garlands and tinsel and mistletoe. Bright, pillowy mounds of snow sit white and untouched on either side, reflecting the glow of Christmas lights strung through spruce trees in the background. Stars shine from above, little celestial ornaments ready to grant holiday wishes. Any picture taken here would put a mall Santa photo to shame.

Kris booked a man named Roger to play Santa. He sits on the throne, looking regal in his maroon outfit. His beard is perfectly manicured, his dark brown cheeks bulging with a pleasant smile. Liam fidgets nervously by his side, muttering to himself like he's practicing a speech.

"Don't worry, Liam," Roger says. "Just let your words flow from the heart. You don't want to sound too practiced. She's going to love this, I'm sure of it."

"Thanks, Rog—" Liam corrects himself with a glare from Roger. "Santa."

Roger nods. "Much better."

I probably have only a minute to stop this thing before everything goes off the rails. I've got to tell Liam to leave before Casey sees him.

I step out from behind the trees, but freeze. Sleigh bells jingle, signaling the carriage's approach. I'm too late. If I run over to Liam now, Casey will see me, and he'll know I had a hand in putting this together. I've never believed in it before, but now seems as good a time as ever to pray to all that is holiday for a Christmas miracle.

"Please let this work out," I say. "Please fall for Liam. Please let Casey down gently." I turn off my phone as I tuck myself back behind a pine. I do not need it to give me away when I've worked so hard to pull the strings unnoticed.

"Here we go," Roger says, looking happily at Liam, whose face is all screwed up in confusion.

Raquel mirrors his expression. "Liam?" she asks as the carriage pulls up in front of Santa's Seat. "What are you doing here?"

Roger, ever the professional, sticks with the script. "He's the love of your ho-ho-whole life! He's giving you the gift of his heart."

Roger truly sells it. In any other setting, this gesture would be sweeping and romantic. But now Raquel looks back and forth between Liam and Casey, indecision written all over her face. My brother, meanwhile, looks like Santa has gone and stabbed him in the back.

"How could you?" His mouth hangs open in disbelief.

That's Roger's first hint that something is up. He turns to Liam, unsure what to do next.

"Raquel, I set all this up for us," Liam says, stepping toward the carriage. "I wanted you to know how much you mean to me. You're so different from other girls. You ask about *me*. You look past my bulging calves and my toned abs and see my *heart*." It takes serious skill to make that statement sound genuine and not prickish, but somehow Liam's done it. "To everyone else, I'm just their social media piece of meat."

He looks like a total Prince Charming. Liam doesn't even question Raquel about who Casey is or why he's here in the first place. He's trusting and vulnerable, and when Liam offers his hand to Raquel, she gingerly places her fingers in his. Casey's wide-eyed with horror. This is not at all his Christmas miracle.

"Raquel," my brother whimpers. "Please."

She looks back at him for the longest pause.

"Choose Liam," I whisper. "Choose Liam."

"Casey," Raquel breathes. "I'm sorry."

My heart soars. "Yes!" I mouth, my coat swishing as I do a little happy dance in the trees. It worked! This is the final goodbye. Casey has to know from here on out that he really has no future with Raquel, and I can rebuild him as a better, independent man.

I expect Casey to deflate. I expect him to trudge alone down the lane back into town, where I will "coincidentally" run into him and pick up the pieces. I'll make him see he never should have been so reliant on another person.

Casey does get down from the carriage, but not at all how I expect. He doesn't seem downtrodden or defeated. He seems energized. He leaps over the side, jostling the carriage so much it makes the reindeer huff in agitation. Instead of moping away, he dashes around the carriage, and just as Raquel's feet hit the snow, he body-slams Liam, all six foot eight of my brother's lanky frame smashing into the Wonderer. They collapse in a tangle of awkward limbs and dancer-toned muscles.

"CASEY!" I yell, not thinking as I launch myself into the clearing.

My brother doesn't hear me. Either my voice was covered by Raquel's scream and Roger's shout of "Ho-Ho-Hold on a minute!" or, more likely, Case is too focused on the fists that fly at his head, Liam swinging wildly as they tumble over and over. No hit has landed yet, but it's bound to happen soon.

Casey ends up on top, straddling Liam and raising a fist high. He's really going to do it. He's going to beat the shit out of Liam.

Casey's fist flings down, and I sprint forward. Liam uses his years of Winter Wonderland choreo to buck like he's doing a donkey kick. The move dislodges Casey, and right in the nick of time too. Case's fist barely misses Liam while my brother flops to the ground. Both are up on their feet in seconds, but there's just enough space for me to wedge myself between these two idiots. Well, mostly my brother—my formerly sweet, gentle brother—is the idiot and Liam's only defending himself.

"Stop!" I face Casey, grabbing his hand as he raises it for another gangly swing. I'm practically on my tiptoes, he's so tall. "Casey, that's enough! Violence is not Christmas!"

For a moment, Casey resists, using his size against me. It's a thing he never did. We were never those cliché older versus younger brothers, the oldest using his physical advantage to beat the crap out of the younger one. Now I realize what a good thing that is. As Casey's body surges forward, I know he's going to trample me. But at the last second, Casey's eyes fill with recognition. He pulls back before I become another casualty to this show of male "chivalry," a.k.a. douchebaggery.

"Aaron?" Casey's lost his animalistic edge. "What are you doing here?"

"I, uh . . ." I search for any excuse, but I'm too disturbed by what I just saw to improvise. If Kris were here, he'd come up with the perfect reason for why we happened to be in the woods. But my mind only echoes with the truth.

*I'm here to betray you.*

I glance at the others, willing them to give me some kind of out. Liam's hands are still clenched in fists, his chest heaving. Raquel has her pristine candy-cane-manicured nails pressed to her mouth. Roger has his hands inches from a walkie-talkie tucked into the big pockets of his red velvet coat. He looks furious. This is so not the Christmas spirit, and I'm sure Casey's display of savagery is an affront to everything he holds dear as a sworn Santa.

I'm silent for too long. It makes me look guilty. And as I stare helplessly into Casey's eyes, I see all the pieces fall into place. He looks to Raquel, to Liam, to Roger and this perfect date setup.

"No one would come out here on their own," Casey says. "It's too far from town. This wasn't a scheduled session for pictures with Santa. You'd need a reason to come out here."

"N-no, I was just out for a stroll." I cringe at the stutter. I'm such a bad liar.

"You hate the cold," he says calmly, smoothly, fitting the puzzle together. "There's no way you'd walk in this temperature, even with all the Winter Wonderland gear. The only way you'd be out here is if you knew something was happening."

"Of course he knew," Roger says. "Aaron and Kris arranged the date for Liam. As a favor to a fellow Wonderer."

And there it is. The truth.

Thanks a lot, Santa.

"Aaron?" There's no more of that sweet, naïve confusion in Casey's tone. He says my name, and I can feel the hurt. I can feel the betrayal.

Yet I still can't say anything.

"How could you?" He whispers it, but I wish he would scream. I wish he would be mad so I could scream back that he's the reason we're in this mess in the first place. With his quiet pain, I'm forced to soak in the fact that I'm the asshole here.

"I swear it was for a noble reason," I say. It sounds weak, even to me.

Casey's eyes well up. He's never been a crier, but here we are, because of me. Those tears are evidence of just how badly I've hurt my one and only brother. The brother who has been nothing but kind and loving to me my entire life.

"I would never do something like this to you," Casey says. "Ever."

"I know you wouldn't, Case. I know it. But I was doing this for your own good. You were just so dependent on Raquel that you completely crumbled when she left. But you're amazing, Casey. Do you know how many people love you? You can't go a single day at work without the kids drawing you something or requesting *you* for story time or bombarding you the second you walk through the door. They adore you. They see your heart. I just wish you could see it too. You don't need Raquel. You're perfect on your own. She doesn't deserve you."

"Hey, now." Liam puffs up, defensive. "Raquel deserves the world."

Raquel doesn't acknowledge him, doesn't take her eyes off *me*. Her expression is blank, unreadable. At least tears aren't pouring down her face, not like Casey. His fall silently, his cheeks getting splotchier by the second.

"You've got it all wrong, bro," Casey says. "*I* don't deserve *her*. Raquel told me she needed to see who else was out there, that she didn't feel comfortable dating only one person her entire life. But I refused to listen. I used our shared love of Christmas to get her to change her mind, and that's so manipulative. It's awful. I'm awful."

A fiery ball of anger bursts in my stomach, melting away my shame. "You are *not* awful. You're entirely too codependent, but other than that, you deserve someone who loves you for *you* and doesn't need to compare you to other guys to know it!"

"We agree on that."

They're the first words Raquel has spoken since the fight broke out. They're barely above a whisper, but she may as well have yelled them. "Casey does deserve someone who loves him for him." She looks my brother in the eye. "But don't you get it, Casey? I never asked for you to prove you love me. I did the opposite. I told you I needed space. And then I got so wrapped up in this place that I thought I made the wrong decision." She's getting louder, more confident with every word. Then she turns that confidence on me. "I told you I was looking for signs, Aaron. Well, this is one massively huge sign, isn't it? A sign that I could never be with someone who would attack another person the way Casey just did." She flicks an angry finger at my brother while she turns to him again. "This trip was supposed to be the start of my next chapter, but it looks like you couldn't even let me have that. I'll be taking that space now, Casey. For good."

She gets back into the carriage and motions for the Elf to drive her away. He looks to Liam and Roger for one second, confused as to what he should do.

"You heard her," Roger says. "She wants to go. On

Dasher, on Prancer, on—well, just the two Cupids, but you get the idea."

The Elf doesn't say another word, just clicks his tongue to get the reindeer moving. Raquel wipes away one last tear but doesn't look back as she hits the road.

Roger walks behind his throne. With an engine rev, he pops out on top of a snowmobile, glaring at us. "You three are certainly on the Naughty List. Treating a young woman like a trophy to be gained? How could you? It's the twenty-twenties, for Christmas's sake! If someone treated my daughter like this, I'd—" He catches himself before saying something I'm sure would be very un-Santa-like. But we'd all deserve it. We can imagine what Roger was going to say as he speeds off, the words he did manage to get out sinking in.

I've done more than just hurt Casey. I've hurt Raquel too. In trying to make my brother a stronger person, all I really did was make both of us look like massive dicks. And made Liam a pawn in all this.

The Wonderer shoves past me. "Screw you guys," he says, then trudges through the snow back to town. Even his glutes bulge angrily.

That leaves the Merry brothers, all alone. Casey looks at me like he has no idea who I am.

"Casey, I—"

He puts up one massive glove. "Don't. I don't want to hear it, bro. I can't believe you did this." He stares at his hands in disbelief, opening and closing them into fists. I don't think he'd ever made the gesture before tonight. But I set off the chain of events that led to his first punch.

With that, Casey traces Liam's footsteps, leaving me out in the cold.

As he should.

# Kris

"He still hasn't called yet. Why hasn't he called yet?"

I've been pacing the same three feet in my room since ten o'clock. The carpet has a dark track where my feet have tread back and forth, back and forth, for over three hours. I called Anjie in hour two, hoping for a distraction. But no matter what she's said, I always come back to Aaron.

The date should be well underway by now. Raquel and Liam should be in each other's arms, basking in their new-found love and the signs from Santa that they're meant to be together. Except I know that's not going to happen, because I got a text from Liam at 8:12 that read, **What the hell, man?** When I texted him back with a **Wait what happened** and then a **????** fifteen minutes later with still no response, I knew something had gone terribly wrong. I could feel it in my bones.

I tried calling Aaron when I got off work, but he didn't answer. Maybe he was with his brother, and answering would blow our cover. I texted him to call me when he could, but he still hasn't called.

One in the morning and still nothing.

"Okay, Kris, I've been trying to keep this in, but you need to calm down." Anjie's exasperation is evident, even over the phone. "This isn't *you*. You're never this frantic."

"But he should have called by now."

"You said that already, Kris," Anjie snaps. "Like twenty-three times. Listen, I know I said you were crushing on Aaron before, but it's more than that, isn't it? You really care about this guy. Like, *really* care about him."

There's no point denying it anymore. I've admitted it to myself, I've admitted it to Uncle Toby, but it's another thing entirely to tell Anjelica or any of the Fling Ring. We've treated the tourists like such chumps for falling for us all this time, so what does it say about me that I've taken the same bait? I can already tell from Anjie's tone that she's going to try to talk me out of it when I tell her the truth. I'm just not entirely sure my wildly beating heart—worried about Aaron—can take it.

"Listen, Anjie, I—" Scratching at my window cuts me off. "I've got to go!"

I hang up and leap onto my bed, then pull back the curtains. Aaron glows under our Christmas lights, his cheeks red and puffy from crying. I don't know how he found me—he's never been to my house before—but with that look on his face, it's the least of my concerns. I push the window open so forcefully that snow flies from the sill and hits Aaron in the chest. He doesn't even seem to notice.

"When I saw your mailbox with *The Brights* etched on it, I knew this was your place." He sounds all stuffed up.

"You've been MIA for hours, and you think that's the most important thing to tell me?"

"I don't want you to think I'm a creep," Aaron says quietly. "I have enough people mad at me already."

That makes my stomach turn. "What happened?"

"He— He— He found out." I don't need Aaron to specify to know he means Casey. "He showed up at the date and got into a huge fight with Liam. I stopped them just in time, but since I was at the scene of this very private moment, he knew I had to be in on it. He's so hurt, Kris. I think I've broken him. For good."

Aaron bursts into tears, deep racking sobs that shake his whole body. He stands there frozen outside, and I know if I ask him to come in he won't be able to move. Not when he's this upset. So I jump down and sweep Aaron into my arms, hold him to my chest, not even the snow soaking through my socks enough to make me want to ever let go.

"I'm so sorry, Aaron," I say. "I should have been there. I should have made sure Casey didn't follow. I—"

Aaron shakes his head hard against my shirt. "It's not your fault. You had to work. I don't blame you, I just . . ."

He shrugs and buries his face in my pajama top. His tears

add to the snowflakes dampening the fabric. "I just need to feel this."

"Okay," I whisper. "Take all the time you need."

I let him cry while we stand in the cold. I don't know how long goes by, the dark sky above looming over us. But under the glow of our Christmas lights and the Hernandezes' next door, it feels like we're in our own special twilight. Aaron's breathing slows as I stroke his back, and his tears dry up. His soft little hiccups get quieter and quieter until we stand in silence, our chests rising and falling in sync.

Finally Aaron glances up at me, a questioning look in his eyes.

"What do we do from here?" he asks.

I shake my head. "I'm used to you being the man with the plan."

"But I don't know what to do."

"I think that's okay. Sometimes you just have to not know for a while before the path forward reveals itself."

"That's stupid," he says, but not in a mean way. More like the concept is stupid, less that I'm the idiot for suggesting it. "Nothing ever gets solved unless I do something about it."

I think back to little fourth-grade Aaron, or at least what I imagine he looked like. It doesn't take much to envision a smaller version of the guy in my arms, realizing his mom left him for good and seeing the pieces she left behind. Knowing that someone was going to have to step in and take her place to make sure all their lives stayed on track. It's a lot of pressure for a nine-year-old. Too much pressure. And now Aaron has cracked under it.

In the quietest whisper he asks, "Can I kiss you?"

Normally, the suggestion would make my heart pick up, my whole body tingle. It really is my favorite thing to do. But for the first time, I think kissing can wait.

"Are you sure that's the best idea?" I ask. "You're in a vulnerable state, and I don't want to take advantage of that."

"It's not taking advantage," Aaron says. "I'm asking. I could use the distraction."

"I don't think that's—"

"Kris!" He squeezes me on either side. "Shut up and kiss me."

I laugh and do as I'm told. I tilt his chin up just so, his splotchy cheeks shining in the light, the tears on his lashes glistening in the cold. As my lips meet his, he releases all his weight onto me, pushing me against the side of my house, keeping him afloat with my arms and our kiss.

I let Aaron take the lead, his lips soft, tender. I can feel the sadness in his movement, and I hope he can feel through mine that everything will be okay. I'm not sure how, I'm not sure when, but it will. I'm Kris Bright, nephew of Tobias Bright, the best Wonderer this island has ever seen. If I can't fix this, no one can.

After a few more minutes of that gentle kissing, Aaron peeks up at me. "I brought you something."

"Your whole plan backfired and your brother is devastatingly mad at you, so you brought *me* a gift?"

Aaron smiles, slow, sad, wiping away a bit of snot that's flecked onto his upper lip.

"It's your Christmas present," he says. "Besides, I started this yesterday before everything blew up in my face, so . . ." He unzips his coat and reaches inside a pocket to pull out a packet of paper that unrolls in his hands. It's three-hole-punched and held together by brass fasteners. "Disregard the tearstains, please. I had to check one more time before I got here to make sure it was perfect."

I flip through the papers to find profiles on Alaskan universities, with lists and lists of scholarships. Every now and then the ink is smeared, but who cares. I can't believe he even had the time to do this in a *day*.

"What's all this for?" I ask.

"You said you didn't have a college counselor here," Aaron says. "And that nobody ever really presents you Wonderer kids with options for a future off the island. So I did some research, focusing on in-state schools that would have the most attainable tuition, especially considering all the scholarships I'm pretty sure you'd qualify for."

This is the sweetest thing anyone has ever done for me. And yet, I'm not sure if I'll even be able to put this gift to good use. "I don't know what to say. This is so nice, but . . . I've been trying to get my uncle back to Wonderland this whole time. This seems kind of like giving up on that."

Aaron doesn't look dejected in the slightest. He nods, hard, some of that can-do attitude he lost clearly coming back. "That's the point! Look, I'm the Robot, right? Why would you want to stick around here when the powers that be are making it clear they don't want you? The best revenge will be showing them how talented you are and how you're winning outside their shitty little island." He catches himself. "No offense. I know this is your home. But there's a whole world out there just waiting for you, Kris. I know you said you and your uncle have always been the best at the holiday, but sometimes I get the feeling that Christmas isn't really your thing. How can you know if you've never tried anything out in the real world? Go see what's out there. *You* get to decide your fate, not the Winter Wonderland board."

"I can't believe you did all this," I breathe, thumbing through page after page. There is so much information on each school, descriptions of their college programs. He's circled dance programs and hockey teams and psychology departments. He seems to think that's the major for me, with notes like *You have the guests on WW pegged. You're born for this.*

It must have taken him hours to put together. *No one* has ever thought of me like this before. They always see me as a side character in their Christmas romance. But this whole time, Aaron's actually listened to me. *Seen* me. I don't know if I'm ready to give up my idea of the future with my family back on the island, but with what Aaron's showing me, I'm starting to feel like there are more options.

"Aaron, I don't know what to say."

He smiles. "You don't have to say anything. This isn't about me. This is for you."

That's all it takes for me to lean in and kiss him again.

# Aaron

This is something I never expected when I asked Kris to help me sabotage Casey's love life. As he presses his lips against mine—soft, slow, and gentle—there's so much more than just my body in it. Sure, I've got tingles up and down my spine, goose bumps rise all along my arms, and I'm getting harder by the second. But overpowering all that is this feeling of warmth blossoming out from my heart.

This isn't just a one-and-done anymore. This isn't just a fling.

I like Kris. *Truly* like Kris. Even more than that, somehow. The longer we stand here, the better I feel, the more grounded I become, ready to figure out how to make things right with Casey.

I don't just *like* Kris anymore. I need him too.

The realization makes me pull back. The frozen air of Winter Wonderland pushes in between us, taking away the warmth of his kiss. It feels like a bucket of ice water was poured over my head. And that's just the sensation I need to bring me back to reality.

I need Kris, but I can't need him. Not when I'm leaving in just two days. Not when our lives have no place for each other. It's impossible, living thousands of miles apart. I can't hinge my happiness on a guy I would hardly ever get to see. We made it to this island on a whim. If it wasn't for that lottery, we never would have been able to afford to come here. We never *will* be able to afford to come here. It's stupid to fall for Kris. So, so stupid.

But even still.

Here we are.

"Aaron?" Kris's voice is laced with worry.

I know what I'm about to ask goes completely against everything I told myself about feelings. But my body is saying now is the time. My heart even more so. Despite constantly telling myself to never listen to this crap because feelings lead to devastation. But how could I ruin my life more than it already is?

I need to feel connected to someone. And right here in front of me, there's a wonderful guy who's showing me he'd like to connect.

"Can we, um—" I nod toward his open bedroom window. "Go inside?"

Kris's eyes light with recognition. He can hear it in my tone. He knows what I'm asking.

"Are you sure?"

I nod. "More sure than I've been of anything all week."

It's true. More than the plans I concocted to make Casey better, more than the surety I felt that this would just be a fling. I know right now that this is what I have to do. As long as Kris is okay with it.

"That is," I add, "only if you feel the same way."

Kris groans, low, deep, and locks his hands together to give me a boost.

I'll take that as a yes.

I'm up and over his windowsill in a heartbeat, Kris just behind. I flop onto the mattress as he lands beside me. Kris swings his feet around to sit up, his right foot hitting my left leg. Cold water seeps from his wet socks through my jeans, making me jump.

"Shit, that's cold!"

Kris smacks a hand over my mouth. "Shhhhh! My parents are upstairs." He says it through a hushed whisper-laugh, his eyes traveling to the ceiling, waiting to hear the hurried footsteps of his mom or dad checking to make sure everything is all right.

Frozen there on his bed, my eyes travel down to take in Kris while he's still occupied looking up. His pajama top hugs him in all the right places. I can see the way it folds around his biceps, his pecs. The bottoms too, a red and black flannel, hug him. Not tight, but enough to see the faint outline of where everything is.

"I think we're good," Kris whispers, pulling his hand

away from my lips. The second he does, I push my face against his and Kris pushes back. Nothing is soft or gentle anymore. We're both hungry, needing this moment.

With one hand, he reaches down and pulls off his socks. With the other, he gently lays me down on his bed. In a heartbeat, he's on top of me, his chest against mine. The weight of him, the warmth of him, that part of him that's *definitely* reacting, all feel right.

I grind upward, making Kris moan again.

"Aaron," he whispers.

That's all it takes. Hearing my name on his lips, hearing that need, that curiosity to know more of me, makes me want to give him more of myself than I ever thought I would.

So I do.

The rest of the night is pure magic. Not Christmas magic, just the magic made from two people connecting through their bodies. Kris was perfect and slow and always checked in to make sure everything we were doing was okay. I was more than happy to say yes each and every time. I'll remember it for the rest of my life.

Already—walking down the dark, quiet Wonderland streets back to my place at six in the morning—I want to do it again. But in just two days, any possibility for a repeat will be gone. Which is probably for the best. I can already feel myself slinking into dependency, which is what I wanted to avoid with this fling. Flings end abruptly, the Band-Aid ripped off, supposedly before feelings develop. Only now I think I'm going to feel the sting in my heart the second our wheels lift from the tarmac at Wonderland Airport.

But really, *It's for the best.*

I need to focus on Casey. I need to be the strong, independent person I was trying to make him this entire trip.

I'm so distracted thinking about last night that I don't soften the jingle bells when I open the front door. They clang loudly, making me freeze.

"Where have you been?!"

Dad bursts from the living room sofa, the plush red velvet keeping the imprint of his butt even as he rushes to my side to wrap me in his arms. He must have been sitting there all night, waiting for me to get home.

"Sorry, Dad, I—" How do I explain that I backstabbed my brother so hard I couldn't come back here to face him? All it does is make me sound like a coward.

Which, now that I think about it, I guess I am.

"I fucked everything up."

Dad doesn't even correct me for language. "I'm just glad you're safe. Don't ever keep your phone off again." He pulls back, the anger gone, settling into his place on the sofa. He taps the cushion beside him, and I take a seat. "Casey told me everything," he says.

"Great."

Dad nods. "Yeah, buddy. He's pretty pissed."

"Where is he now?"

Dad motions toward the street. "He's been out for a walk since four in the morning. Trying to come up with some plan to explain himself to Raquel. You know Casey. Trying to get inspiration from Christmas."

I roll my eyes and scoff. "When will he get that's not how it works? She isn't going to take him back. It doesn't matter if it's Christmas, or Leap Day, or freaking Talk Like a Pirate Day, they're just *days*, not magic!"

Dad pats my knee. It's less sympathetic and more *Are you hearing yourself?* "Give him a break. We've all got to build our own delusions to protect ourselves. Yourself included."

I snap back. "Excuse me? *I'm* delusional? I'm the only one around here keeping things going."

"It's nice that you think that." He says it with no judgment, but I can feel it nonetheless.

"What's that supposed to mean?"

"It means we've all had it rough and coped in our own ways. When your mom left, we leaned on the crutches we needed to get by. I dove into selling more homes, Casey became even more obsessed with Christmas than he already was, and you? You went into your spreadsheets and obsessive planning and need to control."

I feel like I've been slapped. "I made all those spreadsheets because the lights had to stay on. Bills had to be paid. Without me, our lives would have fallen apart. I don't need control."

"Aaron? Have you met you?" But he says it with a laugh, his tone soft. "Do you really remember that time? After she left?"

Now I laugh, but my tone is anything but soft. "Are you kidding me? I'll never forget it."

"Then do you remember," Dad begins, "how you were the one who came to me with all those spreadsheets? How you were the one who brought the bills from your mom's office to make sure they got paid. I never asked you to do it. None of our utilities were shut off. We weren't ever close to losing power or water or our phones. But you came to me—my sweet, loving boy—wanting to make sure that the jobs your mom once did got done. And I knew that it was something you needed to do. You've always liked having everything just so, from your birthday parties to the way we folded your clothes. I saw that day, with that bundle of envelopes in your hand, that this was something I could give you to make you feel like your world wasn't crumbling."

"Wait. What?" This is entirely not how I remember it. "You and Casey were so sad, I just— It felt like no one was moving on."

Dad nods. "We were sad. Sometimes I still have to fight off a wave of hurt that she went away like that. At the time, I blamed myself, wishing I would have seen how unhappy she was. But my sadness didn't mean I couldn't function as your father. And you so badly wanted to keep things under control. I thought letting you have that small responsibility would give you a sense that everything was going to be okay. So I gave you my credit card numbers and let you pay those bills. Then as time went on, you came to me having done more and more: making grocery lists, doctor's appointments, home maintenance requests. It's not that I ever needed you to do that, Aaron. I thought you wanted to. To cope with the loss."

It feels like my world has been turned upside down. Probably just like how Casey felt when Raquel broke up with him. I rack my brain, thinking back to that day I first realized the family was going to need me. I was so sure that if I didn't cover the logistics, everything would crumble. I remember sitting in Mom's chair the day she left, at the desk we sat at together so many times. She'd crunch numbers for bills and taxes while I did my homework or read a book or researched college options even when I was just nine years old. I remember sitting there alone, then opening the top drawer of the desk and seeing all those unopened bills. Water, electricity, garbage pickup. I decided right then and there that I'd do it. I thought that because they weren't opened, they'd never be opened. Maybe a part of me—a much bigger part of me than I ever knew—thought that if I could sit in that room like I did with Mom for hours on end, doing all the things that she used to do to keep our family going, I could bring her back. Like maybe the pressure of it all was too much for her and she needed a helping hand. I wanted to show her I could be that.

"Dad." The tears come hot and fast, my nose clogging with emotion that makes me gasp for breath. "Dad."

I don't know how to say any of these thoughts out loud. They're so clear to me now, after pushing them away for so many years. But still, I can't voice them.

He scoots over and scoops me up, pressing me into his side. "I know, Aaron. I know."

Somehow I still have so many tears left to cry, despite how much I bawled into Kris's chest last night. Maybe it's because these tears are different. These aren't tears of guilt after stabbing someone in the back; these are the tears from being stabbed. I never really knew that's how I felt. This whole time, I closed myself off from letting the pain really sink in when Mom left. I built a wall of control, convinced myself that Mom's stupid memes could count for a relationship. But now that one of my plans has failed like never before, all those walls I built my life inside of are crumbling.

We sit there for what feels like hours, but is really only fifteen minutes. The tears that I've kept locked away pour freely. Dad keeps his arm around my shoulders and doesn't let go. I know that he'd never leave me, not on this couch and not in life. Not like Mom. The universe may have let me down with one parent, but thank god it gave me a monumental dad.

When the last tear finally slides down my cheek, I'm hit with a bone-deep exhaustion.

"What do we do now?" I ask.

"Maybe we should talk to her about it," Dad says. "All of us."

"I meant about Casey."

"I know," Dad says with a small smile. "All this time I thought if I let you have the control you needed, you'd be okay." His own eyes swim with tears as they bounce back and forth between mine. "But you're not okay, are you? Casey's not either. I think it goes so much further than this breakup with Raquel. I'm starting to think his desperation to be with her has something to do with abandonment. They started dating only a few weeks before your mom left. Between their relationship and this holiday stuff, I think he's been avoiding his emotions all along too."

It's just like Kris said. People get so involved with the magic of Christmas because they think it will erase all their problems. But those problems will always be waiting if you don't face them head-on.

I shoot up from the couch. "I need to find him."

Dad stands too, but he's not rushed, not in game-plan mode like me.

"No, Aaron. You're staying here. Casey needs to learn how to solve his problems by himself. Part of that is knowing what it's like to fail. He doesn't need you to get him out of this. And you need to learn that it's okay for things to be outside your control."

He walks to the kitchen while I'm frozen in place, more frozen than I've ever been in the cold beyond our cozy gingerbread cottage. I can hear Dad rummage through the refrigerator as I fight every urge to run out the door and fix the problems I've made.

"I'm going to make us some breakfast," Dad calls. "And you're going to figure out how to apologize to your brother for what you did. It's time you start speaking to people from the heart instead of detaching yourself so you can't get hurt. Don't think I haven't overheard you refer to yourself as the Robot."

Right. That. I guess I was a bit less guarded than I thought. Or way more transparent, at least.

I try to come up with any plan that could truly convey how sorry I am to my brother. But for now, nothing pops up.

Minutes pass, standing there in the living room, waiting for inspiration, until Dad's head peeks around the corner.

"Okay, uh, I know I said I was going to make breakfast, but that's actually the one thing I *do* rely on you for. Unless you're into burnt toast and runny eggs. Want to come in here and teach me a thing or two so I'm not so helpless?"

The tension eases from my shoulders just a bit. "Yeah, Dad. I do."

At least in this case, it's nice to be needed.

The doorbell rings two hours later, "Jingle Bells" chiming throughout the cottage. I don't know who I want it to be more: Kris, to comfort me and maybe just lie next to me while I finally try to get some sleep after the longest night of my life, or Casey, who still hasn't come home and is the reason why I can't get to sleep until I apologize to his face.

Dad's sleeping on the sofa, having finally passed out after a full belly and knowing both his sons were okay even if one was taking a walk to let off some steam. He doesn't budge when the bell rings, which might bode well for me if this actually is Kris. Dad won't be awake to enforce the no-romantic-interests-in-the-same-bedroom-with-the-door-closed rule. If anything could take my mind away from this all-consuming guilt, it would be a lot of making out.

I slowly inch the door open, taking extra care that the jingle bells don't wake Dad up. But when it's fully open, nobody's on the porch.

"Did I just get ding-dong-ditch— *Oof!*"

A snowball hits me square in the chest.

"Get out here, you asshole!"

Casey stands in the front yard, off to the side a bit where I couldn't see him, his chest heaving. He's the maddest I've ever seen him. Cursing would have been enough of a giveaway; he usually keeps things annoyingly PG. There's a mound of perfectly sculpted snowballs at his feet, and it's clear they're all intended for me. He bends down and lobs another one in the blink of an eye. I don't even try to avoid it. I let its cold mushiness explode against my chest, soaking into the onesie Casey insisted we buy.

"We're hashing this out, man to man!" he shouts.

"Casey, you don't want to fight. This isn't you, remember?"

Another snowball smacks me in the shoulder. "This isn't a real fight. It's a snowball fight. You couldn't find anything more Casey if you tried."

He's got a point there.

Another mushy projectile makes its mark. He could give Kris a run for his money.

"You ruined my shot with Raquel, bro! How could you? We wouldn't be in this mess if it wasn't for you!"

I honestly thought I was just going to stand here and take it, because let's face it: I shouldn't have meddled. I deserve this. But his conviction that we wouldn't be here if I hadn't stepped in flips a switch inside me. My blood boils, pushing aside all the biting cold from being outside in only a snow-soaked onesie.

"Are you kidding me?"

I'm off the porch and in the snow in a hurried leap. My bare hands fly into the white powder and craft a lopsided ball that I chuck at Casey. He easily dodges it, which only makes me more pissed.

"We're in this mess because of *you*," I snap. "Because you can't be *yourself* for even a minute. You've got to be her boyfriend. It's like that's the only label you care about. That's pathetic, Casey. You're pathetic!"

His hand freezes in midair, pulled back high to lob another snowball. It makes my heart freeze in my chest too. I've never said something like this to him before. Ever. We've supported each other in everything, all seventeen and a half years of my life. But then his face darkens, and he releases the snowball. It's too fast to dodge, and once again, the powdery projectile explodes in the center of my chest.

"*I'm* the pathetic one?" Casey shouts. "At least I'm actually able to connect with another person. You're so scared of getting hurt that you push everyone away. You burrow inside Excel and don't let anyone in. *That's* pathetic!"

I grab a handful of snow and smoosh it into ammo. "You don't connect, Casey!" I scream. "You're a possessive creep! You couldn't even let Raquel breathe and do her own thing for one second. Do you know how gross that is, *bro*?" I let every ounce of sarcasm I can muster soak into the word.

"You mean like how you connect?" Casey shoots back. "Like how you send stupid texts to Mom and think that counts as actually having a conversation?"

That one cuts me, especially so soon after my talk with Dad. But Casey's right, isn't he? Those texts count as nothing, not compared to the messages Kris gets from his uncle Toby. He actually sends pictures and shares things about his life. All I get from Mom is her face on a turkey's vagina. It's bullshit. It's not even the least she could do.

But while all that may be true, Casey is kidding himself if he thinks his way of handling it is any better.

"Oh, because getting maniacally attached to your

girlfriend to deal with your mommy issues is so healthy!" I say. "You're just sad, Casey. So fucking sad."

"SHUT UP!"

It's the loudest yell yet, one full of rage and sadness and complete exhaustion.

But it doesn't come from me or my brother.

It comes from Raquel. Standing in the walkway leading up to our cabin, right in between us, directly in the line of fire.

Casey surges to her side as fast as the piled-up snow will allow. "Raquel, I—"

She holds up a hand, and he stops suddenly, falling over into the snow, all gangly six foot eight of him.

"Don't," she says. "You're not the same guy I dated for the past eight years. Or maybe you are, and I never saw the real you. That's even more reason why we shouldn't be together."

Casey lies there, a fallen snow angel. "I promise I can be better. I'll do better. Give me a second chance."

"Don't you think eight years is enough of a chance?" Normally, that's a statement I would keep inside, but I'm done protecting my brother from himself. He finally needs to feel this pain. I've been working so hard to shield him from it, but deluding ourselves into thinking we have all our problems handled isn't going to work anymore.

"Bro?" Casey sounds like I've stabbed him right through the heart.

"This isn't about me," I say to Casey, then turn to Raquel. "This is about you. Getting to have the future you want, and no one meddling."

"About time," Raquel snaps. "You know what? There's something that needs to be said." She marches through the front yard, grabbing a couple snowballs left in the pile Casey made. She throws one with expert accuracy that lands right in Casey's face.

"I just came here to say I'm through with signs." She looms over Casey, the first person to ever make my brother look small. "I was such an idiot to think that something greater than all of us was trying to pull me back to you. You don't listen, Casey. I told you we needed our own things, I told you that while we shared so much together, it was important for both of us to have interests that made us individuals. But you wouldn't hear me. I felt *smothered*! And then you're surprised when I break up with you? Even worse, you try to sabotage my new relationship when I'm finally exploring something for *me* for a change? How dare you! I set boundaries, and you refused to listen to them. That is so messed up."

Raquel wheels around, her other snowball raised high. She doesn't attempt to throw it, just stomps over to me and plops it down on my head. "And *you*. Don't go thinking you're any better. You're such a meddler, Aaron. I know you think it's for our own good, but just butt out, okay? I may not want to be with your brother anymore, but that's a decision *I* get to make. You don't get to pull our strings like some obsessive puppet master. If you had let things be, that fight between Casey and Liam never would have happened. My trip wouldn't be ruined. Merry fucking Christmas!"

And that's the end of her speech. She takes off down the road, puffs of breath billowing over her head as she huffs angrily.

Casey and I stare at each other with open mouths.

That was . . . epic.

"I deserved that," I mutter. "I should give it a rest sometimes, huh?"

"Me too," Casey says. "Why would I try to force myself back into her life when she specifically said she needed to see what was out there? I'm such an idiot."

"I think Raquel's point is that you're both idiots." Casey and I look to the porch, where Dad stands with a steaming mug of cocoa in his hands. "My two idiot sons."

I walk over to Casey and offer my hand to pull him up. "I thought it was only you this whole time. But I was also part of the problem. I'm sorry, Case."

Casey takes my hand and pulls me into a hug as soon as he's on his feet. "I'm sorry too, bro."

"Come on, boys," Dad says. "I think we've got some things we need to work out."

And so we head inside, a Merry Mash-Up underway that just might be the most productive one yet.

# Kris

I haven't been able to stop thinking about Aaron the past thirty-seven hours. Who am I kidding, I haven't been able to stop thinking about him since we started this whole scheme. But yesterday was something different. It was more than just a makeout, pushed up against the side of a gingerbread cabin, an ass grab here and there for the fun of it. This is so much bigger than the Race. And honestly, I never thought I'd think something could be bigger than the Race. Or maybe they can share equal importance? For the first time, this has turned into something real. And those real feelings are all I've been able to focus on since he left my place.

Aaron and I have been texting nonstop all that time too. We haven't been able to see each other, though, and I'd be lying if I said it wasn't eating me up inside. Aaron was honest that he needed to spend some time with his dad and brother to work through some family issues.

I've tried to distract myself with helping prepare for the MistleToast—the party we throw on the last night of every Twelve—but I think that's made it worse. I was assigned mistletoe duty, and every single sprig I nail throughout the town square makes me think of how I could be kissing Aaron. Makes me think of every single kiss and touch and gasp we shared and how that experience was unlike anything I've ever done before.

I cannot get a boner when the square is this packed. It's always this bonkers on Night Eleven, but this one in particular is *the real* Christmas night. People are so amped up, it's a surprise that none of their heads explode. Their smiles are eight million times bigger than they've been before, and that's saying something. And knowing that they're leaving in the morning, everyone crowds into Santa's Square with mugs of hot cocoa in their hands, soaking up the ultimate day of holiday cheer before the MistleToast tonight and their final farewell.

Every Wonderer not manning a storefront has helped set up, since the extra-thick crowd makes it take that much longer to get ready. But with all of us at work, we hang the extra garland and mistletoe, and the band Elves get all positioned just in time for the seven o'clock festivities to start. Smells of roasted chestnuts and turkey legs and gingerbread permeate the air while the band plays jazz versions of classic Christmas songs. It's objectively perfect, if Christmas is your thing.

When he was here, Uncle Toby would pull me to the side of the square the minute before the MistleToast started to take it all in. We'd appreciate the hours and hours of Elfpower that went into putting on the celebration, soak in the looks and sounds of pure joy, feel proud that we created the feeling of togetherness for friends and family to cozy up in each other's arms, thankful to be spending the moment together. Uncle Toby would always remind me that this was the reason behind our hard work: this happiness. It had all the trimmings to come across as overly sappy, but it never did. It felt good to be a part of that, even if guests could be annoying or just way too into the whole thing.

Since he can't be with me now, I take a picture of all we've done and send it to my uncle.

**Merry Christmas, Uncle Toby.**

His response is instant.

**Merry Christmas, Kris! That is some view. I may not be able to toast you in person, but here's a cheers to you.**

A picture pops up of him and Jared in matching wool sweaters, clinking mugs of eggnog. For the first time since I learned about him, I'm grateful for Jared. Nothing would be able to lift my spirits if I knew Uncle Toby was spending his favorite holiday alone.

But still, he should be here. With me.

Seeing how deliriously in love with Christmas everyone

is at this event, posing for pictures with any one of our Santas, the glaring absence of my uncle and a gay Santa to boot sticks out like a sore thumb. We're missing one giant puzzle piece, and now I'm not so sure how proud I am to be a part of any of this.

"You've been MIA lately," Anjelica says, clacking next to me in faux-fur stiletto boots. I've been avoiding her ever since our phone call. I know she's going to try to talk me out of my feelings for Aaron. But after what we shared, there's no way that's going to happen.

And sure enough, she gets right to it. "Everyone else is babbling about who's going to win the Race, but you're off in your head. It's about *Aaron*, isn't it?"

Hearing his name brings me out of my mood. The soft smile on my face is answer enough for Anjie.

"What are you doing, Kris?" she asks. Her tone is sharp. Not the genuine concern she shows when we talk about Uncle Toby, or her typical aloofness when the others are around. Normally when we talk about the Race it's all a joke. But this time I know she knows Aaron has gone beyond being some fun byproduct of our competition that we can gossip about later. She's worried. "He's going back home."

"He is." It's not like I have some far-flung dream that Aaron will want to move here or something. Although I'm pretty sure Casey would love that, Christmas is just not Aaron's bag. I can't blame him. I have a hard enough time stomaching the sickly sweetness of this place as it is. And I don't have any sort of delusions that I could afford moving to Southern California on my minimal Wonderland wage.

"Don't you think you're setting yourself up for heart-ache?" Anjie asks.

I shrug. "Maybe I am."

Anjelica stomps so hard, I'm surprised her heel doesn't snap. "Dammit, Kris, this is supposed to be fun. No one's supposed to get hurt! It's what we talked about."

"No one's getting hurt, Anjie."

"*You* are," she insists. "You might not see it, but I can tell you're getting dangerously attached. I've seen far too many googly-eyed boys fall for me, and I see it in you too. You're falling for that mainlander." She grabs my hands, her green nails catching the lamplight. "Don't go think-ing something stupid like you love him, Kris. Nothing can change the reality of this place. We're on an isolated island. If you put hooks into this guy who lives thousands of miles away, all it's going to do is lead to torture."

She bites her bright red bottom lip, anxious, trying to get me not to feel the same pain she does. Not that she has her hooks in any person on the mainland, just that she misses New York more than anything. The one and only time I saw her cry, it was from homesickness. But I can't let her worries get in my way. She doesn't know Aaron like I do. I still haven't told anyone about the packet he gave me, that heartfelt gesture to show me what life could be like outside Winter Wonderland. I worry that if I show it to them, they'll think I'm crazy for even considering a life away from this place. I don't want them to rain on this parade.

If there was anyone I was going to tell about Aaron's gift, of course it would be Anjie. There's a world in which she sees that gesture as a good sign that Aaron is falling for me, that maybe today will be the day he tells me he loves me and I win the Race. I'd get one step closer to bringing Uncle Toby back. But then, that's not what he'd want, is it? His words from our phone call have been a constant refrain in my head since Aaron left yesterday morning.

*If you truly have feelings for someone, you should always tell them.*

I've had a lot of time to think about it, and I know if I followed through with the Race and actually succeeded in getting Uncle Toby back here, he'd be pissed I did it at the expense of finding love. Plus, the likelihood that I could even convince Anjelica's dad of giving my uncle the gay Santa gig is slim to none. How could I be more convincing than Kringle Korp? And the most important thing of all: winning the Race because Aaron fell for me doesn't feel right anymore. He's not a guy to be used . . . he's a guy I love.

I know it's stupid. I know it's fast. I mean, we've known each other for only a week and a half. But after everything he's done for me in that short amount of time, connecting with me in ways dozens of guys haven't, truly seeing me . . . what else could I call it?

So tonight I'm going to break the cardinal rule, and that will take me out of the competition.

I'm going to tell Aaron I love him first.

"Don't worry about me, Anjie." I pull her in for a hug. "I know what I'm doing."

When we pull apart, Anjelica just shakes her head slowly. "Don't say I didn't warn you."

The clock tower looming over Santa's Square chimes seven deep bells. This soon after Anjie's warning, it could seem ominous. But for me, as I look across the square and lock eyes with Aaron, it feels like the start of our next chapter.

# Aaron

There he is. The guy who I thought would just be a flash in the pan. Just a fling. But giving him up tomorrow is really going to hurt. What a Christmas present, huh? Find a guy you actually want to spend time with and realize you can't have him at all. It feels like some kind of cosmic joke.

The last day and a half with Dad and Casey has been a lot of tears, a lot of apologies, but a lot of moving forward too. I know now that I should have just let Casey do his thing and not tried to get in the way. If anything, I should have been much more vocal about him leaving Raquel alone and giving her space.

Casey learned that Raquel isn't just the female lead in the cheesy made-for-TV holiday movie that is his life. She has feelings and doubts and layers too, and her need to know what else is out there romantically is a real one. Maybe someday she'll realize that Casey is right for her and come back to him. But Casey acknowledged that as much as it hurts, that's her decision.

What's that horrifying cliché? If you love someone, you have to let them go? To be honest, I've always thought sayings about love were dumb, but now I'm finally starting to get it. Which leads to the other big topic of conversation we had during our Merry Mash-Up.

Kris.

I shared with Dad and Case how this fling all started because of our meddling, and now my feelings for Kris have catapulted into something I didn't see coming. Casey was ecstatic. The second the words were out of my mouth that I think I more than like Kris, Casey threw his gangly limbs over the table and literally lifted me out of my seat to give me the world's most awkward tabletop smothering.

After a lifetime of keeping my emotions shoved down deep inside, I'm learning that sometimes the best way through a situation is to say exactly how you feel. Or else you have epic breakdowns like I did with Dad. I'm pretty sure I'll have one again if I leave here tomorrow without telling Kris about my feelings for him.

So as the clock tower rings the last of its seven bells and the square floods with tourists dancing to a jazz rendition of "Rockin' Around the Christmas Tree," I run to him. I have to push people out of the way, even shoulder a few. With quick apologies and visitors in such good spirits, I don't think anyone really cares. Or maybe they do, and I just don't notice because I only have eyes for Kris. His whole face lights up when he sees me, his deep brown eyes getting all round like a puppy's, and he runs a nervous hand over his buzz cut before opening his arms wide.

The second his arms wrap around me, I push my lips against his. It feels so good after a day and a half apart, not just because of how perfectly soft and plump his lips are, not just because of the electric tingles his scruff makes cascade down my spine, but because he let me have that time apart and knew how important it was. Absence makes the heart grow fonder and all that. I know it's cringey, but it meant the world to me that he stayed here waiting until I was ready.

Whistles join the jazz music as we kiss. I didn't think we'd have an audience in the hubbub of the MistleToast, but here we are. I pull back, my cheeks blazing, and see a small crowd gathered, probably thinking we've fallen under the spell of Christmas, no doubt like they have. So I guess that means I'm going to have onlookers for this confession, Wonderers and tourists alike. I'd rather it be in private, but this can't wait. Plus, I'm going to have to shout to be heard over the music, so I've got a full spectacle on my hands.

But Kris has something on his mind too. "Aaron, I need to tell y—"

I place my hand over his lips. "Me first, or my stubbornly independent instincts will kick in and I'll never get this out."

Kris nods, his Adam's apple bobbing as he swallows.

"Don't be nervous," I say. "It's a good thing. *You're* a good thing. Sorry, I'm saying this wrong. You're not a thing. A person. And I'm trying to get better at not being a robot and seeing people as complete individuals who aren't just pawns in my plans. Not that you're a pawn. Man, I'm terrible at this." I wipe a bit of sweat from my upper lip. Why am I sweating? "It's just that I've never felt this way about somebody before. All my life I've tried to push others away, knowing I could get hurt if I let them too close. But then you came along and were down to jump right into my plans. You added to them too, and for so long I've felt like I have to be the person to get everything done. I learned recently that that's not the case, and it's nice to know there are guys like you out there who are willing to shoulder some of the weight when things get tough. You made me feel supported, like I could lean on you. I never imagined I could connect with someone like this. In so many ways." *Jeezus, Aaron, get to the point.*

"What I'm trying to say, Kris, is that I don't want this to be it. I don't want this to be the last we see of each other. I know that's so horribly stupid because we live so far apart. Maybe nothing we do can change whether we'd actually ever get to be together, but I couldn't leave here without telling you my feelings."

I take a deep breath.

This is it.

"I love you, Kris." His eyes go wide, and I worry I've made a mistake. "I know that's a lot. I know we just met, and I'm not trying to get too clingy too fast. But these feelings I have for you, they're so much more than like. It's got to be love. I needed you to know before I leave. I love you, Kris. I love you."

God, could I sound any more desperate? I said I love him three times without giving him any time to process. The silence between us is filled by cheering and whistling from the folks who heard my screamed confession. But Kris just stares at me, open-mouthed.

"Sorry, I—I got excited." I've got to fill his silence or else this is going to get even more awkward. "I guess when you're new to expressing your feelings, they all kind of pour out at once."

Kris laughs, and the sound is such a relief. Maybe I didn't scare him off after all.

"Aaron," he says, pulling me close so that my entire body is pressed against him. I wish this could be a whispered moment instead of a shout over jazz music, but it is what it is. This will be one of the little details of our love story, how we literally yelled our feelings at each other. "I was going to tell you the same thing. I lo—"

The music cuts out suddenly, "Rockin'" ending and the jazz band shuffling sheets of music to move to their next piece. Which means Kris is now shouting into the relative quiet. But another Wonderer is too, a hulking guy in mid-convo with the fabulously dressed girl next to him, who looks like she's going to be sick. So while Kris finishes the world's best statement of "I LOVE YOU TOO," this other boy screams, "HE DROPPED THE L-BOMB! KRIS WON! THIS KID JUST TOLD KRIS HE LOVES HIM!"

The girl fumes and stomps on the guy's foot.

"Ouch, Anjelica! What was that for?" That's when he feels all eyes on him and looks around with red cheeks, embarrassed. The music kicks up again, "Frosty the Snowman" saving whoever this guy is as everyone gets back to their merriment. Meanwhile, a pit has opened in my stomach, and my heart falls right into it.

"Kris? What's he talking about?"

Kris's forehead scrunches in a deep scowl. "It's not what it sounds like. It's—"

"*I dropped the L-bomb? You won?* Sounds to me like this"—I motion between us—"was just a game."

Kris looks pissed. He shouts over his shoulder, "What the hell, man!"

"No! Over here!" I grab Kris's cheeks and force him to face me. "What the fuck is going on?"

We're causing a scene again, but this time for all the wrong reasons. People can yell their love for each other in Santa's Square, but they definitely can't fight.

Kris meets the concerned glances of guests nearby. "Not here," he mutters.

"What? Don't want the world to hear what an asshole you've been? What an ass you made of me?"

Kris just shakes his head as he pulls me behind him, into the alley I slipped through almost two weeks ago. The one that led me straight to him. I wish that Advil PM had made me sleep through the whole stupid trip.

"Here's the truth: all of this started out like that. As a game." Kris is such a coward, he doesn't even have the decency to look me in the eye. "Every year people come to the island and get so caught up in the production we create that they profess their love to us. It's like they think we're meant to be their soulmate or something. So we made it a competition—we call it the Race—where whoever gets told they're loved first wins a trip to the mainland."

"*Wins a trip?*" I can't believe what I'm hearing. "So it was all fake. I'm just a mark." Kris reaches out and grabs my hands, but I throw his back at him. "Don't touch me!"

"You're not just a mark, Aaron! That's what I wanted to tell you. Everything I've said to you was true. Because you're different. You saw from the start that this was a production. You knew how much work I put into this place. You knew that nothing here was a sign from Christmas or some mystical holiday spirit. And the longer we hung out, the more I knew I was developing real feelings for you. You care so much about your family, Aaron. You care so much about something that you wanted to see it through to the end. You wanted your brother's happiness to be real and not based on the made-up magic of a commercial holiday. And that made all of this"—his gloved hands whip between us—"the very first time I developed feelings back."

He looks at me expectantly, like I should fall into his arms and tell him everything is okay. But things are so *not okay*. They never will be.

"I don't think you get how captivating it is to see someone want to be the master of their own destiny," Kris continues, desperation tinging his words. "We don't see that here. Not from visitors. And then you go and give me all this information on how I could take control of my future too. That meant the world to me. It made me fall for you, Aaron. No one has ever made me feel this way before. I planned all along to tell you tonight that I love you."

Those words I was hoping I'd hear him say now just feel like pathetic excuses. This could all be another act.

"You were going to tell me so I'd say it back," I snap. "Give it enough time to make it seem believable that you could have developed feelings for me so I'd fall for this trick and you'd win!"

"No!" Kris insists. "It doesn't work like that. If we prompt it, we lose."

I laugh, hard, hoping the anger in it cuts him. "And you win everything, don't you? You're the best at all things Winter Wonderland." He's said it so many times. How he's hoped his and his uncle's talents would someday be enough to convince the Kringle board that gay representation needs to go further in Winter Wonderland. That queer people belong here too. But no matter how noble that cause sounds, it won't come at my expense.

"I can't believe you made me a part of your game," I say.

"It may have started that way, but it's so far past that, Aaron. Please. You have to trust me."

"How am I supposed to trust you? Would you have even hung out with me in the first place if it wasn't for the Race?"

Kris's mouth bobs open and closed. He doesn't have to say a thing for me to know I've hit the nail on the head.

"It wasn't me you were attracted to at all," I say. "I was just a bet."

Saying it makes it real. That's when the knife officially slides into my back, my stomach, my heart. I can't believe I did this. I can't believe I gave in to feelings for the very first time in my life, and they've already made me a chump.

"What a fucking joke," I say.

"Aaron!"

I won't stick around to hear any more flimsy excuses.

"Have a nice trip," I say. "Hope it was worth it."

I run out of there as fast as I can, thanking whatever Elf came through and actually deiced this alley. I don't look back, can't look back.

When I make it to our deserted street, I finally let my tears fall with the snowflakes.

# Kris

I've never cried when my pairing left before. But I guess there's a first time for everything.

I stand on the snow-covered beach outside Anjie's house, watching the lights of the airplane cruise over the island, knowing that Aaron is on it. Knowing that I'll never see him again.

I tried calling so many times after he stormed out of the square, but every single one got ignored. I texted too, but I'm pretty sure I'm blocked now. And I can't say that I blame him. I'd feel used too if I was just some pawn in somebody else's game. That's what's been done to me over and over again, always a pawn to the tourists' desperate need to feel Christmas magic. I can't believe I ever made Aaron feel that used.

"Hey, man, I'm really sorry," Chris says. "I just . . . I got excited, you know, and I blurted, but . . . Fuck, dude, I'm so, so sorry."

Chris's big doe eyes shimmer with tears. He honestly does feel bad. And while I want to blame this lovable himbo, I know it's not his fault.

"It was an accident, Chris," I say. "I know you wouldn't do that on purpose."

"Oh man." He throws his arms around me and pulls me in for a bone-crushing hug. "I'll make it up to you however I can. I didn't expect you to actually fall in love, you know? That's never happened before." He pulls back and looks me in the eye. "To any of us."

"Wild, right?" I say. "I'm just as surprised."

"What does it feel like?"

His question takes my breath away, makes the tears stop. Chris doesn't know. *None of us know*, except for me now. It's just so bizarre that—on this island that's supposedly all about holiday magic and love—we haven't truly felt the emotion. Maybe it's because we've been taught all our lives how to fake it, so now we don't know how to genuinely fall for a person. Or maybe it's because the people who've come here were never really looking to find love in the first place, or wanted it only on their terms, not going through the give-and-take that a real relationship requires. Not until Aaron, that is. He always saw me for me, not as some Elf automaton.

"Mind if I interrupt?"

Anjelica stands in the opening of her sliding-glass doors, giving us the space we need in case we tell her no.

We're supposed to be inside, celebrating the completion of the Race. I should feel excited that I get to meet with Kris Kringle. I was going to give up an audience with him, but now I'll have that face-to-face time to pull on his heart-strings like all the people he chose to move here so long ago. Like Uncle Toby once did. But right now, celebrating is the last thing I feel like doing.

Chris wipes at his eyes. "I'll let you guys talk." He turns to go inside, but before he does he says, "Seriously, Kris. Anything I can do to make it up to you. Just let me know."

I nod. But there's nothing he could do to fix this.

Anjie fills the space Chris left, her gloved hand resting on my shoulder.

"Here to say *I told you so*?" I snip.

She pulls her hand right back so she can point an accusing finger at me. "Don't do that, Kris. You know me better than any person on this island, and you know that's not me."

She glares daggers, and I instantly feel bad. "Sorry, I— It's not your fault. Whatever shit's going down is shit I made happen."

Anjie nods. "Yeah. It is. But I know what stupid things we can do when we're desperate." She waves her phone at me with a small smirk, the crashed Maserati photo set as her background. "But as your friend, I'm here to tell you that you need to snap out of it. This is a win. You're one step closer to getting Uncle Toby back. Dad might listen to you. If I open my mouth, he just assumes I'm some stupid party girl, but you . . . I've said it before, and I'll say it again. You're the best of us. You and your uncle. Dad just needs to be reminded of that by somebody who's not so close to him. Who's not me. Without the board telling him to disregard us as naïve kids."

I can hear the sadness in her voice, but I can't bring myself to say anything. What's the point? I'm not even sure that I'll have the words to bring Uncle Toby back anymore.

Laughs and cheers float through the open doors, coming from Anjie's kitchen.

"I know it's probably not high on your list of priorities," she says, "but you need to do the speech. It's tradition."

*Fuck tradition* is what I want to say. People's obsession with tradition is what brings all those phonies here. Our stupid Race is what blew up my chance with Aaron in the first place. But as Anjie gently tugs me behind her, I don't resist.

"Kris! Kris! Kris!" The rest of the Fling Ring gathers behind Anjelica when we step inside, my name pounding inside my skull. It feels like they're mocking me when I only want to hear my name from the one person who will never speak to me again. Rudy, Dasher, Nicky, Noelle, Chris, and Nick all have cups full of Grinch Juice, Dasher's concoction of lime Kool-Aid and cheap vodka. Dasher shoves a mug of it into my hand, the sticky green liquid sloshing onto my fingers. I can smell the sugar from here.

This one cup seems to perfectly encapsulate what this whole island really is: sickly sweet. Fake. Processed.

"There's no substance," I mutter, not really meaning it to be the beginning of my speech, but everyone's attention is on me nonetheless. So I go with it. What better time than now when they're hanging on to every word I say?

"This place is all just smoke and mirrors. *Creating* a feeling on the surface, but that's so shallow. We never go deep, never find what it is that's preventing our guests from feeling joy in their real lives. Aaron saw how fake this place is from the start. But what he didn't see was how fake *I* am. I'm such an asshole for leading him on like that. And you know what? It's not just me. We're *all* assholes."

"Hang on a minute," Rudy says.

"Yeah, you're being a real downer, dude," Nick adds.

"What? You can't handle the truth? We're no better than the guests who come here and use us. We're using them too, for our own good time, for this stupid competition. Look where it's gotten us! We're so focused on tricking strangers into falling in love with us that not a single one of our group has actually ever felt real love. We see it as a *game*. It's about time we got our heads out of our asses and look around. What are we getting out of this, really? So we mess with some mainlanders. So what? One of us gets a trip to New York. Big deal! What do we win?"

That's the question, isn't it? The one I should have been asking myself all along. I've been so focused on being the best at everything Christmas, at proving my spot here, but what has it really gotten me? Nothing. But something's been taken from me: my favorite uncle, my only gay mentor, the lone Wonderer who gave me hope for Winter Wonderland. I've gone eighteen years being good at this holiday on this stupid island, and it's gotten me nowhere.

It's time I stop relying on everybody else.

I pass my Grinch Juice to Rudy, who whoops, but Nicky and Noelle shush him. They know this is bigger than partying.

"I've got to go," I say to Anjie. "I've got to prep for New York."

# Aaron

"They've mentioned balls dropping forty times in the last fifteen minutes, and you haven't laughed once." Casey nudges my knee with his toe, stretching his outrageously long leg from the other side of the couch. "You can't keep going on like this, bro. Just call Kris and—"

"*Don't* say that name in this house!" I bark, snatching my knee back and scooting out of Casey's giant wingspan. It's been this way ever since we returned to Newport Beach five days ago. Anytime Dad or Casey wants to talk about our time in Winter Wonderland, or mentions Raquel or Kris, I snap at them.

And rightfully so, if you ask me.

"All right, that's enough." Dad gets up from the matching sofa across from us and turns off the TV. Times Square disappears in an instant. "I thought this could wait until the morning, but it seems the New Year's resolutions have to officially start now."

"Hey!" Casey protests. "The ball drops—hehehe—in two minutes!"

"No more stalling, Case," Dad says. "The Merry Men need to start their next chapter right this second."

He grabs his phone from the coffee table before swiping a few buttons and the telltale *swish* of an email being sent reaches my ears. Casey's and my phones ding and buzz with incoming messages, respectively, the subject of Dad's letter loud and clear: *Family Therapists.*

"I spent the week researching psychologists in the area who I think might be able to help us deal with some things," Dad says. "Things we've kept locked inside the past eight years."

Casey beams, like this was the Christmas present he's been waiting for. "I love that idea, Dad. Good call." He scrolls through Dad's list. "Ooh, Dr. Jessica Torres! She's good! She's recommended all the time by the family center. I vote for her!"

Dad looks at me tentatively, like he's waiting for me to snap again. "What about you, Aaron? I made that list because I figured you'd like to see all the options before making a decision."

I get up and grab the remote, not even looking at Dad when I say, "No."

*Click.* The TV's back on, hundreds of thousands of tourists screaming as the ball drops over New York City.

*Nine, eight . . .*

"Aaron," Dad says. "You can't keep doing this."

*Seven, six . . .*

"I'm not *doing* anything."

*Five, four . . .*

"I think Dad's saying that's the problem, bro."

*Three, two . . .*

"Oh, like *you're* the healthiest member of this family?"

*One.*

"At least I'm willing to do something about it, Aaron." Casey gets up slowly. "I wish you would too." He leaves, headed out back to his casita. I can tell from the slump of his shoulders that I've cut him deep.

*Happy New Year.*

"Aaron, come on," Dad says, but I'm saved from having to continue this conversation by another notification on my phone.

It's a text from Mom. This time, she's plastered her head over the Times Square ball, *HAPPY NEW YEAR* written underneath. My fingers move before I even realize it, flying across my screen until I hit call and hold the phone to my ear.

I never call her. Ever.

"Well, happy New Year!" she says, all excited and eager, accompanied by sounds of people laughing wherever she is.

"What the hell is wrong with you?"

"Aaron, I—"

"NO!" I yell, the explosion of anger feeling so, so good. I've been waiting to get this out for the past week, and I've finally found the perfect target. "I said *what the hell is wrong with you*? Who leaves their husband and children for a fucking *cranberry bog*? Do you know how that made me feel? Do you know how that made all of us feel? You were my mother, yet I wasn't even more significant than a *berry*."

"Aaron, this isn't past tense." She's realized how serious this is, her tone now totally at odds with the revelry in the background. "I still am your mother."

"Are you? Being a mom takes action, *Stella*." I let every ounce of disdain I can muster soak into her name. She's not getting *Mom* anymore. She doesn't deserve it. "Your stupid *memes* don't count."

I think back to all the photos Kris showed me of his uncle Toby. They were photos of his actual *life*, and the details Kris could explain of his uncle's new routine showed the messages that accompanied those pictures had to have some substance. Substance is the last thing I ever get from my own mother.

"You're so oblivious to the fact that I don't even know you! Who's with you right now, huh?" I'm on a roll, my words coming fast and feverish. "I've never heard you mention a friend before in all the time you've been in

Wisconsin. What does your house even look like? Where the fuck are the cranberries, Stella? You've never sent us anything! Not a picture, not a gift, nothing!"

"Aaron," Stella says. The background noise is gone now. Maybe she walked outside. Maybe I'm yelling so loud, they can hear it through the phone and I've ruined the entire mood of her party. "I'm coming down there."

"Like hell you are! You don't just get to come and go as you please. You lost that right when you left us. When you abandoned us like we were a burden. But that's the last thing we are, Stella. Dad—" The shift comes on hard. The words that were formerly pouring out in bellowed fury are now stilted, my throat clogged with emotion. "Dad works his ass off to provide for us. He works day in and day out to let us know there's nothing that could keep him from being by our side. He would never leave, not in a million years.

"And Casey? He's the most loving of all of us. He's protective, he's loyal, he just wants me to be happy. He's the exact opposite of you in *every* way. And you don't get to *drag us down* by coming here, Stella. *You're* not good enough for *us*. You can come when I say. And that day's definitely not today. I've already got all the people here I need."

I hang up and toss my phone across the room, not able to get it—or her—away from me fast enough. My face is soaked with tears I didn't know were streaming down my cheeks. My nose is clogged. My breathing comes in harsh, ragged breaths.

Dad stares at me, open-mouthed. "Aaron?"

"I'm o—*hic*—kay, Dad," I say through a hiccup. "I think I'm ready for that therapy now."

# Kris

It's been eight weeks since I won the Race. Eight weeks since I betrayed Aaron. Eight weeks to mentally prepare for what I'm going to say to Anjie's dad, but I still can't think of the words to convince Kringle to change course and tell the Wonderland board to embrace gay Santa.

Drawing such a blank has set my nerves on edge, which is only made worse by the flight to Manhattan. It takes over nine hours to fly from Winter Wonderland to New York, and it's wild to be up in the air for that long. You're so, so high, and with every little bump, I'm sure we're going to die. My conclusion: humans are not meant to fly. It's why we have legs and not wings. I know he's fictional, but jeezus, I feel bad for Santa having to soar across the entire flipping planet.

Even the cushiness of this private plane can't calm me down. The perks include all of Santa's favorite snacks and then some. Halfway through the flight, we're even served an entire pot roast dinner. Apparently normal planes aren't this comfortable, and most have way more than two passengers.

Anjie's in one of her moods as the minutes tick by, which saturates the plane. Between her brooding and my nervous jumping, we're a barrel of laughs. I don't bring it up the first half of the flight, but after our plates with warm apple pie crumbs are cleared away, I have to address it, if only to distract me from being higher than any human has a right to be.

"Want to talk about it?" I ask.

Anjie takes a swig of her eggnog—spiked with a mini brandy when the flight attendant was in the bathroom—before finally sighing. "I just don't know how we got here."

"You mean having all your bank accounts closed so you can't fly your best friend home with you whenever you want to convince your dad he needs to bring my uncle back and hire him as gay Santa?"

Anjie throws her napkin at me while I take a deep breath. "No. How Dad became so heartless that he can't see what's right anymore. How Mom doesn't say anything to him about it. How no one backs me up when I try to tell them there are things that need to change in Winter Wonderland."

"How we have to go to all these lengths just to get an opportunity to talk to Kringle without anyone else thinking we rigged the Race or blasting Uncle Toby on the internet and making him the poster child for queer Christmas discrimination," I add.

Anjie nods. "That part."

"Is there any chance this is going to work?" I ask.

She shrugs. "Dad loves it when teens think they know just how the world should work. Lord knows he took it *extremely* well when I gave him a piece of my mind." She motions around the plane, highlighting that we have to be in a private jet in order for her to even get home. "Cue purgatory. But honestly, it's the only shot we have now." She sighs, sulking in her seat. "Graduation can't get here soon enough. I'm ready to make my own decisions."

I think about Uncle Toby, how he made the decision to move, but it really wasn't his choice.

"I'm not sure it works like that," I say. "I think no matter what age you are, other forces are always going to push against you. They'll try to make us live how they think we should. It's . . . depressing."

Anjie raises her mug. "I'll drink to that." She takes a gulp, and we sit in silence again, my nerves replaced with broodiness of my own.

Finally Anjelica asks, "Anything you want to run by me before you meet Dad?"

I shake my head. "I don't want this to be overpracticed. I've spent my whole life practicing to make Christmas magic look real, but all that does is make it even more phony. He needs to hear this from the heart."

"Copy that."

Four hours later, we finally land at a private airport. If I was jumpy before, it has nothing on the loud and choppy helicopter ride or chauffeured drive with cars practically on top of each other that complete our trip to Anjie's apartment. I'm totally carsick as I get out of the Escalade, and I take a moment to lean on the SUV and settle my stomach. I take deep breaths and gaze at floor after floor of the skyscraper before us. It towers over the rest of the buildings around it, and when we finally go inside and the elevator attendant hits a shiny gold 93, my eyes practically bug out of my skull.

"You live on the ninety-third floor? How can one building be so tall?"

"What?" Anjie shrugs. "There's another penthouse above ours, so it's not like we have the highest unit."

"Oh, right. So down-to-earth."

She laughs as the elevator rockets upward faster than should be possible. When the doors slide open into a sleek modern apartment, her laugh cuts off instantly. Not in awe at the sea of color below us, the entire city lit up with *millions* of lights like a spectacular Christmas tree. The view takes my breath away; I've never seen anything like this. But Anjie has. Her stare is focused on the man sitting at the impossibly long dining table. Kris Kringle, with a binder and a tiny plate of milk and cookies in front of him.

"Hi, Daddy." Anjie sounds the weakest I've ever heard

her. Small, insignificant. Not at all the confident girl I know.

"Sweetheart." Kris Kringle gets up, and seeing him in the flesh throws me for a loop. He really does look like the image of Santa you see the most. White, bulging belly, a full beard, though not quite as full as the real Saint Nick's. He's tall too, taller than me by a couple inches. His whole presence is just large. Boisterous. His smile is huge. I practically get bowled over by his charm. His Christmas cheer. His Kringle Kharisma.

He scoops Anjelica up in a bear hug, lifting her off her Chanel boots. She doesn't smile, doesn't seem relieved to be home. She's distant. I'm in New York, but she's somewhere else entirely.

"This is Kris," she says as soon as her feet touch the marble floor. "My friend from Wonderland."

"Kris! How do you spell it?"

"With a *K*, sir. Just like you. I was named after you, actually. My parents are Marsha and Gary Bright."

"The Brights, of course!" He says it so confidently, so jovially, he'd convince anyone. But I've been taught acting from day one—at *his* holiday immersive experience—and I can smell a fake from a mile away. He doesn't even know their names. Mom and Dad jumped at the chance to work for him, have spent decades making sure his brand of holiday cheer never falters, and he doesn't remember them. When he interviewed them to be there in the first place.

There go my nerves. Right out the window, splatting on

the ground ninety-three floors below.

"It's okay if you don't know them," I say. "There are thousands of employees on the island, let alone the tens of thousands of employees in all your craft stores. That's too much to expect of anybody, so you don't have to pretend."

Kringle's smile wobbles. I can tell he wants to frown, but I think he's even convinced himself that natural human expression isn't okay.

"In the spirit of not pretending, I have something I want to say to you, sir. Something I want to *ask* of you actually. Bring Tobias Bright back." His eyes finally light with recognition. "That's a name you remember, isn't it?" I don't let snarkiness tinge my words, like I want to. I'm trying to win him over. "We need a gay Santa. And it needs to be him. You and the whole Wonderland board saw for yourselves how good he is at Christmas. Hell, you even brought him to the island twenty years ago because he loves it. No one can craft a toy like him, or make a cup of cocoa like him, or remember every lyric to every single Christmas song out there, even the obscure ones."

"Angel?" Kringle's frowning now, suspicious. His eyes wander to his daughter, who smirks back. "Did you put him up to this?"

"No, Daddy. This is all Kris." She puts a hand on my shoulder. "I can say this objectively, he's the best Wonderer we've got. He sees things in ways nobody else does. You need to hear him out."

Kringle opens his mouth to object, but I jump in before he can shut me down when I haven't even really started yet.

"I know all the arguments against it," I say. "So many people would reduce me to being woke or a melty snowflake or appeasing the PC masses. But this is about so much more than that. It's about queer Wonderers seeing ourselves. It's about gay guests truly being welcomed."

"We don't turn away any visitor because of who they are, Kris. That's not the Kringle way."

I nod. "I know that. And I appreciate that. But you include everybody else on the island. There're places for worship for every religion. You have Santas of all races. These are great steps to inclusion that should be there, and I'm thankful that you do that. But by leaving us out, leaving the whole queer community out, our lack of representation says a lot. It's not that you need to tick off boxes in your diversity quota or something. It's just about . . ."

God, why is this so hard? I'm not saying the right things. He's heard all this before, and I worry that he's going to tune me out. I worry that he's going to think I'm just being whiny.

My eyes wander and land on the massive binder next to Kringle's milk and cookies, with *Winter Wonderland Too* scrolled across it in gold cursive. It's stuffed to the brim with papers. It reminds me of Aaron's binder and how he had gathered so many facts about Raquel. He made his plan based on his knowledge of her. To get Kringle to listen, I need to use what I know about him. His likes and dislikes.

"Okay, think of it like this. You're into football, right?" I know he is from all the Kringle football paraphernalia his stores hawk during the Super Bowl.

Kringle grins that charming Santa smile. "It's my favorite pastime, other than crafting, that is."

"So, when you're watching the game—" The words sound foreign and forced even to me, but I've got to continue. "Y-you invite your buddies, right?"

"Always," he says. "It's a Kringle tradition."

There's that word. Tradition. The reason so many want to keep queer people out of things. Because we're not *traditional*.

"Right, and who are your buddies, mostly? Is it a room full of men or a room full of women?"

Kringle doesn't even hesitate. "Always the boys!" He says it so heartily, I'm surprised it's not followed by a *Ho ho ho!*

"But why not the girls?"

He pauses at that, seriously considering it. We might be getting somewhere. "I guess because that changes things," he says. "Men interact differently with their male friends than their female ones." His eyes dart to Anjelica. "But I know that's not right either."

He doesn't say it with suspicion like before. He's not mocking that things are changing. It seems like he actually wants to do good but worries he might misstep.

"That's the thing. Straight men and women often do act differently depending on if they're separate or together. Just like queer people often act differently when we're together versus when we're with straight folks. We're more on guard, more aware when there might be people nearby who want us gone, either out of their space or . . . permanently."

Kringle's eyes widen. "You've felt that? In Winter Wonderland?"

"Mmm." The affirmative makes me think of Aaron. How he can say so much in one tiny sound. He may be royally pissed at me, but I think if he knew what I was saying here, he'd get it.

"Wow." Kringle seems genuinely surprised. Hurt, even.

"It's not that I've ever had anyone be openly bigoted to me on the island," I continue. "But there's always that parent who steers their kid away when they see me holding another guy's hand. Or the assholes who can ruin our social media posts by saying people they perceive as queer should have no place in Winter Wonderland. Or the glaring absence of gay Santa when there are so many others who go against the *traditional* mold. Who go against it in ways they should, to make others feel welcome and included. Yet still, the island has no official gay rep of any kind."

At least Kringle has the decency to look guilty.

"But that's the thing. What can be set in stone about a

tradition that's built on make-believe anyway?"

Kringle puffs his chest, latching on to his argument again. "Ah, that's where you're wrong, Kris. Christmas, Santa, holiday cheer. It's not make-believe. It's real. People feel it. We *make* it. And guests get very defensive when they think the magic they've fallen in love with is changing."

"Yet those people are the ones who don't know what the Christmas spirit is really about." The words fly out of me, and when I realize what I've said, they make me laugh. Who knew I'd be the one sticking up for Christmas spirit, when I've thought it was all a load of crap to begin with. But I feel what I'm about to say in my bones. This is what Uncle Toby was always going on about. When he talked about spreading Christmas cheer, I never really felt it. I didn't understand it.

Until now.

"Christmas is about family," I say. "It's about community. About coming together and making the magic. And since every family is different, who's to say what *their* Santa should look like? Adding another one doesn't mean any guest is required to flock to him. They can continue to visit whichever Santa feels like the best fit for them. But shouldn't everybody have that right? Shouldn't my uncle Toby have the same chance to bring holiday cheer to visitors as any other Santa? Shouldn't our gay guests get to have a figure on the island they can connect with?

To feel safe with like you feel with your football buddies? *That's* what the magic of Christmas is all about. Finding each person's perfect Santa, their perfect family, their own individual holiday traditions. Nobody gets to determine that for anybody else. Except, that's what Kringle Korp has decided to do for the queer community. They've determined who we do and don't get to see in Winter Wonderland. And with all due respect, sir, where's the Christmas spirit in that?"

The silence is deafening. So deafening that I can't help but replay what I said and question everything that left my mouth. I definitely didn't think my heartfelt speech would include the phrase "football buddies," but it is what it is. Kringle keeps looking at me expectantly, and I swear cool, calm, and collected Anjie has a tear in her eye. When neither of them makes a peep, I mutter, "Um. Yeah. That's it."

Kringle doesn't move a muscle. His face is frozen smack in the middle between a smile and a frown. I can't tell if he's been moved by my words or if he's just annoyed.

"Daddy," Anjie says. "Think back to those days when you interviewed all those Wonderers for the first time. You heard for yourself how much Christmas meant to them and awarded them a true gift with their new lives. You gave them a new family. What does it say about us if we let *board members* tell you who can and can't be a part of that family? That doesn't seem right, does it?"

"Angel," Kringle says. "You know how I feel about you

giving me advice about my own company."

Anjelica nods softly, her eyes drifting to the floor when her father adds, "I was wrong."

Anjelica perks back up. "You were what?"

"Wrong, my angel." He pats his ample belly with a hearty chuckle before putting his bear-size hand on my shoulder. "Kris, my boy. You're exactly the kind of person we need as a Wonderer. You understand the spirit of Christmas. Possibly even better than myself."

I'm speechless, but Anjelica fills the silence as she clacks over to her father.

"So you'll change it," she says. "You'll do what Kris asked?"

I feel my heart fly into my throat. Did this actually work?

Kringle scowls, and my heart drops like a stone. "Maybe."

Anjie crosses her arms. "He gave you that Hallmark-worthy speech, and all you can say is *maybe*?!"

"There's a system here," Kringle says. "A method of getting changes approved by the board. I'll address this at our next meeting, but . . ." He slowly walks to the floor-to-ceiling windows, looking down on New York City sprawling beneath us. "I think sometimes it's easy to get caught up in this." He waves his hand toward the skyscrapers and brake lights, to the sounds of the city floating through the air. "Everything is a business. Even

Christmas." He turns, looking that much more Santa-like with millions of lights illuminating his silhouette. But brighter than any of the lights below is the smile spreading across his rosy cheeks. "Yet all it takes is one person to remind us of the magic."

I should feel ecstatic. I should feel like my job here is done. But there's one more thing nagging at me.

"Actually, sir." I glance at Anjie, doubting this will work. But if Kringle was able to hear me out on Santa, maybe he's ready to hear this too. "Two people. I couldn't have done this without Anjelica. I think you might be missing the magic that makes her so unique."

"Is that so?" Kringle says. The smile instantly drops from his face. I think I just seriously overstepped, but I can't back down now.

"Yes." I lace Anjie's perfect fingers through my rough ones and squeeze tight. "Your daughter is one-of-a-kind, Mr. Kringle. We've all made mistakes in the past. Even you, letting my uncle leave the island without so much as a second thought. But I don't think we should be judged solely on our mistakes. Anjelica is so much more than any headline. Her heart is huge. If it wasn't, she wouldn't have stuck by my side, trying to help get Uncle Toby's job back. She's the kindest person I've ever known. Honestly, I think she got that from you."

They stare at me with identical looks on their faces: mouths open, brows furrowed, cheeks reddening ever so slightly. Maybe they're touched. Maybe they're hurt. Maybe it's both.

"Angel?" Kringle says, taking in his daughter.

Anjie worries at her lip before locking eyes with me, unsure.

I give her one tiny nod, certain she knows my meaning. *I've got your back.*

Anjelica lets go of my hand. "Thanks, Kris. For the nudge. I've got it from here." She plants her high-heeled feet firmly in front of her father, and says clearly, confidently, "Daddy, we need to talk. Actually—" She pulls her phone out of her Birkin. "Mami should be here for this too." Her mom picks up the FaceTime almost instantly.

"Mamita, what's wrong? It's so late. Are you hurt?"

"Everything's fine, Mami." Anjie rolls her eyes. "Wait, no. Everything's *not* fine. We need to talk about my exile."

That's my cue. I make my exit, wandering down the nearest hallway that's so much longer than any other hallway I've ever been in. I peek in door after door, trying to find a spot that looks like a guest room. I come across multiple gift-wrapping stations, a sauna, and somehow stumble into Mrs. Pérez-Kringle's closet.

When I finally make it to a bedroom, I collapse onto the red and green duvet. But I can't sleep. We might finally be one step closer to some positive change in Winter Wonderland, and my mind is reeling with possibilities. I need to get out my excitement. I need to share this news with someone who will appreciate it.

Hopefully.

I fish my phone out of my pocket and dial.

It rings only once before she picks up.

"Sweetheart!" I've had a hard time relating to her ever since Uncle Toby left, but she's never lost the love in her voice. "How's New York?"

"It's great, Mom. Could you put me on speaker? I want Dad to hear this too."

Then, for the first time, I'm finally able to put my feelings into words they understand.

# Aaron

Oh, how the tables have turned. All this time I thought it was stupid how many hours Casey spent glued in front of the flat screen, watching couple after couple fall for each other "against all odds" in horribly cheesy made-for-TV movies. Like, why are these so overacted? Why are they all so predictable? Why can I literally guess the lines about 85 percent of the time? That goes for the leads, that goes for the kooky parents, that goes for the zany assistant back in the big city while an outrageously uptight main character realizes small-town living might just be for her. And most of all, why do I find myself loving them?

I figured Casey would be by my side watching, but he's left Christmas in December. Dr. Torres suggested he find things in addition to the holiday to get excited about, and Casey's really responded to the assignment. He's jogging every day, going out to see friends, spending even more hours at the family center, and joining all sorts of school clubs that have nothing to do with Christmas. We've had only five sessions so far, but he's realizing the expectations he set for Raquel were too much pressure on her, and that it maybe wasn't so healthy to get that attached.

I guess that means, in the grand scheme of things, my plan worked. It just involved way more emotional breakdowns than I would have liked, mine included, but I think the lesson here is that sometimes you need to have those big feelings blow up to finally figure out what the problems are and move on. I hate that so much. It seems erratic, illogical, unhinged. Why can't emotional breakthroughs come from clear steps you can follow that lead you to the truth? That would be healthy, logical, helpful.

And yet, here we are. Casey moving forward. Dad and Stella talking again, at Dr. Torres's suggestion, since Stella will have to join these sessions so we can officially move forward. I'm not ready to see her yet, but I think I will be soon.

Yet even with this forward momentum, I still feel like I've failed. I don't need a therapist to tell me it's because of Kris. No, because *I let myself* get attached to Kris. I've known my whole life that attachment would lead to heartache, and I was 100 percent correct. I haven't been able to stop thinking about him despite it being two months since we left the island.

"Bro!" Casey plops down onto the couch in his Christmas casita, shirtless and soaked in sweat after his latest run.

"Case! Go take a shower!" I try to nudge him off the couch with a foot, but that's like an ant trying to move a skyscraper.

"No way, man! There's a big announcement we've got to see." He lunges across the couch to get at the remote, his sweat soaking into my joggers.

"Ew ew ew ew ew! Here!" I throw the remote at him and hop from the sofa. "I've got to change. Then shower. Then burn these pants."

"No, wait!" He uses one of his insanely long arms to grab me before I can go. "You need to see this too."

"Case, you're disgusting," I say, trying to pull back. "Let me go."

"Just watch, bro!" Casey says, flipping to the YouTube app and opening a live stream announcement. From the Winter Wonderland profile.

My heart stops, jumps into my throat, and falls out my butt all at the same time. What in the hell is Casey doing?

"I don't want to see this, Casey," I say quietly, trying to get my tone to convey that I'm this close to chucking one of his precious snow globes at the TV.

Kris Kringle, basically Santa's identical twin, steps up to an ornate red, gold, and green podium outside the Kringle Korp building in New York. I get that prickly feeling someone's watching me and glance over to see Casey's eyes aren't glued to the TV at all. He's looking right at me.

"Why are you looking at me like that?"

"Aaron! Just watch!"

He never says my name. This must be serious. I slowly walk around the back of the couch but only sit on its arm. Seeing the founder and spokesperson of Winter Wonderland makes me want to run.

"Good afternoon, ladies and gentlemen." Kris Kringle's voice is boisterous, full of joy, *exactly* how you'd think Santa should sound. "I've called this press announcement to let you know of some exciting new developments at Kringle Korporation." The assembled reporters all chatter in excited anticipation. Meanwhile, my heart races. Why is my heart racing? "We are extremely pleased with the success Winter Wonderland—our year-round Christmas island—has seen over more than two decades of being the home of holiday cheer. So pleased, in fact, that we are opening a new location." The reporters' volume rises, but I roll my eyes.

"This is the announcement I just *have* to see?"

Casey shushes me. "Keep listening, bro!"

"I know," Mr. Kringle says to the reporters. "I'm positively bursting at the seams. While our new addition will still have all the same Christmas magic, this location will be different from the original in a number of ways. First, Winter Wonderland Too—that's *t-o-o* for all you savvy typers out there—will not be an island, but a community inside Los Angeles County."

That's what's got Casey this amped up. He'll have a

much easier time visiting this place than a secluded Alaskan island. "Who cares, Case?"

"Shhhh! Listen!"

"We're very pleased with this development, as it will be a more affordable and accessible option," Kringle continues. "Visitors can choose between simple day visits or staying in one of the multiple lodging options the neighborhood will provide. I am honored to get to introduce snow to many Southern California residents who've never seen it before. While it may not *technically* be snow, this synthetic and sustainable option created by the Elves at Winter Wonderland will be as close to the real thing as you can get—"

Kringle gets interrupted by shouted questions. I turn to Casey, who's still staring at me so creepily.

"Why should I care that Wonderland is getting another location?" I ask.

"Shhhhh!"

I scoff and turn back to the TV. Doesn't Casey realize how heartless it is for him to force me to watch this when it only reminds me of getting duped by Kris?

Kringle puts his hands up, quieting the reporters. "I promise I'll get to your questions in due time. I have one last announcement." His chest puffs as he takes a deep breath, the glint in his eye just like every image you ever see of Santa. A glint that says he's about to deliver something epic.

"It's recently come to light that we've been letting down an enthusiastic sector of our Wonderland audience," he explains. "And I personally want to apologize to the queer community." For the first time, the waiting reporters go quiet. The press loves nothing more than a scandal, right? "We haven't shown that you are as welcome as any other guest. I was reminded not too long ago that the magic of Christmas can be summed up in one word: family. We don't stand around cooking favorite meals or giving presents from the heart alone. The holidays are about making memories and sharing special moments with the ones we love. A group that we can let our guard down around and truly be ourselves with.

"We're all familiar with the pressures of feeling like we're out of place. Whether it's from walking into a room where no one else looks like us or shares similar personality traits or interests, or sitting in a stadium and realizing you're wearing the wrong team's jersey. It's key for any corporation that prides itself on making sure everyone belongs that there are representatives across the company that signal that belonging. For that reason, all Winter Wonderland locations will be introducing queer Santas, joining our family of Saint Nicks whose sole purpose and intention is to help as many people as possible feel the magic of Christmas. That is to say, the love and community that Kringle Korp is all about."

A wetness seeps through the thigh of my joggers again,

and I push my arm out to get my brother off me. "Case, now is not the time to soak me in your sweat!"

But wait. I glance to the left. Casey's still over on his side of the couch. That spot of wetness building on my sweats is from *me*. From the tears falling silently down my cheeks.

"I know, bro," Casey says. "I know. It's the magic of Christmas."

I laugh, wiping my eyes with my sleeve, while Kringle finishes his statement. "I'd like to thank the young man who reminded me what the true meaning of Christmas really is. Thank you to Kris Bright, who will always be a member of the Wonderland family, no matter where his journey takes him. Now, get ready for Winter Wonderland Too to open this fall, just in time for the holiday season!"

This is the moment in a cheesy holiday movie when triumphant music would play. But here in Casey's Christmas casita, we're silent. I can feel my brother's stare, but I can't look up from the floor. I don't know how to process my feelings. I don't even really know *what* I'm feeling. As Kringle calls on the hungry journalists to finally answer their questions, Casey turns off the TV.

"Pretty big news, huh?" he says, the glint in his eye matching Kringle's.

"Yup." It's all I can muster.

"And that was because of Kris."

"Uh-huh."

"I think you should call him."

A flare of anger burns in my gut. "Casey, it's not that simple."

"Why not?"

"He lied to me."

"So there was some stupid game the Wonderland kids played. It's only because all those idiotic, holiday-obsessed tourists like yours truly confessed their love to them. It's not really Kris's fault."

"But he never would have talked to me if it wasn't for that stupid game."

Casey shrugs. "And I never would have met Raquel if her family hadn't moved to Newport Beach when we were in the sixth grade. That doesn't mean that I loved her any less just because the circumstances that brought us together were out of our control."

"Yeah, but she didn't lie to you. Kris never told me about the Race."

"But he never lied to you about who he was, did he?"

I think back to all the time we spent together. He never made up fake interests so we'd have more in common. He confessed to being over Christmas despite his skills at every holiday-related activity you could name. He admitted he never gave a future off the island any thought because the Wonderers just didn't take that path. He shared with me how jarring it was to see his uncle Toby leave the island. In some ways, I think he was more honest with me than anyone else ever has been. And maybe that's my fault; I've never let anyone in. I'm the Robot. But for some reason, I actually opened up around Kris.

"No," I finally answer. "He never lied about that."

"I've been waiting my whole life for you to fall in love, bro. Not because you need someone else to be a complete person. We all know where that can lead." Casey points to himself with bugged-out eyes. "But knowing there's someone out there who wants the whole you—the good, the bad, and the ugly—is one of the deepest connections you'll ever have. Can you get hurt in the process? Absolutely. But it also means you can forge one of the most monumental bonds human existence has to offer. It's someone who can help you take on your burdens, and who you can do the same for too. Someone who will go to the ends of the earth for you because they know you'd do it for them. You'll get in arguments, you'll drive each other bananas, but you'll also be surprised by how someone can make you truly feel seen, and you'll want to make them feel the same way. Do you genuinely like shouldering everything alone?"

I shake my head before I know I'm even doing it. But the memories of how Kris jumped in so quickly to help me with Casey—even if everything did go haywire—are still so fresh. I felt more relieved and supported than I ever have since Mom left.

"That's what I thought." Casey snags my phone from

the coffee table and holds it out. "You should call him."

For the first time in the weeks since we left the island, I finally feel certain of something.

I grab the phone and dial.

# Kris

When Aaron's name appears on my phone, I think I might pass out. He's calling! Whatever Casey said worked.

I take one last look at Uncle Toby's text on my screen.

**You got this, Kristopher! Just speak from the heart.**

He makes it sound so easy. But it's now or never, right?

I swipe open my phone with shaking fingers and blurt the words I've been dying to say.

"I'm sorry."

Only, through my speaker, it comes out like an echo on an echo on an echo. Because Aaron says it at the same time. And because, standing here in the thin strip of lawn leading to his backyard, my voice carries through the open casita doors into Aaron's phone too.

I watch his back stiffen from the arm of the couch. Then, excruciatingly slow, he turns around. I'm afraid of what I'll see in his eyes: anger, hurt, hatred. But when his finally lock with mine, there's only one thing in his expression.

Hope.

We both hang up, staring at each other, yards apart.

"You're here," he says, not moving from the couch. "Hi."

"Hi."

"How?"

I nod to Casey. "Your brother filled me in on how you've been the past few weeks. The key word he used was *mopey*. I've been exactly the same."

"It doesn't sound like it." Aaron points at the TV. I knew the announcement was coming, but I didn't expect Anjie's dad to give me a shout-out like that. "It sounds like you've been doing a lot of good."

It's still mind-blowing to me that my talk with Kringle led to him addressing the whole board about it. In fact, he had me come with him, to give my same speech. This time when they voted, it was a tie. Kringle was the tiebreaking vote. So with his endorsement, they finally approved including gay representation in their Santa ranks.

"I was just speaking from here," I say, placing a hand over my heart. "I've learned that's really the only way you can connect with someone. Aaron, I'm so sorry. I never wanted you to feel used in that stupid race. I thought things would end up exactly as they had with everyone else: as a fling. But it wasn't until we were deep into it that I realized I had real feelings for you. More than I've ever felt for somebody before."

"That game *is* stupid," Aaron agrees. "But I thought what we had was just a fling too. I guess, in a way, I was also using you. Using you to see what it was like to give in to a crush before heading back home. The perfect scenario for someone who doesn't like attachment. Then it became so much more than a crush. To me."

"Awwww." Casey slaps his hands over his mouth when Aaron shoots daggers at him. "Sorry, bro. It's just—" He waves between us. "This is the kind of thing I live for!"

"Casey." Aaron's got all kinds of warning in his voice.

"Right." Casey springs from the couch. "I'll just see myself out." He heads to the main house, but I'm pretty sure I hear blinds pull up. He's definitely still watching. Hell, he could live stream this for all I care.

"Aaron, I'm sorry I ever made you feel used. But I have to be honest with you. If I could take it all back, I wouldn't ditch the Race." At his angry scowl, I rush to add, "Even though it's so, so stupid, it still led me to you. The guy I was at the start of your Twelve was a jaded idiot. I wouldn't have been able to see how great you were if the game didn't make me so desperate to get to know you. So desperate to make you fall in love with me so that I could finally get a chance to talk to Kris Kringle and convince him we need Uncle Toby back in Wonderland. The thing is, I'm glad I was a desperate jerk. Because I learned how thoughtful and caring and protective you are. I learned that you're unshakable when you set your mind to something. And

I learned, most of all, that I love you. I love you, Aaron. I need you to know that this love isn't fake. It's not some ploy or trick or game. You have to understand that before I leave."

Aaron's face falls. I'm smothering him with this announcement, coming on too hard too fast. I may be good at all things Christmas, but I guess I'm shit at expressing my true feelings. I've never even had true feelings before.

"You're leaving," Aaron says, monotone. "What's the point of giving in to this if you just have to go back to the island?"

A window flies open on the second floor, and Casey shouts, "Tell him, Kris!"

"Casey!" Aaron yells.

"Sorry!" The window slams shut again.

Then, with the smallest smirk, Aaron asks, "What's he talking about?"

"When I said was leaving, I more meant it in the sense of leaving here. Your house. Giving you the space you need to process what I'm saying. But, uh, I'm sort of moving here. Not *here* here, but here to California. Kringle gave me a job. At the new park."

Aaron's mouth drops open. "He did?"

"Yeah. He asked if I'd help make sure this new Winter Wonderland never loses the spirit of Christmas. And Uncle Toby's coming too. The first gay Santa. He's even going to train the others who Kringle Korp is hiring. We're getting a lesbian Mrs. Claus couple, in case you were wondering."

Uncle Toby forwarded me the apology letter he received from Kris Kringle himself, complete with the job offer. My uncle started the email with *I hear you had something to do with this* . . . after which we had a long talk where I agreed never to meddle again. But I spoke from the heart, and he knows I don't regret interfering this one time. Sometimes you just have to go with your gut.

"We'll move right after graduation, and I'll have a whole gingerbread townhouse to myself," I say. "Mom and Dad are getting a spot too. Mom's the new head baker, and Dad says he's been ready for some more routine day and night hours for a long time. What better place to do that than LA?" I'm so freaking lame. Why am I talking about my parents right now?

But Aaron laughs. "You sound like one of my dad's real estate brochures. *The perks of Southern California.*"

"Well, I've left out the biggest perk of all."

"What's that?"

"You."

Aaron slaps a hand over his eyes and groans. "Noooo, Kris! You did not just say that. You're so cheesy."

I shrug. "It's the truth. I feel like it's time I start telling it."

Aaron finally uncovers his eyes. He looks way too stone-faced. "I don't know what to tell you, Kris. You've really let me down."

"I have?" God, I wish I didn't sound so heartbroken already.

"Yes. Because you're not as good at Christmas as I thought. Somebody who was would know this is the perfect time to kiss me."

That's all it takes for electricity to surge from head to toe and jolt me to life. I close the distance between us, lifting Aaron off the couch and pressing my lips to his. I can taste the salt from tears he's shed, but I know from here on out, I'll be able to wipe them away myself. And I'll do whatever I can to make sure he never feels this type of sadness again. I'll always let him know that he is so much more than a fling.

Based on the way he kisses me back, I think Aaron's going to do the same.

He takes my face in his hands, gently running his thumb across my stubble. He looks me in the eye, a small smirk quirking his lips, but doesn't say anything.

I can't take the silence. "What are you thinking?"

Aaron's smile blooms, the biggest and brightest I've ever seen it. "You're the greatest Christmas present I've ever been given."

"Oh, Aaron, now who's cringe-worthy?"

"Gimme a break! I'm just . . . trying to let somebody in for once."

"It's not even Christmas."

He nods. "That's true. But better late than never, right?

Or, it was Valentine's Day a couple weeks ago. Maybe a late Valentine's gift is better?"

"How about we take the pressure off the holidays. Let's just, I don't know, enjoy every day?"

Aaron grins again, so wide, and I can't help but do the same.

"Sounds like a plan to me," he says.

And with that, we seal the deal with a kiss.

# Acknowledgments

I have been robsessed with Santa from the moment I met him. Like, seriously, there's a picture of me at two years old for my debut visit with the Big Man, and I have the most gigantic smile on my face. I was so excited, it seems like I'm ready to leap out of the photo. Needless to say, it's been a lifelong dream to create my own Christmas media. Finally getting to achieve that wouldn't have been possible without my own personal Christmas miracles, a.k.a. the following people:

Megan Ilnitzki, working with you is a true gift. You were like the shining northern lights helping me see the paths Aaron and Kris were supposed to walk. Thank you, thank you, thank you!

Brent Taylor, you deserve your own holiday. You're basically the Rudolph in my life. That's not to say that you have a bright red nose, but to highlight how you always know which directions my career can and should take, and you lead me there with surety and strength. Here's to reaching the highest heights!

The HarperCollins family, you are so much more than Elves; you are indispensable experts of your craft, from marketing to copy editing to the school and library team. I would not be here without each and every one of you, and

I'm so grateful for the gifts your minds, hands, and hearts have brought to my books.

Ricardo Bessa and David DeWitt, the dream team if ever there was one. Ricardo, you brought my boys to glorious life yet again, and I screamed higher than Mariah Carey's whistle-tones when I saw how you illustrated Winter Wonderland. David, your design is always spot on, and this cover truly elicits tidings of comfort and joy when I look at it.

Every reader who has ever picked up a copy of a JJ book. I can't even begin to tell you how happy it makes me when you send messages or emails or comments to share how my stories made you feel. It's sort of like how they say Santa loses his strength if people don't believe in him. I wouldn't be able to do this without your belief in me, and for that I am so, so grateful.

At its core, this book is about family—whether by blood or by shared experience—and the special bonds we make with people who are there by our side as we grow up. In particular, there's something about siblinghood and niblinghood that I wanted to explore, probably inspired by the amazing siblings, aunts, and uncles that the universe gave me. Special shout-out to my big brother, Zach, who's cooler than I ever knew when I was a stupid little kid; to my cousins Ali, Andie, Cam, and Nina, who are as much a part of me as any sibling ever could be; to Andrew, the sister who came into my life thousands of miles from home despite growing up basically down the street (or tractor-packed dirt road) from each other; and to all my aunts and uncles who were there with love and guidance and helped lead their flamboyant, dancing little nephew into adulthood. Of course, my family wouldn't be complete without my parents, who made Christmas and the whole dang year truly magical.

Jerry, the last paragraph is always for you, because it's you I want to end up with each and every day. I know with you by my side, I'll be home for Christmas, for the Fourth of July, for Talk Like a Pirate Day, because home is wherever you are. I love you.